THE MILLSTONE HANGED ABOUT HIS NECK

First Published in the UK 2024

ISBN: 978-1-915953-76-6

The Millstone Hanged About His Neck

By

R. S. Freckleton

Also by the author

Guardians of The Rainbow
The Keepers of The Sunken Way
The Custodians of the Fiery Photons

I

EILEEN PENNYWEATHER HATED BANK HOLIDAY Mondays. This particular Easter Bank Holiday Monday was no exception. As a volunteer for the National Trust, she worked a few hours at the Old Mill at the bottom of the ancient city of Winchester. Her normally quiet and orderly routine in the gift shop was being sorely tested by an unusually large influx of tourists, many with energetic and boisterous youngsters in tow.

"I think it is so important that children are introduced to their heritage at an early age," she heard one woman, sporting an outrageous faux-fur coat, say to her friend.

"Darling, you are spot on – and they are so good at doing activities for the children these days."

Eileen, a woman in her early sixties and glad to have taken early retirement from a tedious job at the earliest opportunity, winced as she saw that neither woman was paying the slightest attention to the activities of the offspring in question, a boy and a girl, both around the age of ten. They were running around the gift shop in an improvised game of tag. Delicate items such as bone china mugs seemed to be in imminent danger. Should she tell them off directly or should she have a word with the two mothers? Eileen had always hated confrontation and was always indecisive at moments like these.

Fortunately, the moment passed as the two children rushed out and down the steps that led to the lower floor where the waters of a branch of the River Itchen flowed through the giant waterwheel providing the power to grind the corn. They were no longer Eileen's responsibility, even though the two mothers were still engaged in lively conversation oblivious to the fact of their children's absence.

"Excuse me," a rather portly man rasped. "I'd like to buy this."

He handed over a tartan rug that you could put over your knees whilst watching the television or indulging in an outdoor picnic on a windy day.

"Certainly, sir," Eileen replied in her best shop assistant's voice. She moved to the till, inspecting the object and searching for the price tag as she went. "That will be thirty-five pounds please."

"What?" the man retorted. "It said seventeen on the shelf."

Eileen sighed inwardly. With so many people about, the last thing she wanted was to be dealing with an awkward customer. She dutifully went to check the shelf and indeed found that a price ticket was advertising seventeen pounds. However, she quickly realised that all the price tickets had been recently moved around, probably by the two young children who had recently exited the gift shop. She hastily put the prices back in their rightful places before any more damage could be done and returned to the till.

"I'm sorry, sir. One of the customers has moved the price tickets. The rugs over there are seventeen pounds. They're very nice – not quite the same quality, of course. Made of recycled material, I believe."

"No, that will not do. That won't do at all," barked the man. "I know my rights. If it's advertised on the shelf at seventeen pounds, you have to sell it to me at seventeen pounds."

Through gritted teeth Eileen responded, "I'm only a volunteer. I don't have the authority to sell goods at less than their retail value. I'll have to call the manager."

"I can wait. I'm in no hurry."

The man was probably older than Eileen and clearly stubborn. It was likely that with retirement time on his hands and nothing better to do today, he could truly wait and wait and wait.

Suddenly a blood-curdling scream could be heard from the depths of the mill. Everyone stopped and turned, forgetting the last thing they were doing. The scream repeated. Eileen moved towards the door leading into the mill.

Everyone else remained glued to the spot. A third scream came, clearly coming from the basement area where the two children had descended just a little earlier. Somewhat annoyed that none of the paid full-time staff had beaten her to the top of the stairs, she cautiously began to descend, one careful step at a time.

Two figures came into view, feet first, then legs, bodies and finally heads. It was the boy and girl who had been running amok a few minutes earlier, but how they were now changed. The girl was deathly pale and shivering. She was the one who had been screaming. The boy was transfixed with an ecstatic expression on his face. "Gross!" he murmured in admiration.

Eileen turned to the thunderous, white-foamed water turbulently rushing through the narrow channel beyond the giant water wheel to see what had caused such dramatic effect.

A hessian sack which had been tied with a rope at the open end, but had since come loose, banged back and forth against the far wall, caught in an eddy of the fast-flowing current. It was shredded and oozed a deep red colour that turned to brown as it diffused away into the surrounding water. There was a substantial object still inside the sack. Protruding out of the sack was an appendage, which Eileen suddenly realised was a human arm and hand. No sooner had the gruesomeness of this registered than she noticed a roughly spherical item bobbing in the water nearby. This rotated as it bobbed and, in a flash, Eileen saw the tortured features of a young man caught in the agony of an untimely death.

A spasm of shock, disgust and disbelief surged through Eileen's body from toe to head in a matter of seconds. Countering the impulse to be violently sick, she shouted at the children:

"Out of here now. Up the stairs, quickly."

Under normal circumstances she would have been surprised at how authoritative her voice sounded. The children obeyed without question. Eileen followed them up, fearing that the shaking that she felt coming over her would cause her to stumble and fall. The two mothers now realising the serious nature of their children's experience, grasped them to their respective bosoms. Eileen broke the glass in the fire alarm at the top of the stairs and started guiding startled visitors out on to the street.

"I'm sorry, there's been an incident. We will have to close."

Eileen shouted this several times as she made for the phone in the gift shop. She clumsily dialled 999 and almost with relief said to the awaiting operator,

"Hello? Can I have the police please. I've found a dead body."

II

DETECTIVE SERGEANT RACHAEL GOODFELLOW KNOCKED on the office door nervously. She had only recently been promoted to her current position with the Wessex Constabulary and this promised to be her first big case. A voice from within beckoned her to enter and she was presented with the sight of a thin, serious man in his early fifties, impeccably dressed with a face etched with the experience of nearly thirty years in the force. He rose from his seat behind the desk and extended an arm to shake the hand of his subordinate officer.

"Ah, DS Goodfellow," he said in a reassuringly friendly but business-like way. "I don't think we've met before. I'm Detective Inspector Towgood."

Rachael was well aware of who this was. Daniel Towgood was something of a legend in the local force. He had been awarded a gallantry medal for outstanding bravery while he was still a police constable and had quickly made his way up the ranks. This was perhaps not surprising as he had gained a first-class honours degree from Cambridge and yet opted to enter the force at the bottom rather than take the graduate fast-track route. The word in the locker room was that he was as honest as any policeman could be expected to be, he would not tolerate shoddy work or unprofessional behaviour and would actively seek to bring anyone down involved in corrupt or criminal practices. He was respected and grudgingly liked by the junior ranks, but the gossip also went that he was not popular with his senior colleagues who felt threatened by someone unwilling to bend to expediency from time to time; maybe this explained why in later years his climb up the greasy pole had stalled. Nevertheless, even the chief superintendent was wary of locking horns with the doughty detective inspector.

"Please sit down," DI Towgood continued. "I've heard good reports about you. I gather you've just been promoted. Congratulations."

"Thank you, sir," Rachael responded, feeling awkward at the unexpected praise.

"Now to business. As you know, a dead body in a state of some decomposition and dismemberment was found yesterday at the mill at the bottom of Winchester High Street. Forensics are still investigating, but it is beginning to look as if foul play was involved. I've already been asked to head up the investigation and I would like you to act as the DS in charge of the incident team. I thought it would be a good idea to have a look at some of the early stuff coming back together before we present to the rest of the group. Let's start with the video of the crime scene."

There was a large TV screen to the right of DI Towgood's desk. He picked up a DVD disk and went across to insert it in a player just beneath the screen. He then closed the window blinds before sitting back down in his seat to control the flow of information with the remote control.

Rachael sat enthralled. The possibility that this might be a murder case was something new and exciting. Yes, she had seen similar images in training, but those were specimen cases, cases that had already been solved by other people.

The video began out in the street showing the mill encased in blue and white police tape with uniformed officers standing guard. The cameraman then moved inside the cordoned-off area and entered the building through the gift shop. A quick pan around showed that this was now deserted but otherwise unremarkable. Then the image focused on the entrance to the mill proper and the eye was led to the stone steps leading to the basement and the millrace. The camera then lingered on the sights that had seared themselves on the memory of Eileen Pennyweather with just a fleeting glance. As the camera panned around, it became clear that it was not pure chance that the body and the decapitated head were still within the confines of the mill. A wooden grill prevented objects as large as these continuing downstream.

There was a break in the broadcast at this point. When it resumed, it was clearly sometime later as the body, and the head were shown laid out on the floor with the blood-soaked sacking in context next to the body. The camera ranged slowly from top to bottom on each object in turn. The sacking was shredded to the point where it was remarkable that it remained as a single entity, the body was lacerated horribly with the left arm below the elbow hanging on by a few sinews, and the head showed features but was shockingly inhuman and devoid of any semblance of having been alive.

Rachael had to close her eyes for a second or two when the facial features came into view. She hoped that DI Towgood had not noticed this and that outwardly at least she had managed to maintain professional composure. He remained apparently detached from any emotion whilst viewing these scenes, calmly pressing the stop button on the remote once the slow inspection by the camera was complete.

"Rather horrible, I'm afraid," he said as he got up to open the window blinds and retrieve the disk from the DVD player. "The forensic labs have not been able to ascertain a cause of death yet. The injuries, I am told, are potentially consistent with the body in the sack being caught up in the waterwheel. The force of the wheel is apparently enough to explain both the lacerations and the decapitation. The death itself may have occurred much earlier. Have you any observations, DS Goodfellow?"

Rachael, rather taken aback at being put on the spot, felt she needed to say something reasonably intelligent if not exactly earth-shattering.

"The fact that the body was tied up in a sack strongly indicates to me that there was foul play, and it was not just an accident. Maybe he was killed upstream, his body bundled into a sack, and then thrown into the river. The current brought it to the mill where it became caught up and mangled."

"Quite so," Towgood said, apparently with approval. "However, let's not be jumping ahead of ourselves on so little evidence. Facts, facts, facts, every assertion must be backed up by facts. We have so few of those at the moment and I fear the watery nature of our crime scene may make fingerprints and extraneous DNA hard to come by. My own view, like yours, is leaning towards the idea that any crime that occurred was committed upstream from the mill and it is probably just coincidence that the body was discovered at the mill. Excuse me…"

Towgood's phone rang, interrupting his train of thought. Rachael waited patiently trying to look as if she wasn't trying to work out what the conversation was about from the interjections at this end of the line.

"That's good news," Towgood said enthusiastically as he put the phone down. "We've been given the go-ahead to set up the incident room. I'll let you go to get things ready. This is by far the most serious case we've got at the moment so if you have any problems obtaining the equipment or personnel you need, let me know and I will shout at a few people. Our first team briefing will be tomorrow at eight. In the meantime, I'm going to check that the river and the banks upstream of the mill are being searched. Happy? I'll make sure you get access to all the notes and forensics data as it comes in."

"Thank you, sir," Rachael responded as she got up to leave the room. She was already looking forward to a very busy day.

III

ON SUNDAY RACHAEL FOUND HERSELF standing outside the elegant portico of a large Georgian house set in well-kept landscaped gardens. It was just after lunchtime and Rachael was a bundle of nerves. The house was now a nursing home, the residing place of her mother who was progressively deteriorating from an Alzheimer's type condition. How was she going to be? Some days she would seem bright and almost normal except for a shocking short-term memory; other days she would be sullen and angry, acting like a petulant child, confusing Rachael with her sister or even her mother, and refusing to cooperate.

She entered into the large hall area and rang the bell for attention. After a couple of minutes, the matron came bustling down the stairs. She was a wonderful woman who seemed to have endless patience and an unbelievably positive and practical outlook on life. Many was the time that Rachael had benefitted from her kind words and advice after a difficult time with her mother.

"Hello, dear," she said cheerily as she reached the bottom step. "Your mother's on good form today. She's looking forward to her trip out with you."

Relieved, Rachael followed the matron into the communal living area to find her mother chatting happily to another resident. She was a small lady, stooped with age and with hair that had not quite all turned to grey. An aura of great intelligence from former years still hung about her; even now you could tell that in her youth she had been considered a great beauty.

"Rachael, how lovely to see you. What are you doing here?"

"Hello, Mum," Rachael replied, "I've come to take you out for a bit."

"Really? That's a surprise. I'll have to let Mrs Merkel know."

Half smiling, Rachael responded, "It's OK, everything is arranged."

The reference to 'Mrs Merkel' arose because when Rachael's mother first came to live at the nursing home, she disparagingly likened the matron to the German Chancellor. Unfortunately, in one of her less sane episodes she thought she was being held prisoner by the Germans and so the matron was always thereafter referred to as 'Mrs Merkel', even though her real name was Betty Smith.

Twenty minutes later Rachael's mum was safely belted up in the passenger seat of Rachael's small but reliable Japanese car. Rachael, with a sense that stage one of the operations had been safely negotiated, engaged first gear and drove off.

"I thought we'd go into Winchester. We can have a look around the shops and then go to evensong at the cathedral."

"That sounds nice," Rachael's mum responded approvingly.

The month of May was just around the corner, and they were lucky that afternoon to have the first hints of summer sunshine and warmth. Rachael's mum seemed to straighten and lose several years as she wandered around old familiar territory with her daughter. Rachael in turn relaxed and they were able to chat comfortably and reminisce without any stress or anxiety.

Rachael's mother needed a few items of clothing, which were obtained from the department store which still had fragments of William the Conqueror's castle in its walls. There was just time for a cup of tea and a slice of cake in the café before heading across to the cathedral.

"Do you remember the first time we came in here, dear?" Rachael's mum said, smiling while sipping her tea from an elegant teacup. "It was your first day at secondary school."

Rachael did indeed remember. The day had been almost overwhelming. Although the Queen's School was not huge by national standards, it was immense by comparison with the tiny village primary school that had struggled to have a total intake of fifty young souls. The concept of a form and a timetable, moving every forty-five minutes when a bell went, and having different teachers for different subjects was all bewildering. Everyone seemed very stern and there were lots of things she was told she mustn't do. How glad she was to see her mother at the school gate! That wonderful woman who was always right, always dependable and who unconditionally loved her. Rachael, even now after all these years, could almost taste the cream cake she had had while her mother sipped tea in exactly the same way as she was doing now. The only difference was that Rachael now had to be the dependable rock and her mother was the 'child' seeking reassurance. She suddenly felt rather lonely and sighed.

Her mother, however, had moved on to other topics and seemed energised by giving a fulsome account of incidents from Rachael's childhood and teenage years. A discerning listener would have noted that amongst the outwardly happy conversation there was no mention of more recent years, or of Rachael's father.

A short walk from the back of the store took the two of them to the west door of the cathedral. Even in this day and age, the mighty Norman edifice dwarfed the shops and buildings in the town's High Street and stood as a symbol of utter permanence. Once inside, they made their way slowly up the long nave to the choir where they found seats amongst a small congregation of no more than fifty. Gone were the days when the size of the building could be justified in terms of the number of worshippers. One or two laggardly tourists were politely ushered out into the spring sunshine by stewards and then the great organ commenced a voluntary. Rachael smiled as she remembered how, as a child, she had been terrified when the cathedral organ had been played loudly. The low pedal notes caused the stones to vibrate, and she had been convinced that the whole building would collapse and fall down on top of her. The choir and clergy processed in, the choir with their red cassocks and white surplices and the clergy in their extravagant vestments. Both the bishop and dean were in attendance on this occasion, with the bishop giving the sermon. It was very erudite and intellectual, but half an hour after the service, Rachael would have been pushed to tell anyone what it was all about.

She had lost any religious faith she may have had when she left school. Yet childhood experiences of going to Sunday school and singing in the church choir had given her a sentimental attachment to the Anglican Liturgy. As the light poured in beams from Heaven through the plain glass side windows, just for a moment everything seemed right, correct and in order. Peace and hope existed as the pure sounds of the boy sopranos drifted effortlessly upwards as the choir sang an unaccompanied anthem.

Rachael believed that her mother experienced similar emotions. She was calm and almost like her old self in the car on the return journey.

"The bishop is a sweet old thing," Rachael's mother opined as if she knew the man well. "I don't trust the dean though. He has a sneery face and his eyes are too close together."

Rachael smiled. Her mother had always made snap judgements about people on the slightest acquaintance, either hating or loving people within moments of meeting them. Rachael knew this was a tendency she had inherited too, often wondering whether some of her failed relationships had been due to an over-eager tendency to like people too soon.

"I'm sure the dean is a perfectly nice man, if you got to know him," Rachael responded diplomatically.

"There's something not right about him, dear, mark my words."

At this, Rachael changed the subject and they spent most of the rest of the journey talking about what her two brothers and sister were up to.

Not this time was the difficult parting. Rachael's mother gave her a hug, and with a smile on her face, she went to talk with Mrs Merkel about her afternoon trip out with her daughter.

IV

"COME IN."

Rachael responded to this command and entered DI Towgood's office.

"Ah, take a seat, DS Goodfellow. It looks as if this unsavoury death is going to be a tricky one to solve."

In front of him on the desk were two photographs, one of a small piece of hessian sacking, and the other of a key.

"As I said in the briefing this morning, forensics have confirmed that this sacking matches the material around the body at the mill. The key was found in the bottom of the river nearby. As you can see, it's a car key and has a Toyota logo on the end. Frustratingly, we can't identify the precise vehicle from this alone, and in any case, we can't be sure that the key has anything to do with the incident. It may have accidentally dropped into the water at any time. That's it! Nothing more has come to light. The mill has been thoroughly checked but everything confirms the idea that the body was in the sack floating downstream when it was caught in the waterwheel while the miller was grinding flour first thing this morning."

DI Towgood, tapped his fingers on the desk and then added, "I think it would be a good idea to go and see the area where the sacking was found. The forensics team have finished their investigation, and the land is now open to the public again. It's a nice day and the location is only a five-minute walk from here. Shall we take a stroll? Bring the case file with you and pop these two photos back in."

They left the building and walked the quiet, uninspiring residential back streets until quite suddenly they were in a semi-rural spot with a row of cottages on one side of the street, trees and open fields on the other. A board with the inscription, 'Welcome to Deanside Country Park', stood by a gravel track leading away from the road opposite the houses. They walked along it for about a hundred yards and came to the river. The visitor was then given the option of either walking left or right along the riverbank.

"According to the files, the sacking was found here," Towgood announced while picking up a twig and sticking it in the ground to mark the spot. He then moved a few paces to the side of the river and pointed directly down through the water: "The key was found just here, very close to the bank."

Rachael looked down through the crystal-clear waters, filtered by the chalk at the river's source. Everything looked so pure and clean, she could even see some large fish swimming happily around without a care in the world.

"And that was everything they found here?" Rachael queried.

"Apart from all the litter which the teams have had to spend several days sifting through without any successful outcome. Have you noticed how clean it is?"

Rachael had a look around her and noticed not a trace of a crisp packet or plastic bottle. It would not stay like this for long.

"The initial post mortem suggests the body was in the water for between twelve and twenty-four hours. The experts informed me this morning that the body could have been dumped in the river here and the current could have carried it down to the mill at the right time to fit the events we know about already. There's less than half a mile's distance between here and there."

"What do you think might have happened then?" Rachael asked.

"Ah, now you are asking me to speculate," Towgood responded with an amused smile on his face. "Facts, facts, facts – we must always have facts before we jump to conclusions. However, just this once I will indulge your curiosity.

"Let us assume that our unfortunate young man was killed by one or more assailants. If the deed was done here, it would be extremely unlikely that it would have gone unnoticed in daylight hours. Remember, we are looking at the Easter weekend for the time when the crime was committed. This area is extremely popular with ramblers and dog walkers and from what I remember the weather was good on Easter Sunday, although to be fair, the previous couple of days had not been so good.

"If the deed were done at night, then it was a very meticulous and swift dispatch. Any disturbance or shouting would have been heard by the occupants of the cottages. Besides, would the killer have a sack to hand specifically for disposing of the body? I think it is most likely that any murder took place elsewhere and the body was brought here to be disposed of in the river, probably in a van or the boot of a car."

"Have we any impressions of tyre tracks near here?" Rachael asked.

"Far too many to be of any use, I'm afraid," Towgood answered with a sigh. "In any case, a potential criminal could have parked on the road or in the car park fifty yards down the road without being noticed in the dead of night."

He paced backwards and forwards and looked upstream then downstream, as if expecting some divine inspiration. Eventually he stopped and said to Rachael rather unexpectedly, "Now it's my turn to ask you to speculate, DS Goodfellow. Assuming there is a murder here to investigate, what are your thoughts on the nature of the murderer? I believe you did some work on psychological profiling in your last post?"

Rachael paused for a moment giving the matter some thought before continuing.

"Well, sir, if we say that the murderer brought the body in a van or car and dumped the body in the river in haste, then that all sounds a bit desperate to me and also very unprofessional. Why not bury the body? Or better still why not cut it up and dissolve it in acid? I would say that the murderer was not used to murdering. Maybe it was all a terrible accident. In a blind panic he or she threw the body in a sack that was to hand, dumped it in the boot of their car and drove around wondering how to dispose of it. Maybe stopping here and throwing it in the river was the first thing they could think of. They will know that it's been found now with all the publicity in the press, and I guess they will be pretty twitchy and behaving rather oddly."

"Interesting," mused Towgood. "An incompetent or accidental murderer, and yet by design or chance they seem to have pulled off the near-perfect crime. We don't know who the victim is, we don't know how he was murdered, we don't know where the crime was committed and most importantly, we don't know who the murderer was. Just two clues, and one of those may be a red herring – a small piece of sacking and a key for an unidentifiable car.

"I think the only thing we can do for the present is organise interviews with all the residents of the cottages opposite and hope that someone heard or saw something unusual. Can I leave that with you? I have to give a briefing to the chief superintendent and I'm not looking forward to having so little to tell him about this case. Oh, and by the way, there is a new man, DS Martin Hall, starting today. You could get him involved in the interviews and generally make him feel welcome."

Rachael's blood drained from her cheeks. Surely this couldn't be the Martin Hall she had been relieved to be rid of when she had left her previous post. Had a nightmare returned to blight the prospects of happiness in her work?

"Yes, sir, I'll get on to it straight away," she managed to say through gritted teeth.

* * *

To be fair, the blame did not all lie with Martin Hall. He certainly had done nothing criminal. He and Rachael had worked together when they were both newly-trained police constables. Martin was unquestionably good looking, and Rachael made one of those hereditary snap decisions that she liked him. Martin in turn was intoxicated with desire for this clever, determined young lady who seemed to have eyes only for him. Not surprisingly, it only took a couple of dates before they were spending the night together. Initially the sex was great, and something new for Rachael as her previous experience had been furtive fumbles with hopeless boys when the parents were out of the house. Alas, she soon realised that Martin was very selfish in his love-making, only being concerned with his own gratification. She also soon realised that they had very little in common once the lust had died away. She wanted a soul mate, someone she could have an intelligent conversation with, who would be empathetic to her needs and would be a true life-partner. He (at least according to Rachael) was emotionally immature. He was a 'lad's lad' and would spend most Saturdays at the rugby club. His tendency to get blind drunk after the game with the rest of the boys became more than a minor irritation and she really did not like the sexist and supremacist attitudes of many of his rugby-playing friends.

In the end she decided to call it a day, being very matter-of-fact about the situation with Martin at the end of a Friday shift. She had expected that Martin would shrug his shoulders and say, "OK, it was fun while it lasted". However, she was totally perplexed when he burst into tears and begged her to reconsider. She stood firm, despite the embarrassment of the situation, and made it clear that there was no going back.

Martin spent the next two weeks desperately trying to win her affections back, bringing her flowers and chocolates and begging her to go out on a date with him again. Colleagues started to notice, and they were called separately into their superior's office. Rachael was given a somewhat stern and paternalistic lecture about not letting relationships interfere with the smooth running of the department. By all accounts, Martin was given a much more severe dressing down and told in no uncertain terms that if he didn't desist from pestering Rachael, he would be out on his ear. After that there was just sullen silence from Martin; a blessed relief at first, but eventually it became a deadening weight on all aspects of her working life. In the end she just had to escape. Her promotion and redeployment, first as a detective constable and then as a detective sergeant, had been akin to salvation.

* * *

When Rachael arrived back at Headquarters, it was as she feared. There, without any shadow of a doubt, were the handsome features of DS Martin Hall.

"Do you mind if we have a quick chat in private before I assign you to duties?" she said, with forced civility.

Martin with just the faintest nod of recognition acquiesced and followed Rachael into the corridor.

Looking both ways to make sure that no-one was looking, she launched forth, "What the hell are you doing here? You know I took the post so I could get away from you and start over again. Are you deliberately trying to sabotage my career and ruin my life?"

Maintaining his equilibrium and a dignified demeanour he responded, "Look, it isn't all about you, you know. I want to make progress in my career too. This job came up, I was ready for it, and I would have been stupid not to apply. I'm sorry it means having to work together again. I'm not absolutely thrilled about that myself. I hope you're not going to make a fuss and make things difficult. Let's just behave professionally and get on with things."

This mild rebuke rather took the wind out of Rachael's sails, and she ended by lamely saying, "Well, as long as we understand each other."

The afternoon was spent, with the team, going from house to house along the row of cottages opposite the country park taking detailed statements from the inhabitants. Those houses which were empty, were returned to in the early evening or the following day. Eventually, statements given correlated with all occupants on the electoral register.

On the face of it, the results from this task weren't very encouraging. Rachael and DI Towgood sat down in his office a week later to review them.

"Mm... well, I suppose it was too much to expect that anyone would see the murderer lugging a sack-filled load in broad daylight and then dumping it in the river," DI Towgood mused. "However, there were two things that did strike me as worth further investigation. I see that Mr Smith in number one mentioned hearing an argument in the street between two men on Saturday night sometime between eleven thirty and half past midnight. Who took that statement?"

"Gavin did, sir," Rachael replied.

"I see that Mr Smith thinks they'd probably just come out of the pub. 'The Red Lion' is only fifty yards up the hill from the cottages. Perhaps you could go and have a word with the landlord on Monday? I don't think they open at lunchtime in the week, so it's best to go as soon as they open in the evening;

there aren't as many customers about to cause a distraction. Have a word with DC Trueman before you go and see how he rates the credibility of the witness.

"Now, the second thing I noticed was that Mrs Shepherd in number 23 heard a car screeching away at speed at about 2am on Easter Sunday and there's half a confirmation of that from number 22. Who took that statement?"

"That would be DS Hall, sir," Rachael responded icily.

DI Towgood momentarily raised a glance in Rachael's direction before continuing. "I think I might go and have a word with Mrs Shepherd myself. I might take DS Hall along with me to get some experience. We can both report back to the team briefing meeting on Tuesday morning. Do you think I missed anything from any of the other statements, DS Goodfellow?"

"No, sir."

V

"HELLO, SIS. ARE YOU GOING to meet me at the station before we go and see Mum?"

"Can't you go and see her by yourself just for once?" Rachael responded curtly down the telephone.

"Come on, you know she's much better when you're around. You can manage her when she gets... difficult."

Rachael sighed and responded almost with resignation, "Oh... I'll think about it. Just because I'm here on the spot, the rest of you seem to think I can cope with anything."

She terminated the call to James, her second eldest brother who now lived in London doing some IT job she didn't understand. He was the closest of her siblings in age, but that did not mean she had a particularly close bond with him. He was a remote figure with seemingly few friends, very intelligent with interests such as chess and computer games, but socially awkward and unwilling to open up about feelings and relationships. In fact, Rachael was unaware of any relationship he had ever had, and although he was two years older than her, he seemed destined to lead a solitary bachelor existence for the rest of his life. Naturally, he was hopeless with their mum in her present condition, and as a result, kept his visits to a minimum and always in the company of at least one other person. However, his conscience meant that he did make the effort from time to time, unlike her eldest brother, Matthew, who lived in Birmingham, was married, and had two kids. It was all too difficult for him to visit, what with the children, the distance and his hectic work schedule (at least that was his excuse). As for her sister Ruth, who was two years younger than Matthew, she was of no use whatsoever, having migrated to Australia with her partner when she had qualified as a doctor and got fed up with the NHS after ten years' service.

Anyway, enough of that for the moment. She was putting on some nice clothes to go out in. Gavin Trueman had asked if she would like to go out this evening. Was it a date? Rachael wasn't quite sure. She found Gavin to be a friendly and unusually interesting man for a police officer. He read quite a bit and enjoyed a broad range of music. They found they had quite a lot in common. He wasn't in the drop-dead gorgeous category of men (at least in Rachael's eyes), but he was the sort of person you noticed more and more as you got to know them. She was definitely beginning to find him quite attractive. The invitation had been a rather matey and casual one.

"Hi, Rachael, I'm at a bit of a loose end this weekend. Do you fancy going to see that film we talked about this Saturday?" he'd announced out of the blue at the end of a shift during the week.

"Yeah, okay. Why not?" she'd responded, in an equally off-hand manner – or so she hoped.

They'd arranged to meet at 'The King's Head' which was just around the corner from the Odeon cinema. On entering she immediately saw Gavin dressed casually but quite stylishly, propping up the bar with a half-pint in his hand. She was not pleased to see that the person he was talking to was Martin Hall, who she soon realised was out with some of his rugby club friends.

However, before she had time to think, Martin noticed her and announced in a clear voice, "Ah, there she is, right on time as usual. How are you, Rachael?"

"I'm fine thank you, DS Hall," she responded in a deliberately frosty manner.

"Hi, Rachael," Gavin intervened. "Can I get you something to drink? We've got twenty minutes before we have to go."

"I'll have a small gin and tonic, thanks."

"Are you two on a date?" Martin asked mischievously. Rachael bit her lip and Gavin noticeably reddened.

"We're just having a night out and going to see a film that we're both interested in," Gavin responded as he took his change from the barmaid. "Shall we go and sit over there, Rachael? There's a table free in the corner."

"Yes, I think that's a very good idea," Rachael added pointedly.

Gavin and Rachael retreated to the corner table while Martin returned to his friends on the other side of the room. Gavin inquired about Rachael's mother and there followed twenty minutes of inconsequential small talk. She couldn't help feeling that all the time Martin was watching them and as they rose to leave, she noticed him look over with an unpleasant smirk.

The film was long and, to be honest, something of a disappointment. Rachael was also distracted by wondering how Gavin would react when sat in close proximity in the dark. He made no attempt to put his arm around her or to hold her hand at any point. She tested the waters a little bit by deliberately grabbing his arm in a scary scene. The response was neither one of alarm or reciprocal embrace, but rather an indifferent and ambiguous acceptance that it was an okay sort of thing to do.

They had some more to drink after the film ended at a wine bar in the city centre. Rachael could feel her head beginning to spin just a little. She sensed she was staring into Gavin's eyes and chuckling at his jokes rather too obviously. She still couldn't tell whether there was any mutual feeling in return. It was all rather frustrating.

Gavin chivalrously offered to walk Rachael home (her flat was only ten minutes gentle walk from the city centre). The talk on the way back was all about the film and what they each thought about it, still nothing to encourage any romantic notions. At the front door, Rachael decided to give it one more shot.

"Do you want to come in for a coffee?" she asked, embarrassed at the cheesiness of the invitation.

"No, I'd better not. I've got to walk back to the station to get the train to Southampton. It's been a good evening though. We should do it again sometime, and maybe go for a meal too."

He held out his arms to give Rachael a friendly hug. Rachael misinterpreted the gesture and went in for a full-frontal kiss on the lips. Gavin immediately recoiled and said, "Whooah… hang on a bit."

Rachael immediately realised she had crossed the line and said rather incoherently, "I'm sorry… I'm sorry…"

She rushed inside the house and slammed the front door shut. Gavin stood bemused for several seconds and then hurriedly moved away, hoping that nobody had noticed.

* * *

Rachael stood at the bar of 'The Red Lion' waiting for the landlord to make an appearance. It had only just opened and the only other person in the room was an elderly gentleman sat in a corner nursing a pint and staring vacantly out of the window. It had been a trying Monday. She had done her best to avoid DC Gavin Trueman after the embarrassment of Saturday evening, and as for DS Martin Hall, he seemed determined to make little comments filled with inuendo that made her blood boil. He'd obviously found out that the 'date' had ended disastrously. What had Gavin been saying to the rest of the team? She dared not think about it. She was glad to get away from the office for an hour.

"What can I do for you, luv?"

The landlord emerged from the cellar and entered the room behind the bar.

"Sorry to keep you waiting, I had to change one of the barrels," he continued.

"DS Rachael Goodfellow, Wessex Constabulary," Rachael announced, flashing her warrant card as proof. "I wonder if you would mind answering a few questions."

The landlord suddenly looked very serious and acquiesced immediately to Rachael's request.

"Now I'd like you to think back to the Easter weekend and Saturday evening in particular," Rachael began. "We've had a report of an altercation in the street around midnight. Is that when you would have been closing?"

"We had an extension to two that night, but people did start to leave about then. I'll confess that one or two were a bit rowdy, but it seemed good-natured."

"Did you notice anyone having an argument before then which might have developed into something more dramatic?"

"Well, as you mention it, Ryan was having a bit of a heavy session with someone in the corner. They might have been arguing about something."

"Ryan? Do you know his surname? What does he look like?" Rachael asked, suddenly showing a lot more interest.

"Sorry, don't know his last name. He comes in occasionally. I wouldn't call him a regular. Some of the customers know him. He's fortyish and got a workman's build. Not much hair left on top."

"Ryan Fielder's his name," said a voice from over by the window. It was the old man who had been slowly sipping a pint by himself.

Rachael spun around and looked at the old man, "You don't happen to know anything about him or where he lives, I suppose?"

"He lives on the Meadowcroft estate. I don't know the exact number. I wouldn't be surprised if he was involved in some dodgy dealing. He doesn't seem to have a regular nine-to-five job."

Rachael was immediately a bit wary. This was exactly the sort of thing her mother would say on the basis of no evidence whatsoever. However, she continued her questions.

"Do either of you know the person he was talking to that evening?"

"No, I'm afraid not," the landlord replied, speaking first. "He was a young man, in his early twenties, I'd say. He's not been in before, but there's plenty of pubs in the city centre, so it doesn't necessarily mean he was a stranger in these parts."

The old man by the window simply shook his head with a gesture of resignation and resumed his watch on the world outside.

Rachael thanked the two men for their help. She took the details of the old man and advised him that the police might need to ask a few more questions in the future. She then informed the landlord that a police constable would return the following day to get a detailed description of the unknown young man and that they would be asking customers in the next few days for any witness accounts. At least they had something to go on now. It shouldn't be too difficult to trace Ryan Fielder.

Half an hour later, with the help of a detective constable and the internet, she had established an address and also a previous conviction for Fielder. Nothing terribly serious, a sentence for handling stolen goods. He had got away with a fine, although a fairly hefty one for someone without a regular income.

Just as she was about to leave the office for the evening, there was a knock on the door and Gavin popped his head around. Rachael's heart sank.

"Are you off duty now? Can we have a chat?" Gavin pleaded.

Rachael could hardly say no, so she beckoned him into the room and reluctantly sat back down behind her desk. Gavin sat down opposite her.

"Look, I think I owe you an apology," Gavin began.

Rachael was taken aback by this as she was about to say the same thing to him. He continued,

"When I said I was at a loose end this weekend, it was because my partner was away visiting his parents. I should have told you about that first, but I have to say all this 'coming out' stuff when you meet a new colleague or make a new friend becomes pretty tedious. I'm sorry if you feel I've accidentally led you on."

Rachael sighed. Of course, Gavin was gay. It all made sense now. She was being unrealistic to expect a straight police officer to be sensitive and caring, interesting to talk to and cultured. Hopes dashed again. Rachael put a brave face on it and smiled.

"I'm sorry too. Whatever your sexuality, I was a bit premature in jumping on you like that."

"Don't get me wrong," Gavin hastened to add. "I was extremely flattered. If I'd been straight and unattached, I think I would have been very interested. I like hanging out with you. I don't want this to spoil our friendship."

Friends – that was the best Rachael had been able to manage since the breakup with Martin. However, Gavin was a sweet guy and someone she would rather have in her life than not. She laughed and said,

"I've forgotten about it already. I'm glad we've cleared the air."

Relieved, Gavin got up and left. As Rachael, also rather relieved, left the room Martin just happened to be passing on his way out of the office to go home.

"Rachael, how did your date go with the lusty Gavin Trueman?" he asked with mock casualness.

"Shut up," said Rachael, testily. "You knew all along that he was gay. That's why you were grinning like a perverted Cheshire cat in the pub on Friday."

"My dear, unfortunately *everyone*, except you, knows that Gavin is gay. Hard luck – perhaps you shouldn't have thrown away the opportunity to be with a real man."

Rachael bristled at this and with a caustic laugh replied, "Gavin is a better human being than you'll ever be. Go away and play with your moronic rugby chums."

VI

TUESDAY MORNING SAW THE USUAL daily briefing with the whole team waiting for instructions for the day ahead. Rachael looked around. There were ten of them altogether, seven men and three women. Even though things were a lot better these days, she often felt besieged and outnumbered, battling with the testosterone-filled attitudes of her male colleagues. She therefore sought the consolation and solidarity of keeping on good terms with her female colleagues whenever possible. Roshni was somewhat older than her. She was settled and married with one child in what seemed to Rachael a fairly traditional westernised Sikh family. Rachael got on perfectly well with her, but they were hardly best friends. It was clear that her priority was her family; her career path had consequently stalled at the level of detective constable. Rachael suspected that if she had another child, she would quit the force altogether. The other female member of the team, DC Hyacinth Jones, was a lively girl of West Indian origins. She was much more on Rachael's wavelength. Still only being semi-attached to her boyfriend, she was free to go out and do things by herself. She and Rachael had already spent a fun afternoon going out shopping in Southampton.

"Right, we'll begin by reviewing yesterday's work and then we'll see where that tells us we should pursue our inquiries," DI Towgood commenced. "I'll begin by updating you on my interview with Mrs Shepherd at N° 23, Deanside Lane."

DI Towgood explained that Mrs Shepherd could give a very accurate timing to hearing the car go by as she had noticed the time on her digital alarm clock/radio. It was exactly two in the morning. On closer questioning, he had worked out that the car could not have been in the public car park at the bottom of the road as Mrs Shepherd had heard the car go past the house from right to left. It may have been parked on the verge at the entrance to the country park, but that was a bit speculative.

Rachael then outlined her findings at 'The Red Lion'. Towgood seemed impressed that they finally had a name; something concrete to investigate.

"Thank you, DS Goodfellow," DI Towgood said at the end of the briefing. "We'll put all our resources into that line of inquiry for the time being. I've got to go and supervise a robbery investigation in Basingstoke today, so DS Goodfellow will be in charge. Let's see if we can make some progress."

He left the room and Rachael began to designate tasks. The regulars at 'The Red Lion' were a key priority and several members of the team were tasked with getting posters printed which were aimed at anyone who had heard anything outside the pub around midnight. Distributing them in the pub and the local area was then an urgent matter. Others were detailed to interview any of the regulars who were in the pub that night. A couple were tasked with going through the statement from N° 1, Deanside Lane, and then going back to clarify one or two points with both Mr and Mrs Smith.

Rachael had reserved for herself the job of going to see Ryan Fielder. She had already discussed her plans with DI Towgood who had sternly insisted that she was not to go alone for this interview. She decided to take Gavin with her as he had taken the original statement from Mr Smith and so could spot any anomalies in what Ryan might say about the incident in question.

The estate where Ryan lived was as depressing as Rachael expected; row upon row of soul-destroying box-like structures which resembled terraces of rabbit hutches. They had been thrown up in the late nineteen seventies and the lack of quality was now evident with the rotting wooden facia boards and the peeling off-white paint. The house that matched the record of Ryan's abode was one of the worst examples. The small patch of grass looked as if it had never been cut and rubbish of all sorts lay strewn around the bins. An apology for a porch hung precariously from one side only.

Rachael knocked on the door with as much authority as she could muster; there was no doorbell. A long wait ensued. Just as she was beginning to think there was no one in, sounds from inside became clearer as someone moved to the door from the inside. Suddenly the door swung open and an unkempt man wearing grey flannel track-suit bottoms and a dirty tee-shirt came starkly into focus. The landlord's description of him being fortyish was probably correct but he looked older. He had certainly let himself go.

"Wacha want?" he asked without ceremony or politeness.

"Ryan Fielder?" Rachael inquired.

"Who wants to know?"

Both Rachael and Gavin simultaneously flashed their warrant cards and Rachael said, "We have some questions we'd like to ask you. I'm Detective Sergeant Goodfellow and this is – "

She was not able to finish her sentence. She momentarily caught sight of panic on Ryan's face and then things became confused as Ryan pushed her violently into the rubbish bins and made a dash for it.

Gavin looked at her for a moment. Rachael was dazed and began to have a throbbing head. She was composed enough to say to Gavin, "Go after him. Go – I'll be fine."

After a final moment of hesitation, Gavin turned and did as he was commanded leaving Rachael perched awkwardly against the plastic recycling bin. She reached for her phone and immediately called for back-up.

Considering the police headquarters was less than a ten-minute walk away, it seemed to take an age for a police car to arrive. Rachael was up on her feet again with her second wind when a police car with two constables in screeched around the corner.

"Are you alright?" the first constable out of the car said as he approached Rachael. "You've got a nasty bruise on your head."

"I'm fine," Rachael responded. "It looks worse than it is. Quick, one of you needs to stay here and guard the house. It could well be a crime scene and we'll need to get a warrant to search it. Who's driving? Come with me. We need to find where DC Trueman has got to. He's chased after the suspect."

She hurried to the car with the constable who had been driving and they set off in the general direction that Ryan Fielder had gone. There was no point in going fast. It was a case of cruising around the estate looking out for clues. Rachael requested a call to all available cars to come to the Meadowcroft estate and look out for Ryan. Rachael's head was starting to throb again, and she was finding it hard to concentrate. She tried to contact Gavin several times on his phone, but without success.

Just as it seemed that they would never find a trace of either of them they turned a corner and saw two men brawling outside a shop. One of them was DC Trueman.

"There they are," shouted Rachael.

The constable pulled the car up sharply. Another marked police vehicle rounded the corner from the opposite direction and came to a halt at almost exactly the same time. Out jumped the officers, with Rachael leaving more gingerly, clutching at the door for support.

Ryan was a burly man but not that fit. Whilst he was a handful for Gavin, who was slim and only average height, he could not withstand three additional officers weighing in too. By the time Rachael had crossed to the melee, Ryan had already been bundled into the other police car, charged with assaulting a police officer and his rights were being read to him.

The car sped off to the police station to dispatch its criminal contents with all due haste.

"Are you okay, DC Trueman?" Rachael asked.

"I'm fine, but you don't look so good yourself. There's a nasty bruise beginning to develop and you're going to have a black eye too. I think you ought to go to A & E to be checked over."

Normally Rachael would have protested, saying she was fine, but at that very moment a surge of pain crushed her forehead. Back at the station, a police constable who was on his way to the Royal Hants Hospital to take a statement from a patient, gave her a lift. He very gallantly made sure that Rachael was settled comfortably in the waiting area before going about his business. The wait was long and tedious. Rachael wished she had got something to read. At least she was able to catch up with emails and messages on her phone.

Eventually she was given some routine checks by a junior doctor who was probably younger than her. Everything seemed to be in order, so she was dispatched with a proviso that she was to come back if she started having dizzy spells or blackouts, and was to take paracetamol if the headaches became a nuisance.

The police constable had rather sweetly waited for Rachael when he had finished his tasks and took her to the door of her house. Rachael half felt she ought to ask the PC in for a cup of tea by way of recompense for his attention. However, after her misunderstandings with Gavin, she did not want to give this young fellow the wrong idea. She did not have a comfortable night. Her throbbing head became more noticeable as she tried to sleep, and the bruises started to ache. She drifted in and out of sleep uneasily, having bad dreams about being chased by villains trying to beat her to death.

In the morning she found a message on her answerphone. It was from DI Towgood saying she was to take the day off and only come in the following day if she was feeling a hundred percent better. She felt somewhat deflated. This was her first big case since being promoted and through her own physical frailty she was now side-lined as the investigation was inevitably evolving without her. She had wanted to be in on the search of Ryan Fielder's house, she had wanted to be involved with the interview with him and she had wanted to be at the hub directing operations and deciding what happened next. She felt peripheral, useless and frustrated.

By the afternoon, she was feeling considerably better. Some time to tidy up the house and put some washing on had made her feel in control of her life again and by the evening she was relishing getting back into the fray the following day.

VII

"AH, GOODFELLOW – COME IN," TOWGOOD said in response to the knock on his door. "How are you this morning? Not feeling too sore I hope."

"Much better, thank you, sir," Rachael replied.

They were about to have a regular meeting held occasionally after the general briefing for everyone in the team. Rachael was anxious to get back on terms with the case after her enforced day off.

"The team is working well. I was particularly impressed with how well DS Hall stepped into the breach yesterday and directed the teams you had set up. I feel we are beginning to get somewhere at last."

Rachael was not entirely happy to hear this. As well as her natural antipathy towards Martin, he was also of equal rank to her, and she held seniority by only a matter of a few weeks in position. She felt threatened. However, she managed to nod approvingly.

"Right, let's review what we've got," Towgood continued. "The posters and the interviews at the pub have already yielded three statements. As you can see from the folder, statement 'A' confirms the landlord's description of the young man Ryan Fielder was talking to; average height – probably about five foot ten, early twenties, brown eyes, slim build and casually dressed. Again, it confirms the landlord's assertion that they were having an argument and that they both left together around midnight. In addition, the witness definitely overheard Fielder saying something like, 'I've paid twenty percent of the money. Where's the goods? You promised them today'."

"So, it looks as if the argument was over a business deal that the young man failed to honour. It doesn't sound as if it was a particularly regular or legal arrangement," Rachael interjected.

"Indeed," Towgood concurred. "Now let's consider statement 'B'. This witness left the pub at about the same time as Fielder and his young friend, but he went to the gents' toilet first before leaving the premises. When going out onto the street, he saw Fielder and the young man by the side of the road still arguing. He says he heard Fielder shout at the younger man, demanding his goods or his money back. He also says he saw Fielder physically lay his hands on the young man and aim to throw a punch. The witness hurried away at this point not wanting to get caught up in a fight."

"Some evidence for a possible physical assault then."

"Possibly, but the witness would not swear to seeing a punch actually being thrown. Statement 'C' probably covers a period twenty minutes or so later, but the witness here can't be sure of the exact time. He was taking the dog for a walk and was passing the cottages opposite the country park. He saw a slim man in his early twenties run by on the other side of the road – or at least trying to run. He apparently had a pronounced limp and may have had blood on his shirt. It was obviously dark at the time so the witness could only make things out by the lamplight. A few minutes later an older, more portly man came by as if in pursuit of the first one. Neither of them said anything to the witness. Indeed, the two men may not even have noticed that the witness was there. The two men passed into the darkness of the night. Any thoughts, DS Goodfellow?"

Rachael had already had a chance to read the three statements, so she had considered some of the possibilities.

"How about this? Ryan Fielder arranged to meet the unknown young man for some kind of dodgy business transaction. The young man was unable to come up with the goods, despite Ryan having already paid some money upfront. Ryan got very angry and went outside to beat the young man up as a lesson not to mess with him. It got out of hand. The young man escaped and ran off as best he could, despite having hurt his leg. Fielder pursued him, caught up with him and finished him off. He then dumped his body in the river and, hey presto, we find it at the mill the next day."

Rachael was disappointed to see that Towgood looked very doubtful.

"It is a possibility that needs to be followed up," he said after a moment's reflection, "but we mustn't be blind to other options. Although the description of the young man could fit that of the corpse, we have no definite proof that they are one and the same. We could do with finding some names. To that end, one of the jobs I want organised today is to get the photofit guys to pool the descriptions of the young man and to issue some images throughout the Force. He may be alive and well. If so, we need to find him. Where does the sack come into your theory? It's not the sort of thing you'd find just conveniently lying around. I think we need to find out more about Mr Fielder and consider whether he is capable of murder. Let's have a look at the results of the search of his property next."

Very soon after Fielder had been arrested, blue and white police tape went up around the front of his house. As soon as a search warrant had been obtained a team went in to methodically search through the house. It was an absolute tip, with clothes and belongings lying haphazardly on the floor or on tables and chairs. The kitchen hadn't been cleaned for months and plates, cups and dishes lay on the work surfaces crying out to be washed up. A computer had been found, wrapped up and taken away to be investigated. Apart from this, the search proved disappointing. The highlight was a small plastic bag containing hash.

"So, we learn that Fielder does not have much in the way of domestic skills and smokes a little bit of cannabis to drive away the pain of everyday life," Rachael commented dryly after reviewing this information with Towgood.

"You sound almost sympathetic, Goodfellow," Towgood responded raising an eyebrow.

"Well, there doesn't seem to be enough stuff there to accuse him of dealing and let's be honest, half the population of Winchester under the age of thirty have tried it at one time or another."

"We'll have to see if the computer and his mobile phone yield anything interesting. We haven't got anything back from the IT labs yet. Let's move on and have a look at the interview from yesterday."

Towgood moved to the chunky looking DVD player and inserted a disk. The screen above immediately responded by showing the inside of interview room one. Fielder was there on one side of the desk with the duty solicitor sitting next to him. On the other was DC Michael Yapp, one of Rachael's team and DC Hyacinth Jones. DC Yapp was the first to speak doing the honours by introducing all the participants and stating the interview had commenced at 18.45 hours on the previous day. The formalities over, DC Yapp commenced his questioning.

"At 11.10 am, two days ago, two officers called around at your house to ask you some questions. Why did you respond by assaulting one of the officers and running off?"

"'ere – don't give me that. I only gave her a little push," Fielder responded. "T'weren't my fault she tripped up and fell in the bins. That's no assault. You're not getting me on that."

"And why did you run off?" DC Yapp persisted.

"Don't like police very much. They've fitted me up once. Probably goin' to do it ag'in."

"So where were you planning to go?" Hyacinth asked.

"Nowhere. Just hang about the estate 'til you was gone."

DC Yapp continued the questioning.

"You were seen having an argument in the street outside 'The Red Lion' public house at around midnight on the Saturday before Easter. Who was the person you were arguing with?"

"Don't know," was the curt reply.

"Come on. You don't expect me to believe that? You were seen talking to him in the pub by several witnesses for at least half an hour before you went outside. Who was he?"

"I don't know. I dealt with the guy's boss on the internet. He was just a contact. Was s'pposed to arrange delivery of the goods, but said there'd been a problem."

"…And this made you angry?" Hyacinth interjected.

"Angry? Bloody livid, darling, I'd already paid two hundred quid as a down payment. I've been bloody shafted."

"Were you angry enough to hit the other man? Did you injure him?" Hyacinth asked again.

"Look, I shouted, put my hands on his collar and threatened him, but I didn't hit him in the end. Honest truth."

Michael now took over the questioning. "So, can you explain to me why we have an eyewitness account of a man trying to run away from the area with a pronounced limp and blood on his shirt pursued by someone who looks uncannily like you?"

"He was limping when he came in the pub. Don't know about the blood. I was chasing him 'cause we had unfinished business."

"Did you catch up with him?"

"Nah. He was too quick for me. Haven't seen him since. Can't get in touch with his boss neither."

"What was the business you were conducting?"

"Garden gnomes and other outdoor ornaments. I was tipped off that a whole stash was going cheap. I was going to buy some and flog them off at car boot sales now the summer months are here."

"Why such a cloak and dagger business? Why couldn't you deal with the boss directly?" Hyacinth asked.

On the video Ryan could be seen shrugging his shoulders at which point the solicitor leant over and said something to Fielder. This seemed to act like a trigger to end proceedings and DC Yapp went through the closing protocol before the screen went blank.

"Not really giving much away, is he?" Towgood commented. "We'd better send out a request to check for any reports of gnomes being stolen from garden centres in the county."

Rachael was about to chortle at this but then throttled it back to a cough when she saw that Towgood was deadly serious.

"Right, so there's the photofit to organise and distribute and the garden gnomes to investigate. Should we carry on looking for witnesses to Fielder's argument outside the pub?"

"I think so," Towgood responded. "Look out especially for anybody who heard any of the conversation going on between them. Oh, and there's one other thing. Forensics came back with a rather odd finding this morning. The fibres of the sacking around the body are a match for the type of sacking used by the miller at the city mill to store his flour. I'd like you to go and interview him as I've got to go back to Basingstoke again to supervise this robbery case."

He gathered together some papers as Rachael rose to leave the room. As she was detailing tasks to the team, he swept out of the office altogether. She wondered how he managed to keep on top of this investigation while having to supervise others at the same time. It must be confusing.

It was a glorious sunny day, so Rachael decided to walk down to the mill which was only five minutes away by foot. The building was an oasis of idyllic calm with the water burbling happily through the millrace. There was not the slightest sign that this had been the spot where a brutal murder had been discovered so recently. She entered the gift shop area where there was a small sprinkling of mainly elderly visitors. She showed her warrant card to the volunteer on the admissions desk and asked to see the miller. She was directed to the upper storey where the continuous low grumbling sound told her that the mill was operating and grinding corn.

"Hello," said the miller, "I can't stop the milling once it is going. Do you mind if I carry on while we talk?"

Rachael did mind as she would have to shout uncomfortably to be heard, but at this preliminary stage she was prepared to be flexible.

"I'm interested in the sacks that the corn comes in," she boomed.

The miller raised an eyebrow, obviously not understanding what Rachael was getting at. "What do you do with the sacks when you've finished with them?" she continued. "Is it usual for the sacks to be made out of Jute in this day and age?"

The miller smiled as he crossed the room to check on a feeder which was passing the corn down to be ground between the massive millstones.

"You know what the National Trust are like. They always want things done the traditional way and are keen to be seen protecting the environment. Modern commercial milling would probably use polypropylene sacks. As to what we do with them, we return them to our suppliers if they are in good nick. If not, we let local schools and charities have them. If they are full of holes, we compost them."

"Can you recall specifically which organisations you've given empty sacks to in the last six months, say?" Rachael asked hopefully.

"Oh, that's a very tall order. It's done on a very ad hoc basis. I don't always know when my colleagues have given them away. I remember giving some to St Aethelberga's Primary School a few weeks back so that they could use them to do the sack race on sports' day, and I remember letting the cathedral have some to make a nativity scene and use for general storage just before Christmas."

Rachael took the miller's particulars and thanked him for his help. She was glad to get away from the noisy confined space and head back out into the fresh air.

VIII

IT WAS SUNDAY MORNING. RACHAEL was not looking forward to the day. She was on the platform of Winchester railway station waiting for the London train to arrive. Much against her better judgement, she had finally agreed to meet up with James before going and seeing their mother together. The snake-like train slowed to a halt and Rachael looked up and down the platform hoping to catch sight of James. There he was, emerging from the final carriage. An emaciated figure, as thin as a beanpole, with curly fair hair that was beginning to thin, caught Rachael's eye and started to move towards her as the train set off again. They embraced formally and James said to his sister,

"Hi, sis. How are you keeping?"

Rachael politely replied that she was in good health, and all was well. She suggested going to have something to eat in town before heading to the nursing home to see their mother. James concurred and they made their way on foot to a pub that did a Sunday carvery in the centre of town. Rachael had no interest in James' geeky IT job and James had no interest in Rachael's adventures in the police force. Conversation was therefore somewhat stilted with plenty of head-nodding, but very little listening to each other. With relief they settled the bill and headed for Rachael's flat to pick up her car.

The day was overcast and grey and although it probably wouldn't rain, Rachael felt the weather mirror her sense of foreboding about the afternoon.

"How's she been?" James asked as the car entered the long drive that wound its way around to the entrance of the nursing home.

"She was on good form the last time I saw her. I took her to evensong at the cathedral. That always seems to calm her."

Mrs Merkel was in the foyer and looked a bit more serious than usual.

"Your mother has had a bit of a difficult night, dear," she said to Rachael. "She may be awkward to handle today. You've got my number if things get really difficult."

Rachael's heart sank. This was the last thing she wanted to hear. Her mother looked sullen and grumpy as she was led into the foyer area.

"Look who's here. It's Rachael and James," Mrs Merkel said brightly. "They've come to take you out for the afternoon."

"Huh, I wish they'd come to take me away from here for good. I want to go home. I don't like it here," Rachael's mother replied testily. She did, however, greet James and Rachael with a hug but said to James, "Why are you looking so old? You're not feeding yourself properly. What happened to my beautiful boy?"

James just turned red and opened and shut his mouth like a goldfish. He hadn't a clue how to respond. Rachael became cajoling and led her mother out to the car. Rachael's mother was deliberately placed in the front passenger seat and James sat in the back. Fortunately, she cheered up a bit as they drove off and she started to reminisce with Rachael's encouragement. James remained fairly taciturn.

They had planned to take their mother into town and just have a wander around the shops. Their mother had always been keen on getting bargains when she was younger, and still enjoyed rummaging around to find the best prices. This went fairly well and despite some grumpy comments about the rate of inflation, their mother was duly entertained for a good hour and a half. The sun even broke through the clouds to give a more optimistic perspective on the world.

Rachael risked going for a cup of tea in one of the cafes at the far end of the High Street. It was a little quieter there and it was now nice enough to sit outside away from too many people. The waitress brought a big pot of tea with three teacups and saucers. They each had a slice of cake too (Rachael was careful to choose something for her mum which she knew to be one of her favourites). James relaxed a little and he and Rachael talked for twenty minutes or so about the other members of the family and shared childhood memories while their mother listened in, sipping her tea. Then out of the blue she suddenly said,

"I don't know how I can afford to live at that big house, I haven't got any money."

"Don't worry about that. We are sorting that out for you," Rachael replied.

"Really? I don't know where all my money went. I used to have a lot."

"Mother, don't worry about it," Rachael pleaded, knowing exactly where this conversation was heading.

"I think someone has stolen my money."

"No-one's stolen your money."

"Yes, they have, we must contact the police immediately."

"We're looking after your money for you, so you don't lose it."

Rachael knew this was going to lead to a very awkward exchange as she and her siblings had taken out an enduring power of attorney to manage their mother's finances after much arm-twisting and reluctance from a proud and independent woman.

"Has that awful man stolen my money? I bet he's spent it on that floozy."

'That awful man' was Rachael's father, an inadequate and devious individual who was incapable of keeping Rachael's mother satisfied and in the end was forced to divorce her. Whether there was any adultery involved was a matter of conjecture.

"No, your ex-husband has not stolen your money."

"Then someone else in the family has stolen it. Has Matthew taken it? Is that why he never comes to see me? He's run off with it."

Rachael's mother was becoming extremely agitated and people on neighbouring tables were beginning to stare.

"I think it's time to go," Rachael announced. "Can you go and settle the bill, James please?"

"I don't think I've got enough change on me, sis," James said rather pathetically.

"For goodness' sake, James. They take plastic," she snapped at him. James duly went to pay with his head hung low. Rachael fussily got her mother's coat from the back of the chair and started to help her put it on, just as if she was a little toddler needing help with dressing. She could feel her mother shaking. James returned and they began the awkward journey back to the car. Rachael tried to set a bold pace with her mother trailing behind and James acting as backstop. Rachael was on edge as she heard her mother chuntering behind her, but at least she was still following.

"Who's stolen my money? .... Why am I being held prisoner by the Germans?... Your father's responsible for stealing the house."

Rachael ignored these comments, but she could have throttled James for not trying to engage with his mother more. He couldn't accept that he was no longer the child and that he now had adult responsibilities to other members of his family. As always, it was Rachael who had to take on the burden of carer. They got to the car somehow, but then all of a sudden, their mother stopped short as if stuck to the ground.

"I'm not going back to that prison," she said adamantly. "You can't make me. I want to go back to my house."

"You can't, Mother," Rachael responded, really anxious now. "We explained that we had to sell the house so you could be looked after by all those nice people at Rose Hill Lodge."

"They stop me going out. I hate it," her mother squealed.

"You like it there really," Rachael said desperately. "You don't have to cook or clean, and everything is organised for you."

"If I can't go home, why can't I come and live with you?"

Rachael's mother looked with desperate longing in her face. A tear came to Rachael's eye. This was unfair. It was unintentional emotional blackmail. Rachael loved her mother, but she had her life to live. She loved her job, and she loved the freedom it gave her to live in an independent and fulfilling manner. Why should she give all this up to be stuck as a carer to an ungrateful and increasingly difficult woman when her three siblings expected to carry on with their lives as if nothing was amiss? She wasn't prepared to do it.

"Don't be awkward," Rachael shouted, as if speaking to a naughty child. "Get in the car and don't be so stupid."

Rachael was terrified, James was taken aback and remarkably their mother did exactly as she was told. She obediently got into the front passenger seat and put on her seat belt, but Rachael could sense she was a broken soul. James, without saying a word got into the back seat, like a ghost who was trying not to be noticed. Rachael stood still for a moment, breathing deeply, trying to compose herself. She then opened the driver's door and settled herself in. Before setting off, she reached across for her mother's hand and held it firmly. It was of some solace to find that her mother responded by squeezing hers in return.

The journey back was thick with silence. There was nothing to say. Only the constant hum of the engine and the noise of the tyres on the road accompanied the gloom. Rachael didn't even attempt to lighten the atmosphere by putting the radio on. What was the point? When they arrived back at the lodge, she sternly told James to stay in the car, swiftly moved around to the passenger's side and helped her mother out. Thankfully, all resistance seemed to have been spent. Rachael's mother meekly got out of the car and with Rachael's guidance moved towards the front door. Mrs Merkel, as if by some sixth sense that all was not well was at the door to greet them.

"Did you have a nice time, dear?" she inquired jovially.

"Yes, thank you," Rachael's mother responded formally.

Rachael followed her mother into the hall, but at a sign from Mrs Merkel she stopped. Mrs Merkel said to her mother, "Edna has been asking after you today, why don't you go and have a chat with her in the lounge? She's had some visitors today. You can exchange your news."

Rachael's mother went off as if she didn't have a care in the world. The afternoon's outburst seemed completely forgotten.

"I take it you had a difficult afternoon?" Mrs Merkel said, taking Rachael's arm sympathetically. Rachael was now desperately trying to hold back the tears.

"Try not to take it to heart," she continued. "You will still have some good days too."

Rachael composed herself enough to thank Mrs Merkel for everything she was doing for her mother. She then walked back to the car to take James to the station. She didn't feel like talking to him, so the funereal atmosphere persisted.

At the station while they were waiting on the platform for a train back to London, James muttered thanks to his sister for accompanying him today. For no apparent reason this acted as the trigger for Rachael to vent forth.

"Yes, well don't ever ask me to do that again. Next time have the backbone to go and visit Mother by yourself – or perhaps take that no-good elder brother who can't be bothered with you too. I'm sick and tired of having to carry the burden of caring for her. Just because I'm here on the spot, it doesn't excuse the rest of you from taking your share of the burden and the responsibility."

She went on in a similar vein for several minutes. Did it make her feel any better? Not really. She had wanted James to respond robustly, to defend himself and to clear the air between them. However, he just stood there, taking the full force of Rachael's tongue, with tears welling up in his eyes.

"I'm sorry… so, so sorry," he mumbled as the train pulled in and he stepped pathetically into a carriage to find a seat.

As she drove the short distance back to her house, tears welled up in Rachael's eyes. She now understood how sad and lonely a figure her brother really was. Unable to cope with the world, unable to form meaningful relationships even with his family, he was drifting through life just hoping to get through somehow. No joy, no hope, he would end his days alone, friendless and with no-one to care.

She got her mobile phone out as soon as she got in and sent James a text apologising for her rant and assuring him of her love. The response was simply, 'Thanks x' – but that was enough.

IX

RACHAEL WAS RELIEVED TO HAVE the distraction of work on Monday. It turned out to be a very intense day. DI Towgood was planning to interrogate Ryan Fielder himself. There was some urgency to the matter as the offences he had been charged with so far were fairly trivial and would not justify a request for bail being turned down. Towgood and Rachael spent a good couple of hours planning how the interview should be conducted. Towgood wanted Rachael in with him, principally as an observer to gauge Fielder's reactions at key moments when it was hoped he might be caught off guard. As it turned out, it was the early afternoon before Fielder with his lawyer sat opposite Towgood and Rachael in the interview room with Towgood going through the formalities for the recording machine. Towgood then went through much of the questioning again that DC's Yapp and Jones had already conducted. When he was happy that he was getting consistent, if unhelpful answers, he branched out a little further.

"Since your last interview we have had an opportunity to look at your phone and computer. You stated that you did not know the young man who you were arguing with on Easter Saturday evening but were in contact with his boss. Would you mind looking through these numbers that you called in the last month and tell me which one corresponds to your contact?"

Towgood slid over a sheet of paper which contained a list of dates, times, telephone numbers and durations of calls. Fielder eyed it suspiciously, and then said very defensively, "Can't remember."

"Let me try and help you," Towgood responded dryly. He pointed to the sheet of paper and continued, "This number here seems to have been rung at regular intervals over the last few months. Could that be your contact?"

"Might be," Fielder mumbled, "but as I said last time, nobody's answering these days."

"Fortunately for you, we've already checked that number and discovered you are telling the truth. No-one appears to be answering."

There was a long pause before Towgood continued.

"Look, we are not overly concerned with your petty criminal activities handling stolen goods. Admittedly you run the risk of a small custodial sentence with your previous record, but you are here principally to help in a murder investigation."

She had been expecting Towgood to say this. Rachael looked at Fielder intently and noticed a flicker of surprise and disconnection when murder was mentioned.

"On Easter Monday, the body of a young man was discovered badly mangled at Winchester Mill. You've probably heard about this from the radio and TV. What you don't know is that we have compelling evidence that the body was dumped in the river just yards from where you were having an argument with this young man who has apparently gone missing. From witness statements, it seems he is about the same height and build as the corpse we have. I think you can see where I am going with this. We have no names or means of identification yet, but we do have this coincidence of circumstances." Leaning over the desk to emphasise his point, Towgood continued, "You, my friend, are the prime suspect in a murder investigation. I would therefore suggest you should be a bit more cooperative and provide us with some hard facts and information which will clear your name."

Towgood deliberately sat back and folded his arms, saying nothing but fixing Fielder with a stare that challenged him to remain silent.

Rachael, again expecting this, was watching Fielder's reactions as the bombshell was delivered. He seemed genuinely taken by surprise at the mention of the murder investigation and showed real signs of panic when it was implied that he was the chief suspect.

"Look, I ain't a murderer," Fielder blustered. "I admit I've done some dodgy deals, but I don't deserve to be fitted up for murder."

"Then we need some information. You can start by giving me the name of your contact who you can no longer call."

Fielder's lawyer whispered something in his ear which he apparently didn't like. He responded to Towgood hesitantly, "I can't, I'd be wrecking my chances of getting any more work."

Towgood raised his voice slightly, "I don't think what you do can properly be described as 'work'. A name please."

Silence.

"... a NAME!"

"Alright, alright... It's a guy called Gus Kenwood. He runs a house clearance business and well... maybe handles a few dodgy items on the side."

"Would you like to elaborate on the nature of your business with Mr Kenwood? Perhaps there is more you'd like to tell us now."

"Honest, Guv'nor – I've been telling the honest truth about that. He had this bulk order of garden ornaments he wanted to shift. He was going to let me have them for a knock down price so I could flog them at car boot sales and the like."

"Why not just go and collect them from his shop?"

"He didn't want them on the premises. He didn't want to be seen to be connected with them in any way. This guy I met, the one you think I murdered, was supposed to bring the stuff to me, but he didn't have it... Said that he couldn't get into the warehouse to get the boxes. He didn't know why there was no-one there. He couldn't say when I would get the goods. I'd already paid money upfront. You can see why I got angry."

Towgood looked at Fielder very intently for a few minutes and then continued. "Tell me again, very carefully, what happened when you and the young man went outside the pub – every detail you can think of please."

"The young guy who was supposed to bring the goods was leaving. I went outside with him to protest. Yes alright, I'll admit I did grab his shirt and shaped to hit him, but I didn't lay a finger on him otherwise, I swear. He broke free and ran off down the road. I tried to catch up with him, but even with his limp he was always going to outrun me."

"How far did you get before you gave up the chase?"

"Not far, the end of that row of cottages opposite the river. He was nowhere to be seen by then anyway."

"Did you hear a car drive off?"

Fielder was surprised at this question but considered carefully. "No. I didn't hear anything especially. He might have parked in town, though."

"Now, one final question. Are you absolutely sure you have no idea who this young man was?"

"Honest to God, Guv'nor, I never saw him before or since – complete stranger."

Towgood paused, considered and then said, "Thank you for your cooperation. You are free to go for the moment. Check with the desk about your appearance at the Magistrate's Court and stay in the area as we may well want to speak to you again."

Fielder, rather surprised that the interview had ended so abruptly got up and left with his lawyer.

Half an hour later, having had a chance to have a cup of tea and a biscuit, Towgood and Rachael were seated in his office.

"Well, what did you think?" Towgood asked.

Rachael was convinced that Fielder had been genuinely surprised when the question of murder had been raised. He had become increasingly fidgety afterwards. She thought it was probably because he felt uncomfortable at being caught up in a crime way beyond his depth, although it was not inconceivable that he realised he'd been rumbled.

"I don't think he's a murderer, sir, and unless he is a very good actor, I don't think he knows anything about it."

"I'd tend to agree, DS Goodfellow, but it worries me. The more we investigate this line of inquiry, the more I feel we are being taken down a blind alley. Anyway, we must discover what has happened to the young man with the limp and we do now at least have a name that we can follow up. Let's put our energy into pursuing that."

It was not particularly difficult to track down Gus Kenwood. He had a stall in the local market which traded under the sign, 'Gus Kenwood's emporium of quality trinkets and knick-knacks'. Most of the objects were of little value and little use either. There were novelty bottle openers and pencil sharpeners in the shape of the Eiffel Tower to name but two. Rachael took a stroll down to the market in the city centre with one of the duty PCs where the stall holders were beginning to clear away their stock in the late afternoon spring sunshine. Gus was a small man who was looking after the stall by himself. He wore a flat cap, and his clothes indicated a tradesman's demeanour. He was initially helpful when Rachael started questioning him, but became more edgy and evasive as it became clear that the police were interested in his dealings with Ryan Fielder.

Gus finally admitted to having several boxes of garden ornaments in the shed at the bottom of his garden, but insisted that he had bought the merchandise in good faith through a third party. Rachael radioed for a police car so that she and Gus could travel to his house to inspect the goods. Reluctantly, Gus allowed the boxes to be removed and taken away as evidence, making it clear that he expected everything to be returned in good order. He also admitted trying to sell some of the boxes on to Fielder, and, most importantly revealed the name of the go-between, one Michael Bakowski.

"At last," Towgood expostulated when Rachael reported back to headquarters. "A name that we can actually go looking for. It's not a common surname either, so it shouldn't take too much tracking down. Well done, Goodfellow, nice work."

Towgood paced across the office to where four shabby cardboard boxes that contained garden ornaments sat stacked one on top of the other. These were the boxes that until recently had been in the possession of Gus Kenwood. Towgood lazily caressed the top box and then decisively removed a garden gnome at random from it.

"Oops!" he said, as almost accidentally, he dropped the gnome on the floor and watched it shatter into a thousand pieces. Rachael looked on horrified.

"That's all got to be returned intact to the owner."

"They're not valuable," Towgood responded casually. "I'll pay for a replacement out of my own money."

He crouched down on his haunches and began sifting through the debris with his right hand. A frown crossed his brow. "Well, that's extraordinary," he said almost in a whisper.

Rachael was dying to know what was extraordinary but did not dare ask directly. Fortunately, an explanation was forthcoming.

"I would have put money on finding little plastic bags of white powder inside each of these, but there's nothing there," Towgood explained as he rose to an upright position. "It really does look like it's a rather feeble, barely illegal attempt to get rid of stolen garden gnomes."

A rather more orthodox method of X-ray scanning later revealed that none of the figurines had any drugs lurking inside of them, so the consignment was clean from that point of view.

Towgood, with a rather apologetic gait wandered over to the cupboard where the cleaners' equipment was stored. He took out a dustpan and brush and swept up the mess he'd made and deposited it in a metal waste-paper bin by the door.

Half an hour later, one of the PCs came in with rather better news regarding Michael Bakowski. His mother had been traced to a small flat above a shop just off the High Street.

"Right, I think you and I ought to deal with this one ourselves," Towgood said decisively to Rachael. "Let's go."

X

THE FLAT WAS INCONSPICUOUS. A passer-by would probably not even have noticed that there was a residency above the chemist's shop. The entrance was a ramshackle doorway immediately to the left of the pharmacy. It was unclear whether the doorbell had worked, so Towgood rapped the wooden door with a determined fist. After a while, faltering steps could be heard approaching from inside. A woman in her late fifties with a care-worn demeanour appeared. Towgood made the introductions, and with just the merest flicker of surprise she led Rachael and himself up a dark and narrow staircase to the first floor flat. Once upstairs, however, it was clear that Mrs Bakowski took a pride in keeping her flat clean and tidy. There were two bedrooms, a bathroom and a large room that doubled as a kitchen and a sitting room. Mrs Bakowski beckoned the two officers to a sofa by the window and offered them a coffee. Towgood accepted the invitation and taking her cue, Rachael did the same. While Mrs Bakowski was filling the kettle and getting out a jar of instant coffee, Towgood started engaging in seemingly inconsequential conversation.

"Bakowski – that's an unusual surname, isn't it?" he inquired.

"Not really," Mrs Bakowski responded. "It's the usual story. My husband's father was a Polish airman in the war. He stayed on in England and married a local lass."

"Is Mr Bakowski still around?"

"No. That is, he's still alive but he lives up north in Manchester. We got divorced a long time ago. Myself and Michael are far better off without him," she added darkly as she brought a tray with the three cups of coffee and some biscuits across. She sat herself down in a chair adjacent to the sofa. Towgood continued the conversation.

"It is Michael we have come to talk to you about. Is he your only child?"

"No. I have a daughter who is older. She's very successful. She's got a well-paid job in the City and is hoping to get married next year. What's Michael done?"

"When was the last time you saw Michael?" Towgood asked, not directly addressing Mrs Bakowski's question. She stopped in mid-action and concentrated fully on the conversation.

"A few weeks ago; over the Easter weekend I think."

"…And you haven't seen or heard of him since?"

"He comes and goes. He's still got a room here, but he travels all over to find work; it's not unusual for him to be away for weeks at a time."

"Mrs Bakowski, it's important to know exactly when over the Easter weekend you last saw your son," Towgood insisted gently.

Mrs Bakowski paused for a minute and then said, "It was Good Friday. Yes, I'm certain of that. He said he had an important job to do on Saturday."

Towgood gave a look to Rachael, who understood the significance of this information.

"It is important that we track down Michael. Do you know where he is?"

Mrs Bakowski gave a deep sigh that betrayed a whole range of emotions including despair, disillusionment and disappointment.

"He comes and goes these days. He won't settle to anything, and he doesn't listen to my advice. He treats the place like a hotel, except he doesn't pay the going rate for board and lodging."

"Is it usual for him to be away so long, though?" Rachael commented. "It's been a few weeks now."

"No, he's usually off for a few days at a time. It's not unheard of, though. He sometimes gets seasonal work at the seaside at this time of year, and he may be away for as much as a couple of months. I've given up trying to make him stay in touch. He just says he's a grown man and I should stop fussing."

Towgood then intervened, saying, "Have you got any contacts for any of his friends or former employers so we can try to find him?"

Mrs Bakowski was now beginning to put two and two together, realising that the police were looking for his son for a serious reason.

"What's the matter?" she asked. "Has he finally done something really stupid? Has he got himself into real trouble at last?"

Towgood pursed his lips for a moment. Rachael could see he was making a mental calculation. He spoke slowly and precisely.

"Mrs Bakowski, we are investigating a murder. You may have seen some information in the news. It is the young man whose mutilated body was found at the city mill on Easter Monday. Your son was last seen being pursued by an angry man at exactly the time and place where the victim's body may have been deposited in the river."

"Oh my God!" Mrs Bakowski screamed, turning as white as a sheet. "Are you saying, he was the murderer? ...Or are you saying that he's the one that was... murdered?"

She lost all composure and burst into tears. "Why couldn't he behave himself? Why couldn't he be more like his sister? I blame his father." She sobbed at irregular intervals.

Towgood looked at Rachael and asked her to make another cup of coffee or find something a bit stronger for Mrs Bakowski. He then said he would give Mrs Bakowski a few minutes to compose herself and stepped outside.

'Thank you very much for that!' Rachael thought to herself as she heard Towgood's footsteps heading down the stairs. She did her best to calm Michael's mother, making it clear that everything was hypothetical at this stage, and they were just making routine inquiries. Eventually, Mrs Bakowski calmed enough that the questioning could continue. Rachael headed downstairs to find Towgood gazing thoughtfully into the middle distance, leaning against the wall.

"That was a bit brutal, sir," she said with a degree of irritation. "Was it really necessary to tell her we were investigating a murder?"

Towgood raised an eyebrow in surprise, but answered Rachael with a smile, as if he were pleased that Rachael had questioned his judgement for the first time.

"Yes, I agree that was harsh, but if she thinks her son has been murdered, it's likely she'll be more open with us about what he's been up to. Is she ready to carry on?"

Rachael nodded and the pair of them reclimbed the stairs to continue the interview.

Mrs Bakowski didn't know much. She had a couple of possible contact numbers, but she did not divulge any startling revelations as a result of knowing the link with the murder inquiry. Perhaps now feeling guilty at having upset Mrs Bakowski for little or no reward, he concluded by saying, "Now, Mrs Bakowski, you must try not to worry. It is highly unlikely that your son has been murdered or was the murderer, but I'm sure you understand we must follow all lines of enquiry."

As he turned to go, a thunder of racing footsteps could be heard on the wooden steps and a young man burst into the room.

"Hello, Mum…"

Four people stood looking at each other in stunned silence with their mouths opening and closing like goldfish.

* * *

After the shock had worn off, Michael was asked to help the police with their enquiries down at the police station. He accompanied Towgood and Rachael on foot through the narrow streets of the old mediaeval town. Despite initial reserve, Michael was fully cooperative. He convincingly corroborated the testimonies of both Gus Kenwood and Ryan Fielder. Michael Bakowski had been spooked by his encounter with Ryan and had gone to ground in Cheshire with an old school friend.

The outcome of all of this was that Gus Kenwood's contact at the garden centre was sacked for pilfering stock, Gus Kenwood himself was given a fine for handling stolen goods, Ryan Fielder was given a six-month suspended sentence for a number of minor misdemeanours, Michael Bakowski received a caution, and the gnomes were returned to the garden centre.

There was absolutely no connection to the death of the still unidentified young man whose remains rested unquietly in the mortuary based at the hospital. The investigation had been led up a completely blind alley. Rachael did not envy Towgood having to explain the state of play of the murder investigation; an eventuality that occurred the very next day as the chief superintendent himself with a small entourage accompanying him swept into the office and demanded an audience with the detective inspector.

The chief superintendent was a crude and caustic man who had worked his way through the Force the hard way. He had had little formal education and adhered to traditional views of policing. He was extremely determined and self-aware, however, and was able to bend with the times and say the right things to the right people. His ambition was to get to the top, whatever the cost. He would show the doubters that he was worthy of their respect even if he had to sell his soul to do it. He had a terrible chip on his shoulder because he'd not been to a good school or had the opportunity to go to university, and loathed the confident, socially adroit graduate types who had fast tracked through the system. He loathed even more those who had zoomed up the promotion ladder and then turned their nose up at the compromises and effort needed to get to the very highest ranks, making great play of their intellectual superiority and maintaining their ethical integrity – people like Daniel Towgood.

The DI's office was merely a plywood partitioning of the corner of a large room. It was far from sound proof. Any raised voices could easily be heard and understood. Those in the main part of the office, including Rachael, pretended to busy themselves with various tasks, but were really solely concentrated on hearing as much of the sparky interchange between Towgood and the chief superintendent as they could. They were not disappointed.

"How am I going to justify this shambles of an operation to the police and crime commissioner? He's already told me I've got to cut £10 million from the budget this year," boomed the voice of the chief superintendent.

Towgood, maintaining a calm and reasonable manner was inaudible.

"What?" thundered the chief superintendent. "Do you honestly think that finding a few stolen garden ornaments justifies the expense and effort that's gone into this investigation? Garden gnomes for fuck's sake – not even good ones. We're the laughing stock of the tabloid press."

(Again, inaudible murmuring from Towgood.)

"It's no good. You've got nowhere. The murder investigation will have to be wound down and reclassified as a cold case. No arguments – you don't have any other evidence to go on and there's plenty more crime to be solved."

Fairly soon after that, the chief superintendent rushed out of the office, his cronies desperate to keep up behind. Towgood emerged at a more amiable pace and announced that there would be a briefing in half an hour. He beckoned Rachael to come back into the office.

"I guess you heard most of that. We've been ordered to close the case down for now. Oversee the return to normal operations, would you, DS Goodfellow?"

There on the desk were the case notes and forensic photos, and in plastic bags the only two solid clues to the mystery: the hessian sacking fragment and the key.

"Ah well," Towgood said philosophically, "you win some and you lose some."

He scooped up the items and placed them in a filing cabinet drawer, shutting it firmly with an air of finality and resignation.

XI

THE NEXT FEW DAYS WERE very sombre. Much of the time was spent dismantling the operations' room and returning the ten officers in the specialist unit back to normal duties. A sense of failure and frustration hung in the air and people talked to each other less than normal. At least Rachael felt encouraged that DI Towgood specifically requested that she should remain working with him and an additional silver lining was that she saw far less of Martin.

After a few weeks, life settled into a fairly mundane routine of solving burglaries and assaults of varying degrees of seriousness. The occasional murder that required solving was blindingly obvious and only needed careful gathering of the forensic material and meticulous attention to filling in paperwork.

Rachael was eventually due some leave but had no obvious idea of what she wanted to do. She was still single and didn't really fancy the idea of going away on her own, but on the other hand she didn't want to simply fester at home. Gavin suggested that she should join him and his partner for a week in a cottage that they had booked in Wales. Rachael said it was a kind offer and she'd think about it. She was going to politely decline, but then when she was out on a shopping expedition with Hyacinth and the subject was raised, Hyacinth was quite emphatic.

"Are you mad, girl? You need a break. Will do you good to get away and get some clean country air in those lungs of yours. Gavin's a nice guy, isn't he? You can have a nice time without all the stress of trying to seduce each other."

"Yes, but I don't want to be playing gooseberry. He'll have his other half there," Rachael protested.

"Darling, if that was a problem, he wouldn't have asked you in the first place."

So, in the end with some misgivings, Rachael told Gavin she would be happy to go along with them. Gavin seemed genuinely pleased and when the day came for them to go, her first sight of the cottage filled her heart with ease and contentment. The two-bedroomed cottage was built of stone with a slate roof, and was full of character. The owner had tended the garden lovingly and a variety of different coloured roses bloomed prolifically. The cottage was sited halfway up a mountain side with an awe-inspiring view over the sea and as they got out of Gavin's car, the deep orange sun was setting in the west, causing diamonds to sparkle on the water's surface after a roasting hot day and crystal-clear skies.

Rachael was to have the smaller room while Gavin and his partner were to share the master bedroom. Her bedroom was cosy with unfussy white painted walls interspersed with exposed timber beams. Simple pine furniture sufficed for storage and the bed, which was a small double, felt comfortable enough.

Rachael had offered to cook on the first evening and Gavin and his partner, Jacob, joined her in the kitchen when they had finally unpacked and got their room sorted (Rachael suspected that it had taken them so long because they had been making out in between putting their socks in the drawers).

Jacob was a firefighter and had met Gavin at a gruesome pile-up on the M3 when they were both attending in an official capacity. He was muscular and tall, as you might expect, but like Gavin he had an unusually sensitive side to his character. He had a kind, noble face, yet strangely vulnerable. Rachael took an instant liking to him (the family genes kicking in yet again).

It was already late by the time they had finished eating and done the washing up, but they sat up late getting slightly drunk on red wine and whisky and they felt they all knew each other a little better by the time they went to bed.

On their first full day together, they walked along the coast path for a fair way. The weather was still very good, and they were able to dress in tee-shirts and shorts. It was one of those rare occasions when the whole of nature seemed to be on their side. The sun shone, but a breeze from the sea wafted around them keeping the temperature just right. Birds sang and performed acrobatics in the air for them. The sea rippled a beautiful deep blue and the mountains and forests put on their most regal and majestic demeanour.

Inevitably, Rachael and Gavin gossiped about colleagues and work, including the disastrous investigation into the 'Watermill Mystery', as it was now referred to in the office. Jacob was very gracious about this and accepted that he was going to be out of the loop in these conversations. By way of recompense, Rachael made a point of being curious about Jacob's background and asked why he had wanted to join the Fire Brigade. It turned out that his father had also been a firefighter and that Jacob had wanted to follow in his father's footsteps from a very early age. He was unexpectedly open about the difficulties he had had coming to terms with being gay. Not surprisingly, he had a hard time at school. He hung around with a group of very alpha male boys and had to pretend to be interested in the opposite sex to the point of inventing pretend girlfriends. In the end, forced by family and societal expectations he found himself in a real relationship with a girl who had stereotypically good looks but with whom he had nothing in common. It even got to the day of their wedding when he finally cracked and realised it would be madness to go ahead with married hell. He fled the scene twenty minutes before he was due in church and left his poor distraught bride alone in floods of tears, jilted at the altar.

"It was like I'd been looking through one of those clouded glass windows you find in bathrooms and toilets all my life, and suddenly it had smashed and the light from outside poured in, and I could see the world clearly for the first time. I realised I had to stop pretending and be who I really was," Jacob explained to Rachael as they were walking along the top of a cliff at the sea's edge.

"So, what happened next? What happened to your fiancée?" Rachael asked, unable to curtail her curiosity.

"Well, I basically ran away to Scotland for two weeks, not knowing what to do. My best man came looking for me and wasn't judgemental. In fact, he was very sympathetic. That surprised me and gave me the confidence to come back and sort out the mess. As for Amanda, my bride, I was dreading having to explain why I had done such a horrible thing to her, but I had no option. I had to face her screaming at me and breaking down in tears."

"That's sad," Rachael interjected. "I guess you two have never spoken again?"

"Oh no, on the contrary. We're the best of friends now. She always knew deep down that I couldn't love her properly. She's happily married now with two kids and always jokes that I did her a massive favour by leaving when I did. After all, she may never have met the love of her life had I not abandoned her, and she would certainly have been very miserable married to me."

As they walked casually but purposefully along the scar in the landscape that was the path etched out by walkers, probably for centuries, Rachael was quiet for a bit and allowed Gavin and Jacob to talk to each other while politely listening. She couldn't help but contrast Jacob's openness about his past life with Gavin's reticence. Not once had Gavin mentioned any coming out stories or talked about past boyfriends or girlfriends. Indeed, if she hadn't made such a fool of herself after the ill-fated cinema trip, she might not know even now that Gavin was gay. Still, it was a personal matter and not her business to pry.

They ended their walk in a small coastal village which had a very quaint tea shop, just back from the beach. After tea and cake, they were able to catch a bus almost back to their house. They did not feel like cooking that evening and walked down to the local pub for an evening meal and one or two drinks.

Whilst lying in bed that night, gently drifting off to sleep, Rachael thought she had just had one of the nicest, calmest and stress-free days in a long while.

Unfortunately, the rest of the holiday didn't quite work out so well. The second day was wet, pretty much from dawn to dusk. They had planned another walk and foolishly went ahead with it. Even with waterproofs on they were like drowned rats by the time they had finished. Somehow, although the weather improved for the remainder of the week, it had already set off negative thoughts in Rachael's mind that spoilt her time away. She again felt like a spare part, intruding on Gavin and Jacob's happiness as a couple. How odd that she had always imagined having a holiday with her partner and inviting her sad, lonely, best gay friend to join them. Never in a million years did she think that she would be the sad, lonely, best straight friend. It irked her in a totally unreasonable way. Also, she started being fixated on Gavin. She knew it was ridiculous and simply a matter of wanting something she couldn't have, but that didn't matter. He grew more handsome, sexier and more desirable every time she looked at him or spoke to him. It started to make her feel sick in the pit of her stomach to know there was absolutely no hope that they would ever get together. By Friday, she had to work very hard to hide her jealousy of Jacob. The two of them were so easy in each other's company, caring and considerate of one another and not afraid to show affection either. Rachael so desperately wanted this but could never seem to find it for herself.

"You seem to be very quiet," Gavin said to Rachael as they were making the long car journey home back to Hampshire.

"Oh, don't mind me. I'm just a little car sick," Rachael lied.

"Do you want to stop for a bit?"

"No, it's OK," Rachael responded. "I'll take an aspirin and I'm sure I'll be alright in a minute."

The only good thing to be said about hopeless crushes is that they tend not to be severe for long, even if they last for years. Within a fortnight of resuming work, she was able to speak to Gavin again without having butterflies in her stomach, although she was left with an overarching sense of sadness which left the world feeling grey and uninspiring for a while.

XII

SEPTEMBER ARRIVED AND ALTHOUGH IT was still warm, there was a whiff of autumn in the air. Towgood and Rachael were going through the laborious exercise of preparing to give evidence in court for what should have been an open-and-shut case of assault. The accused, however, insisted on pleading 'not guilty' and was wealthy enough to employ a pretty decent legal team. Towgood was uncharacteristically restless. He had been morose since the case of 'The Watermill Mystery' had been abandoned, but he had maintained his usual dignified professionalism. Today it was almost as if he was coming to the end of his tether and required something a bit more exciting in life. He frequently got up while looking through the notes and paced around the room.

"It's no good," he blurted out at about eleven in the morning. "I'm going to get a coffee. Do you want one, Goodfellow?"

"No, I'm OK thanks."

Towgood left and was gone some time. Rachael was somewhat relieved as Towgood's constant restlessness, interjections and sighing had become an irritating distraction and she was at last able to focus on her work. When he did return, it was as if he had been transformed. There was a twinkle in his eye.

"Do you fancy a trip out?" he asked. "I've just been tipped off in the front office about something that might be quite interesting. There again, it'll probably turn out to be nothing." Rachael decided she might as well.

The clouds were thickening and by the time they were on their way in

Towgood's car, spots of rain were beginning to appear on the windscreen. They soon reached the outskirts of town and rather surprisingly, Towgood took a turn onto a small country lane that used to be the main Roman road between Winchester and Old Sarum. The road was surrounded by hedges and trees almost giving the effect of passing through a tunnel. Rachael realised they were heading for the Farley Mount Country Park. They pulled off into one of the car parks slightly away from the monument itself; a shrine to a horse of some rich landowner. 'Not surprising,' thought Rachael, 'in a country that cares more about animals than it does children.'

She was none the wiser about why they had journeyed to this bleak and remote spot, but dutifully got out of the car and followed her boss. A uniformed police constable was waiting for them.

"Is this the vehicle in question?" Towgood asked the officer.

"Yes, sir, just over here," the officer replied, pointing to a sorry-looking car that must have been at least twenty years old.

"How long has it been here?"

"It's hard to say. A member of the public phoned in to say they had been walking their dog up here for several weeks and had noticed that this car had always been here and never seemed to have moved. No one pays much attention to vehicles out in the wilds. The car parks aren't regularly inspected; it could have literally been here for years."

Rachael looked at it carefully and noticed that it showed signs of not having been driven recently. One of the back tyres was nearly flat, a wing mirror was missing and there was a layer of dirt that could have only settled if the car had remained static for a considerable time.

"So, it's an abandoned car," Rachael said with some incomprehension. "Surely just some joyrider who's nicked it?"

"Ah, but no one has reported it missing," Towgood responded.

"I'm not surprised. The owner was probably glad to see the back of it."

"Even so, I have a wild hunch that there is something more to this than meets the eye," Towgood persisted.

Rachael was then taken aback to see Towgood put on some plastic gloves and take a plastic evidence bag from the boot of his car. In it was a key.

Rachael immediately recognised the Toyota symbol. Before she could comment, Towgood had already inserted it into the driver's door of the abandoned car. He turned it and the door responded. He then carefully put it in the ignition and turned it again without disturbing anything in the car. There was a spluttering, an attempt to start, but enough to convince all three who were present that it was the right key for the right car.

Towgood was now fully energised. "Right, Constable, blue incident tape around the whole car park. I'll get forensics out here immediately. It'll need the full works: fingerprints, tyre prints, blood stains, DNA swabs, and anything else you can think of. You didn't touch anything while you were waiting for us?"

The constable looked a bit uneasy and said, "Well... I might have accidentally leant against the car while I was waiting for you to arrive."

"That's a shame. You'll have to give samples of everything tested to be eliminated from inquiries. Let's hope they don't find traces of faeces."

The constable went red and shifted awkwardly from foot to foot as Towgood moved briskly on.

As soon as they were back at headquarters, Rachael was tasked with tracking down the owner of the car from the number plate. Towgood told her that it was to be her number one priority ahead of any other task. Before he could say very much more though, he was summoned to see the chief superintendent who had somehow got wind of Towgood doing something unusual. Rachael sensed that yet another unholy row between the two of them was about to take place – and she was not wrong.

A row between the chief superintendent and DI Daniel Towgood was always experienced by staff in the surrounding offices as a booming rant containing every swear word in the dictionary followed by silence as Towgood presumably replied calmly with reason and logic. The chief superintendent was a natural bully and this sort of response only seemed to make him more and more angry and aggressive. Rachael knew that a colleague some time ago had asked Towgood why on earth he put up with this treatment. He had replied that the chief superintendent was a dull and unimaginative person, and, at the end of the day, he could always get what he wanted from him, whereas if he complained about his behaviour, someone else would come along who was likely to be far more subtle and intelligent and difficult to manipulate.

On this occasion, Towgood didn't quite get what he wanted. The chief superintendent allowed Towgood to reopen the murder investigation but did not allow him to reassemble the team until he had more persuasive evidence that was likely to lead to a conviction. He would allow Towgood to work solo and have access to the services and then review where they had got to in a month.

Rachael soon realised that 'working solo' included her as Towgood's assistant.

"Don't worry," Towgood had casually informed her. "If there is any flak, I'll deal with it. There's no need to worry about the chief superintendent."

Rachael hoped he was right. She didn't fancy having to face a barrage of abuse from the chief superintendent, whom she had studiously managed to avoid so far.

A couple of days later, they were reviewing the fresh evidence they had garnered so far. Rachael had discovered from the DVLA that the vehicle had been deregistered a couple of years ago, but that its last owner had been a Mr Daniel Jarvis, living at an address in Peterborough. From his recorded date of birth, he would be twenty-seven years old now, if he was still alive, that is, and not the mangled corpse that was found in the mill.

"There were plenty of different fingerprints in the interior of the car, but of course the body was so badly lacerated we were not able to take a set of prints from the corpse," Towgood reported. "There was no sign of a blood stain so that's not going to be helpful. There were a few hairs, which might be human, under the driver's seat, a possible semen stain in the back and a few globules of what might be dried up snot. If we are lucky, we might get some DNA from that. I know we weren't able to find any extraneous DNA from a potential attacker, but there's plenty of the victim's own left to identify the corpse. The trouble is that that is going to take time. One more concrete development though, the casts of the tyres don't match any found down by the river, so we know that it wasn't at our potential crime scene at the time we were interested in. What are your thoughts, DS Goodfellow? It's time for a moment of speculation."

Rachael paused, then spoke out loud the things that had been going through her head.

"Well, we certainly have got an interesting link between the car and the possible crime scene. One possibility is that the driver is the murder victim. Maybe he parked there, walked into Winchester and then confronted his murderer. As the killer was about to dump the body in the river, the key fell, unnoticed, into the water. Another possibility is that the driver is the murderer, only he or she went to find his victim and dropped the key while disposing of the body. I also have to say in light of what's already happened that the whole thing might be yet another red herring. Someone may have deliberately abandoned an old piece of junk up on Farley Mount and then just happened to drop the key by the river while walking the dog."

"You put the possibilities very succinctly, Detective Sergeant. I hope to God that it's not another false lead; my career won't survive the further disgrace I would suffer. Let's take your first possibility; there are two things I'm not convinced by. Why did he park all the way out here, why not park in the town centre?"

"That does seem odd," Rachael responded. "Maybe he didn't have enough money to pay car parking charges."

"That's a bit weak."

"…or maybe he didn't want the car to be discovered. After all, it's not registered so it won't be taxed, and he won't have insurance. It's far less likely to draw attention out here than in town."

"That's more convincing."

"…and of course, we don't know that he wasn't killed out here; his body may have been taken by the murderer in a different vehicle to be deposited elsewhere. The victim needn't have walked anywhere."

"Yes, that's certainly worth considering. I'll ask the forensic team to widen their search area just in case. That will please the chief superintendent. Right, my second issue is why did only the key fall out of his pocket? What happened to his wallet any loose change, handkerchief and so on?"

"Well, I do have a thought about that," Rachael continued. "Do we know if the victim's shirt had a breast pocket?"

Towgood couldn't answer from memory, so they opened up the files and had another look at the photographs of the body taken at the scene of the crime. The clothing like the body had been horribly lacerated. However, enough of it had survived to show that the victim had been wearing a conventional button up shirt (probably white) and yes, there was a flap of material hanging loose which might have suggested a breast pocket.

"Right, well suppose the victim had put the car key in his breast pocket and everything else in his trouser pockets? The killer emptied the trouser pockets before disposing of the corpse, but didn't think to check the breast pocket. The key may well have dropped out without the murderer even noticing."

"That's feasible," Towgood responded. "A bit far-fetched but feasible. Well, there are still far too many 'what ifs' about this situation. Facts, facts, facts – that's what's going to allow us to make progress. We have only two new ones at the moment and those are the ones we shall have to follow; an address and a name. How are you fixed for the next couple of days, DS Goodfellow? Can you manage a trip up to Peterborough to investigate?"

"That should be OK, sir. I haven't got anything important down on the calendar. When are we leaving, in the morning?"

"I'm going to let you do this one on your own. I've got to catch up with a few other cases while we're waiting for the DNA to come in. I'll phone ahead so that they can lend you a constable to help out. Make sure I get a daily briefing though."

XIII

AFTER A LONG AND TEDIOUS journey, which involved crawling around the M25 in a slow-moving traffic jam for an hour and a half, Rachael finally arrived at the police headquarters in Peterborough; a modern, clinical complex of buildings on the outskirts, just off the ring road. When she arrived at about 2pm, it was clear that messages about her arrival hadn't filtered down and she wasn't expected.

The duty sergeant was a surly man and wasn't best pleased at having his daily routine disturbed. "This is most irregular," he kept muttering under his breath as he rang around various of his colleagues to try and make some sense of the situation. All of this took another hour and a half which left Rachael boiling with frustration. 'No wonder the crime detection rate is going down,' she kept thinking.

Eventually a woman, perhaps a little bit older than Rachael, came to greet her.

"Hello, sorry to keep you waiting. The request for assistance from your detective inspector didn't come through the usual channels. I'm Detective Sergeant Karen Oakley. I'll act as your liaison officer while you are here. If you need to access any of the services you can do it through me."

"Thanks very much. I'm Detective Sergeant Rachael Goodfellow, by the way."

Another half hour was spent being familiarised with the office and procedures, being given accreditation and access cards to enter the premises.

Rachael was itching to get to the address where the abandoned car had last been registered and finally by half past five, she was able to be on her way. She had a very junior constable, PC Jeremy Black, assigned to her. In fact, it was only his second day in the job. He was tall with a mop of dark brown hair, ridiculously young and somewhat chirpy for one so inexperienced. She would have much rather done this job on her own. However, following one or two recent incidents, the rules had been tightened so that no officer of any rank was allowed to attend an unknown address without a second person being present.

The address took them to the New Fletton area and a perfectly decent two-up, two-down terraced house. The front had been completely concreted over to allow for extra parking, but there was no sign of a car when they arrived.

"Now, we'll go to the door together, PC Black. It would be good training for you to take notes of our conversation. I will do the same and we can see if we agree in the car afterwards. I don't expect you to say anything unless it's a matter of life and death and don't contradict me in front of the public."

"Yes, ma'am."

"Detective Sergeant Goodfellow will do…"

"Yes, DS Goodfellow…"

Rachael led the way and rang the doorbell. An elderly man, possibly in his early seventies, with wispy streaks of white hair on an otherwise bald head opened the door. He had a fine military-style moustache, completely white now, and an organised and orderly demeanour.

"Sorry to disturb you, sir. I am a police officer with the Wessex Constabulary," she announced holding up her warrant card. "Inquiries into a recent crime have led us to this address. Can I ask if a Mr Daniel Jarvis lives here? He would be in his early to mid-twenties now."

"No, I'm sorry," the old gentleman replied, "it's just me and my wife Margaret who live here now. You'd better come in if you are going to ask me a few questions."

It transpired that the couple had been living in the house for about two years. The house had apparently been repossessed by the Building Society from the previous owner and so they never knew who that was. The house was completely empty when they moved in, but things were in good order, and they had no complaints. To be honest, they had got the place for a bargain price.

Rachael was a little dispirited at what seemed like another dead end, but at least she could follow up with the Building Society. On the way out, she noticed a nosey neighbour peering at them through the curtains of one of the adjoining houses. Normally she was wary of involving curious onlookers, but today she thought it would do no harm to have a chat. She went to the door and knocked assertively. This time an old lady with a fearsome blue rinse answered. When Rachael introduced herself and PC Black, she could see the eyes of the old lady light up with excitement. The two of them were almost forcibly ushered into the house before they could change their minds and escape, and were made to sit down in the lounge. In the course of their discussions, Rachael discovered that the old lady lived on her own and probably had a very lonely and humdrum existence. Rachael was providing the most interesting diversion she had had in years.

"We are looking for someone called Daniel Jarvis. We have reason to believe that he lived next door at one time. The people who live there now don't know who lived in the house before them. I don't suppose you can remember who was living there previously?"

"Oh yes," the woman responded enthusiastically. "You must be referring to Dan – a nice young man. He didn't live there long – maybe a year, maybe a little more."

"Do you know where he went?" Rachael asked eagerly.

"No, I'm afraid not, dear. He left quite suddenly."

"Oh well, not to worry. Can you give us a picture of him? What was he like? What did he do?"

The old lady was now in her element. She was the centre of attention, probably for the first time in years, and she made the most of it.

"Well, he was a very handsome young man; tall with tidy dark hair, muscular (I think he went to the gym a couple of times a week) and well-spoken. He had no obvious accent. He must have been straight out of university. I think he had a professional job; he dressed in a suit and tie every day when he went to work. My, he looked so adorable when he was dressed for work! He reminded me of my Lenny when we first started courting.

"I also thought at the time he was rather young to be buying a house. I wondered whether he'd overreached himself financially. He had to have a lodger to help pay the mortgage. Oh, my goodness, did he have trouble with his lodgers! They came and went, and some were really very suspicious types. Finally, he couldn't find anyone who would live with him. I wonder if that's why he couldn't pay the mortgage at the end of the day?"

The old lady continued talking and gradually wandered off the theme to talk about crime in the neighbourhood and how things weren't as good as in the old days. Rachael sympathetically allowed her to ramble on, thinking of her own mother's plight and how lonely and isolated she must feel at times. She scowled at PC Black when he yawned and looked at his watch. Eventually Rachael decided enough was enough. She got up and said,

"Well, you've been very helpful, thank you so much. We must get on with our inquiries now."

"Anytime, do call again," responded the old woman, almost pleadingly. "What are you investigating?" she added as an afterthought.

Rachael hesitated. The usual response was to be non-committal, but why not make it a day to remember for this poor old lady? It really wouldn't do too much harm.

"We're investigating a murder, but I must stress that we have no evidence to suggest that Daniel Jarvis was in any way involved. We just need him to help us with our enquiries."

The old lady's eyes almost popped out of their sockets as the door closed behind DS Goodfellow and PC Black.

Back in the car, Rachael was secretly impressed with the grasp of the facts that Jeremy had recorded from their two visits. She grudgingly told him that his notes were 'quite good' for a first case. She then told him to be in bright and early tomorrow to spend the morning going through telephone directories, electoral registers, Facebook and Twitter accounts and anything else you could think of until they had found Daniel Jarvis.

The nights were already beginning to draw in and by the time she had booked into a hotel and got something to eat, it was already pitch black. When she finally got back to her room, she spent fifteen minutes checking her notes and collecting her thoughts before initiating a video call to DI Towgood. She gave an account of the day's interviews and her follow-up intentions for the next day.

"That's all very good," Towgood responded at the other end of the phone. "It was too much to hope we would hit the jackpot so easily. Carry on and try and track down Jarvis, or at least see if you can trace his timeline. There has been a development at this end. The DNA results have come back quicker than expected. There is a strong positive match between the victim's body and DNA found in the car. In particular, the sources seem to be concentrated where the driver would sit. So, we know that the victim was in the car at some point and probably drove the car there."

"So, it's also a possibility that the victim is Dan Jarvis?"

"…Which is why the timeline from when he moved out of the house to the murder may be just as important as trying to track him down. Contact me tomorrow about the same time and let me know of any further developments."

Rachael signed off. She couldn't help but be a bit curious about the background behind Towgood's head. There seemed to be a bookcase with shelves filled with volumes that seemed to be arranged haphazardly. Was this his study at home? She knew next to nothing about his personal life.

XIV

RACHAEL RATHER ENJOYED THE FEMALE company of Karen Oakley the following morning. While they were getting on with their respective tasks, they were able to chat about their experiences in the Force and found that they had had similar ups and downs along the way. Karen had endured an unhappy relationship with a male colleague, similar to the one Rachael had had with Martin. Fortunately for Karen, her ex had not continued to linger on as a colleague and had promptly moved to another area of the country. Perhaps wisely, she had married outside the Force to a curate who was hoping to progress to being a vicar with his own parish fairly soon.

Soon after lunch, Jeremy marched into the office triumphantly.

"I've made some progress, DS Goodfellow," he announced as if an inaudible trumpet fanfare was accompanying him.

"Well okay, let's hear it then, PC Black," Rachael responded with a hint of irritation.

"The Building Society has copious records about Daniel Jarvis' mortgage and the foreclosure. It all pretty much fits in with what the old lady told us yesterday. He couldn't keep up with the payments and by mutual consent he allowed the Building Society to dispose of the property. But here is the interesting thing, about a year and a half ago they allowed him to take out another mortgage."

"That's rather unusual," Rachael interjected. "I would have thought the Building Society would have been very cautious about lending to a defaulter."

"Exactly what I thought," responded Jeremy. "It turns out that he put up more than half the value of the house in cash and so the amount he wanted to borrow was really very modest. As he still had a regular job, the Building Society reckoned he wasn't much of a risk. Anyway, the important thing is that I have an address and it's not too far away."

"Well done, Constable Black. Good work." Rachael could hardly believe she was saying this, but she was fair minded and warming to this young man who did seem to have some impressive qualities. "Now we mustn't be too hasty. If he's still alive he will be at work, so we'll aim to go about six and catch him when he's just got in. What time does your shift finish? Have you got anything on this evening or is it okay to request overtime for you?"

"No that's okay. Will I get time and a half?"

"I don't know, you'll have to sort that out with your manager."

For the rest of the afternoon Rachael tried to look calm and relaxed and went through Jeremy's notes and rehearsed the questions she would ask Daniel Jarvis although she half expected that they would find the house empty and abandoned as the rotting corpse of Daniel Jarvis would be lying in the morgue in Winchester hospital. In reality she was as anxious to get to the address as Jeremy was.

Eventually, when the clock had achingly worked its way around to the appointed hour, they found themselves outside a very respectable house in the Dogsthorpe area of the city. It was certainly a step up from the house they had visited yesterday. It was a neat three-bedroomed semi-detached house, probably built within the last twenty years. The front was completely paved, but there may have been a small garden at the back. Rachael rang the doorbell with Jeremy standing a few paces behind.

The door opened and a young man in his mid to late twenties stood before them.

"I'm looking for a Mister Daniel Jarvis," Rachael announced.

"Yes, that's me. What can I do for you?"

Rachael was slightly surprised to get this response and she took a moment to find her warrant card and explain that she was a police officer pursuing her enquiries. She noticed a worried expression pass fleetingly over the young man's face as she explained who she was, but he nevertheless invited them in and led them into a small, sparsely furnished, yet tidy living room. Rachael sat in the one armchair and declined an offer of tea or coffee. Daniel perched on the small two-seater sofa and Jeremy, dressed in his everyday constable's uniform, felt obliged to remain standing as it would have been inappropriately cosy to snuggle into the second seat on the sofa.

"Now, we have found a car abandoned just outside of Winchester and we have discovered that you were the last registered owner." Rachael handed Daniel a photo of the car as they had found it abandoned on Farley Mount.

"Ah well, I got rid of it in a private sale. The new owner must have failed to register it."

"Have you any documentation to verify the sale? Do you know the name of the person who bought it?" Rachael retorted.

"No. It was a while ago now, so I threw any paperwork away. I can't remember the name. He came to the house, gave me cash and took it away."

There was something about the fidgety way Daniel answered the questions that made her suspect he wasn't being truthful. She decided to apply some pressure.

"You do realise it is a serious offence to drive an unregistered vehicle and not to keep DVLA informed of the ownership status. I hope you are telling me the truth. However, whether or not the car was being driven illegally is not the issue we have come to see you about. You see, the car has become entangled in a murder investigation."

Rachael paused and saw that she got a very obvious reaction from Daniel. He hadn't been expecting that. She decided to lay her cards on the table in the hope that she might shock Daniel into telling her the truth. She continued,

"A young man's hideously mangled corpse was found in Winchester on Easter Bank Holiday Monday. His DNA was subsequently found in the driver's seat of your former car when it was found. This strongly suggests that the deceased, who we've been unable to identify so far, drove that car, and explains why we must find out what happened to the car when it left your possession. If…" Rachael needed to say no more. She had been going to finish, 'If you are trying to protect someone then you are doing them more harm than good by not telling us the truth,' but the colour had instantly drained from Daniel's face the moment she had mentioned the word murder, and he was now holding his head in his hands trying to disguise the fact that he was close to tears.

"Jack, Jack... what the hell have you got yourself involved with? ...you poor bastard..." Daniel muttered incoherently. Then with an effort of will he continued more clearly, "Okay, okay... I'll tell you everything. When I thought it was only about the car, I was only trying to protect someone who has had enough grief in life already without getting in trouble with the police.

"When I left my first house, I didn't bother to update the registration details. I couldn't afford to run a car and it just sat on the driveway. I thought I might want to use it again in the future though, and kept hold of it. Apart from moving it from one property to another I've kept it off the road. I had been looking to sell it, but no one was interested in buying it and so I was toying with the idea of selling it for scrap. It's pretty old and I wouldn't get even scrap value if I sold it through one of these 'buy any car' websites. I can get by without a car these days, anyway."

"Tell me how you came to be able to afford this property?" Rachael asked, trying to probe whether she could now trust what Daniel was saying. "We went to your first house yesterday and know that you struggled to fund the mortgage then. This house is a step up from that and you're managing to pay for it relatively easily I assume. How come?"

"Two reasons; firstly, I'm on a considerably higher pay grade these days (I'm good at my job) and secondly, my mother passed away and left me roughly £200,000 in her will. That's why the Building Society were willing to give me a second chance. I could have bought the property outright, but I didn't want to sink all that money into one house."

"I'm sorry to hear about your mother. Is your father still alive? Have you got brothers and sisters?" Rachael enquired.

"No, my father died some time ago. He had a job in the City and worked all the hours possible to make as much money as he could. He died of a sudden heart attack at the age of forty-five. Poor bastard, he was never around to see his family grow up and didn't live long enough to enjoy the fruits of his labour. Still, I should be grateful as I'm sure he's the reason why there was so much money in my mother's will. I have one sister. She is married with two kids. My mother left her the family home."

Rachael decided that this all seemed plausible and, although interested to learn more of Daniel's past, she needed to refocus on the car for the time being.

"Now, I think you know something about how your car ended up on our patch."

"Yes, I know something, but not all. About a week before Easter, Jack got very jumpy and said he had to go down south to sort something out. He pleaded with me to let him borrow my car. I said it was illegal and I didn't want any trouble from the law. I even offered to pay his train fare, but he said he needed to have the flexibility to move around when he went down there. He applied every emotional lever he could. He said if I was really the only friend he'd got in the world, I'd let him have it without any questions asked. Reluctantly, I let him have it in the end and gave him the keys. I haven't seen him since."

"Weren't you worried about Jack when you heard nothing from him?"

"Yes, of course. I've been more and more worried each day that has passed, but what could I do? If I started making enquiries, I could have got him into serious trouble over the car. I just had to hope he was all right and was just taking his time sorting out whatever needed to be sorted out."

"...And you have no idea what was so urgent or what it was he planned to do?" Rachael intervened with urgency.

"No idea at all, but something triggered it off. One minute he was fine, as happy as I've seen him in his adult life in fact, the next he was back to being an angry, difficult human being seeking revenge for some hurt in his past."

Rachael paused for a moment to think. After gathering so little evidence for months on this case, information was now flooding in faster than she could keep up with. Secretly she was hoping that Jeremy was paying as much attention as he had done yesterday. She continued,

"We need to know more about Jack. Tell me everything you know about him."

"Ah, Jack Nobel… where to begin? We were at school together – primary school then secondary school – you could say we were best friends for much of that time. I'm probably biased, but he was the nicest person you could wish to know: kind, intelligent, funny and unbelievably energetic. He was one of those amazing people who did everything right and yet was still popular. He wasn't considered a nerd or a geek, because, of course, he was one of the best sportsmen in the year. He also had the voice of an angel and sang in the local church choir every Sunday morning. Everyone thought he had a bright future ahead of him – and then something happened.

"It was probably just around the time of his fifteenth birthday – yes, it was towards the end of year 10 – he was away from school for a week, which was most unusual. When I rang to find out what was wrong his mum said he'd had some kind of a breakdown. He was away for the rest of the term, and I didn't see anything of him during the summer holidays. Whenever I called at his house, his mum would say it wasn't a good idea to see him just at the moment.

"It wasn't until we started school in September that I saw him again. My God, how he'd changed! He was sullen and withdrawn, difficult to talk to and became uncooperative with the teachers. He had several flare ups over assignments that weren't done or flippant or sarcastic remarks that he made. He dropped out of the football team and left the church choir. He lost most of his friends, particularly when he got hideously drunk at several classmates' sixteenth birthday parties. The girls who had been flocking around him hoping he'd choose them to be his girlfriend now studiously avoided him. By the time we came to take our GCSEs, I really was the only friend he had left, and that was only out of loyalty to the times we'd had in the past. I asked a couple of times what the matter was and why had he changed so much. He would never say, but would get angry and aggressive, so I left it, and we became more and more distant. He got a reasonable set of results, but nothing like the ten A* grades that everyone had been expecting.

"He started the sixth form but struggled to cope and became, if anything, even more reclusive. Halfway through the lower sixth he dropped out of school altogether and I saw nothing of him for several years. In fact, it wasn't until I moved into this house that I suddenly got a message from him that he'd like to meet up. I went to see him in one of the coffee shops in the town centre. I remember thinking he looked thin and gaunt, and he'd obviously been through a difficult time. He would never tell me exactly what happened in that period between when he left school and I met up with him again, but I suspect he had problems with drink and drugs and may have even been homeless for a while. I asked him what he was doing now. He said he'd got a permanent job at a supermarket and was looking for somewhere to live (I'm not sure what his living arrangements were at that time). In a moment of supreme generosity, I suggested he moved in with me. He cried and took my hand and said that if he still believed in such things, he might think I was an angel sent to help him on the right road. I'd never seen him cry before, even when he went through his difficult phase at school. It was quite a shock. I offered to come over and pick his stuff up, but he declined and said he hadn't got much and would turn up after work the following day. He obviously didn't want me to see his current living conditions, and he was quite right about not having much. He turned up with a rucksack and a couple of plastic bags and that was that.

"I have to say I was worried at first, wondering whether he might still be doing drugs or drinking too much, but actually he turned out to be a model lodger and helped keep the house tidier than I would have done on my own. It was nice to have the company and we gradually re-established the relationship we had as kids. We'd often reminisce about the old days, but never about the times after he had his breakdown. He put on weight and gradually became more confident again and was even talking about plans to do a university course so he could get a more interesting job. And then he suddenly decides he needs to sort something out and take my car…" Daniel drifted off into silence as he contemplated that this really was now the end of his relationship with Jack.

Rachael was rather startled by Jeremy suddenly coming forward at this point with an object in his hand.

"Is this you and Jack in this photo here?" he asked.

"Oh yes, I'd forgotten that was on the window sill. That must have been taken no more than a couple of weeks before he left."

Jeremy handed the photo to Rachael who gave him a slightly stern look in response. She had told him in no uncertain terms before they entered the house that he was to observe only and not intervene. However, she had to admit that she may not have noticed the photo herself. "Thank you, PC Black, perhaps you would like to put the kettle on and make a cup of tea for Mr Jarvis. I think he has had quite a shock."

"Ah, the lot of the rookie constable, despatched to make tea just as things get interesting. Would you like one too, DS Goodfellow?"

"PC Black! No thank you. We are on duty and please maintain a proper tone."

"Sorry."

When Jeremy left the room, Rachael returned to the picture and stared at it, mesmerised for several minutes. She obviously recognised Daniel straight away, but he was standing next to another young man, arms around each other's shoulders. The photo was a good one, well composed, showing their shoulders and heads. They were both smiling and obviously good friends. It had been taken on a sunny day, probably outside a bar or coffee shop. There were two quite different things that whizzed around Rachael's mind. Firstly, the death had now become personal, and she couldn't help but compare this handsome, happy, lively man in the picture with the grotesque features of the severed head found at the mill. Secondly, she couldn't help but compare the two easy-going figures in the photo with Gavin and Jacob. They looked very happy and easy in each other's company, you could almost sense that they loved each other.

"Forgive me for asking, and this is totally off the record, but you two... you weren't an item, were you?"

Despite his sad demeanour, Daniel gave a little chuckle.

"No, no... NO!" he said. "Don't get me wrong, I loved Jack like a brother, but I had no sexual feelings towards him. I have a girlfriend who I'm plucking up the courage to pop the question to." He hesitated for a second or two and then continued, "...As for Jack, I'm not sure. He was pretty fucked up when it came to relationships. I'm not aware of him ever having a serious girlfriend... or boyfriend for that matter. I was worried that I seemed to be his only real friend. He certainly hero-worshipped me a bit. I sometimes did wonder whether he fancied me a bit too. I hated the prospect of having to have a really difficult conversation with him when I finally asked Julie to marry me. I wasn't sure how he would take it. Still, I won't have to worry about that now…"

He put his head in his hands and left it there as Jeremy returned with a mug of rather weak and insipid tea. Rachael carefully laid the photograph in a light spot and took a photo of it with her mobile phone. She then enquired about Jack's room.

"It's all as it was when he left," Daniel replied. "I respect his privacy."

"Good. Don't go in there. I will get forensics out in the morning, and they will need to go through it with a fine toothcomb. We are likely to be causing a lot of disturbance for the next few days; can you go and stay with Julie? I'm thinking it would be best if you had some company anyway after such a shock."

"Yes, I guess so."

Twenty minutes later Daniel had a bag packed and Rachael drove him to his girlfriend's address. Daniel was obviously quite distressed and was quiet for most of the journey. When they got to the house, his girlfriend came out to meet him and they embraced in a way that convinced Rachael that they were genuinely in love with one another. Rachael returned to Daniel's house to find that Jeremy had been joined by two other constables who were already putting blue and white police tape across the front door.

"Well done, folks," Rachael said. "The property will need monitoring overnight and if any of the neighbours get nosey, be non-committal. Make it clear, however, that the owner has done nothing wrong. Gossip can be poisonous for many years. PC Black, your shift's almost up. Do you want a lift back to the station?"

"Yes please."

As they were driving back, now quite late in the evening, Rachael asked Jeremy what he thought of Daniel's testimony. She was pleased to hear that he'd been listening intently, and he highlighted one or two points that she had not considered important. She asked him to start tomorrow writing his version of the interview so she could compare it with hers.

"You're still very new to the Force, aren't you? How are you finding things?"

"It's great," Jeremy replied. "I didn't expect to be involved in a murder enquiry so soon. It's really exciting."

Rachael couldn't help but smile at Jeremy's youthful enthusiasm which she knew would evaporate soon enough. "Don't get carried away. This is exceptional. Most of the time you will be doing admin and dealing with unpleasant people out on the street."

That night Rachael returned to her hotel room absolutely shattered, but she still had one more important task to do. She put in a video call to DI Towgood and rehearsed the whole day's events over again.

Towgood came alive as he listened to Rachael's account. She could literally see his eyes twinkling in her phone, especially when she downloaded the photo she had taken of Daniel and Jack together.

"Facts, facts, facts; we finally have some meaty facts to get our teeth into. Well done, DS Goodfellow. I'm coming up in the morning. I think we have enough information to pursue our investigations up there now."

Rachael finally got off the phone at two in the morning. She didn't worry too much about the niceties of preparing for bed and was asleep within fifteen minutes.

* * *

Rachael struggled to get up the following day and was about fifteen minutes late getting to the police station. Karen, who was already at her desk, observed, rather unhelpfully, that Rachael looked 'rather rough this morning' and asked whether she was alright.

"Anyway, there is someone to see you in the DI's office."

Rachael went across and opened the door and was stunned to see DI Towgood there, fresh as a daisy. Rachael calculated that he must have set off for Peterborough more or less as soon as he'd finished his telephone conversation with Rachael and driven through the night.

"Ah, good morning, DS Goodfellow. I hope you slept well. Let's start by going through everything that you have found out in the past two days, and I'll also bring you up-to-date with what has happened at our end."

Rachael couldn't supress a sense of déjà-vu as she repeated, sometimes word for word, her account from the previous night. After a couple of hours Jeremy popped his head around the door with a copy of his account of the interview with Daniel the previous day. Towgood was clearly impressed with this and immediately started another round of discussions, forensically examining any differences or discrepancies between Rachael's and Jeremy's account.

Towgood did not have much to add in return from his end of the investigation. The forensic tests had all come back. They confirmed the DNA link between the corpse and the car. There was clear evidence of a second person in the car at some time (but Towgood now suspected that this would quite innocently turn out to be Daniel rather than the killer).

One rather interesting discovery, however, was a small patch of hessian sacking found caught on a yew bush not more than ten yards from the abandoned car. By its side, a short length of rope had been found that may or may not have been linked to it. The sacking was the same type found with the body and matched the fragment found by the waterside with the car key.

"Well, that's all very good. You've done extremely well, DS Goodfellow," Towgood finally said. "After lunch I think we should go and see Mr Jarvis again. I'd like to ask him a couple more questions and we will need to take the test kit to get a DNA sample and his fingerprints to eliminate him from the investigation anyway. Do you think he'll be at work? We can check at the local government offices first and if he's not there he will probably be at his girlfriend's house."

He paused, and then on reflection added, "After that, we'll go around to his house and see if forensics will allow us to have a poke around in Jack Nobel's bedroom."

So just after 2pm Rachael and Towgood found themselves entering a functional, no-nonsense brick and glass building. It took them no time at all to locate Daniel Jarvis, who was immediately able to find a small interview room for them to conduct their business.

Rachael was business-like and efficient in taking Daniel's fingerprints and a DNA swab. Towgood had explained that it was to eliminate him from the investigation and Daniel was totally compliant with that.

Towgood then moved on to interview him and struck an emollient tone when he began.

"Mr Jarvis, thank you for helping us yesterday and seeing us again today at such short notice. I'm very sorry for your loss; it must come as a great shock. I can assure you we will do everything possible to get to the bottom of this mystery."

Daniel nodded his approval of these comments. Towgood continued,

"There are just two further questions I need to ask you for the moment. You said that you and Jack Nobel grew up together. I know that both your parents are dead – and I'm sorry to hear that, but are Jack's parents still alive and do you know where they live?"

"His mother is still alive. I think she still lives in the family home where Jack grew up. As I said to your partner the other day, we lived in the same village and went to the local primary school together. Here, I'll write the address down."

Towgood examined the piece of paper carefully and then folded it away in his wallet for safe keeping.

"Thank you," he continued. "Now my second question is this; can you remember more precisely what day it was when Jack suddenly started talking about taking the car and doing whatever he had to do? In your previous statement you said, 'about a week before Easter'."

"Oof... you're asking a lot there. Let me think. Well... it wasn't the weekend because I remember coming home from work. It was probably a Tuesday or Wednesday. Oh yes, I remember him saying something odd about the irony of resolving the problem in Holy Week, so it would have been the week before Easter. Sorry, I can't be any more precise than that."

"Not to worry, that's actually quite helpful. Now we are going over to your house to see how the forensics are doing next. If they've finished, we would quite like to have a little sort through Jack's room. Technically we need a warrant, but if we can do it now with your permission that will allow you to move back home far more quickly."

"Yes, sure."

"Good… and one last thing. We'll need to take that photo of you and Jack so that we can process a proper image of Jack. We'll take good care of it and return the original as soon as possible."

"OK, just make sure you get the right image. The last thing I need is to see my face labelled as a murder victim."

Rachael and Towgood made their way across the city in Towgood's car to Daniel Jarvis' home. Towgood was in a chatty mood and made various comments about how things were progressing back at the station in Winchester. He was obviously enjoying finally making some progress on this case. When they got there, the blue and white police tape was still in place across the front door, but otherwise the place seemed deserted.

"Hello? Anyone there?" Towgood shouted through the front door which was slightly ajar. A rather frail white-haired man in full protective gear, who could have easily been in his mid-seventies, came to the door.

"Can I help you?" he asked in a weary tone. Towgood introduced himself and showed his credentials.

"Are you here on your own?" Towgood asked with a mixture of surprise and concern.

The man snorted in derision and responded, "You're lucky there's anyone here at all. You'll only get the full works if there is a body. I retired five years ago, but I'm sure you know the forensic service is a complete mess these days. I keep getting asked to come in and cover the gaps. One day I'll say no."

"Have you found anything?" Towgood asked anxiously.

"Depends what you are looking for. As usual I haven't been told very much. I'm just giving the house the standard sweep for fingerprints, blood stains, human detritus and anything that's oddly damaged or out of place. Look, I know it's not standard practice but if you put on the gear in the back of the van, I'll walk you through the house; you can fill me in on the details I ought to know and in return I'll let you have a little nose around, which I'm sure is why you are really here."

Rachael and Towgood found white plastic protection suits in the back of the 'Friendly Forensics for You' van (the current forensic service of choice) along with plastic shoe covers, gloves, masks and goggles. Inside, the house looked much the same as Rachael remembered it. The forensic technician became less downbeat and more interested as Towgood, rather freely to Rachael's mind, unfolded the mysteries of the case so far. This in turn led the technician to open up and point out particular features that might be relevant to the case. It was Rachael's job to note down these points, a job that was becoming more difficult as the dialogue became less formal and more conversational.

It was Jack's bedroom that held the most interest for them. It was a tidy room with a single bed in it. There was nothing on the cleanly-painted walls, except an oblong mirror opposite the window that looked out onto the main street; the remaining furniture consisted of an old-fashioned Victorian wardrobe, a pine set of drawers, a bedside cabinet and a small, not particularly comfortable-looking chair.

Towgood checked the bedside cabinet first. There wasn't much in any of the drawers, but the top one did provide him with the most interest. He found a newspaper there, a copy of the Peterborough Telegraph dated Tuesday 10th April. It had been folded so that page ten was visible and in biro, a particular article had been aggressively highlighted. Rachael watched as Towgood skimmed through the article, his eyebrow raised a notch or two. He passed it over to Rachael who was quite curious herself by now. The article seemed innocuous enough. It was a typical local paper story about a clergyman, Reverend John Randall, who had recently been promoted to the position of archdeacon of Winchester, having previously been a rural dean within the Peterborough diocese. The article went on to say that Randall had previously been a Parish priest in Fenton St Mary, a moderately large village nine miles east of Peterborough and three miles west of Wisbech. Towgood showed Rachael the piece of paper that Daniel had written Jack's mum's address on. Lo and behold, it was an address in Fenton St Mary.

"Do you think we might at last have a connection to Winchester? It looks promising," Towgood suggested to Rachael. He then asked the forensic practitioner to bag up the paper as evidence and to forward a copy of the article as a matter of urgency.

After an hour and a half, they had exhausted all the possible insights that the forensic scientist had to give them and they had peered into every conceivable nook and crevice and found nothing to match the significance of the newspaper article. It struck Rachael that there was so little here to mark the life of the poor unfortunate young man. How easy it seemed to be, even in the modern world, to drift through life unnoticed, uncared for and unremembered. A tear momentarily came to her eye, but she consoled herself by noting that at least he'd had one good friend. The forensics man was itching to pack up and go home so they took their cue to leave.

Towgood was unusually quiet on the way back to the station as his earlier joie de vivre had turned into a more uncertain, pensive state.

"I guess the next step will be to go and break the bad news to Jack's mother?" Rachael ventured.

Towgood didn't answer immediately and then cautiously replied, "No, I think we'll leave that just a little bit longer. It is going to be a terrible shock for the unfortunate woman and I want to be able to release the body for burial when she's told, if possible. I think I'd also like to talk to John Randall back in Winchester first. He might be able to give us some useful background information and I can weigh him up as a potential suspect at the same time.

"You're due some time off in lieu I think, DS Goodfellow. Head home tomorrow and we'll discuss the next steps when you're back."

XV

HAVING ARRIVED HOME JUST AFTER midday, Rachael spent the rest of the afternoon tidying the house and putting on some washing. Her mind was somewhere else though. As well as turning the recent events in the case over and over trying to search for a solution, she was plagued by consequent questions about the meaning of life and therefore her own effort at it. Here she was fast approaching twenty-nine, without a steady relationship, struggling to pay the mortgage on a two bedroomed flat which was hardly bigger than a rabbit hutch and being the one on whom all the unpleasant family duties fell. Was this all life had to offer? The surprising conclusion to all this angst was that she should go and visit her mother tomorrow on her day off.

Arriving at the nursing home at two-thirty on the afternoon, Rachael noticed that at least it was a warm sunny afternoon which would give some cheer to the proceedings. Mrs Merkel was her usual bright, breezy self. How did she do it day in day out? Rachael knew she would be in a state of abject depression doing that job even for just one week.

"Hello dear, hope everything is alright? Your mother is in one of her grumpy moods, I'm afraid. It's probably best not to take her out today. She's sitting in the garden. Why don't you go and join her and have a chat? I'm sure she will cheer up a bit."

Rachael wasn't convinced, but followed the now familiar route through the house to the spacious landscaped lawn and gardens at the back of the house.

Her mother was sat in a deck chair with a large straw sunhat pulled down over her eyes. It was hard to tell if she was awake or asleep.

"Hello, mother," Rachael said with forced cheerfulness. She bent down and gave her mother a kiss on the cheek.

If her mother had been asleep, she now woke up and briefly smiled. "Ah, Rachael my dear. I haven't seen you for such a long time."

"Don't be silly, it's not been that long. In any case, I've been in Peterborough for the past few days with work."

"Aren't there enough criminals around here for you to sort out? Why do you have to go meddling in crime all the way up there?" Rachael's mum commented, rather testily.

"It's a big case which involves a crime in Hampshire. We have to be prepared to investigate all over the country. Anyway, you know I can't discuss the details of individual cases with you."

Rachael's mother made a sound a little bit like a balloon being deflated. "Oh, I do wish you'd done something more respectable with your life," she continued. "Your sister is a doctor; your elder brother is important in finance and even James has a respectable job in IT. Why on earth you had to join the police and spend all your days with low-life scum – and that includes your colleagues as well as the criminals – I do NOT know."

Rachael wrestled with her rising anger to maintain control. "Mother," she said firmly, "you know very well it was the one thing in life I really wanted to do. I'm making good progress and I think I'm going to be very good at it. I know for a fact that Matthew is bored rigid with his job at the insurance firm. He may be well paid, but he's as miserable as sin. Anyway, let's change the subject. How's your week been?"

"Oh, as exciting as ever," came the sarcastic reply. "Things never change here. It's so dull. That new assistant over there is getting on my nerves. I suppose that's a development."

Rachael looked over to where her mother was pointing. She saw a slender young man in his mid-twenties talking to one of the other residents sitting on the other side of the garden. She vaguely remembered seeing him on previous visits, but now she had a really good look. He had short, dark hair and brown eyes, and a well-maintained beard that was just a bit more than stubble but not so much that you couldn't see the skin on his neck. When he stood up straight, he must have been about six foot two with a well-toned body that was fit and proportioned without being over developed. In fact, he was a damned fine specimen of a man. Suddenly he looked in her direction and gave her a smile which was enough to melt her heart. She smiled and rather idiotically waved before going red with embarrassment. Fortunately for Rachael, he was on his way inside for the moment.

"What's the matter with him? He looks like a decent sort of fellow."

"He's Spanish!" exploded Rachael's mother.

Rachael was aghast. "Mother, what difference does that make? Don't be so racist, for goodness' sake."

"I'm not a racist. I'm sure the Spanish are very nice people in their own way. It's just at my time of life I want my own people around me; people who understand my ways; who share my culture. It would be nice if my family were prepared to look after me too, rather than locking me up in this prison."

There was a stony silence. There was nothing more to be said. Both Rachael and her mum stared across the lawn into the middle distance. Finally, Rachael's mum said, "I'm tired. I'm going up to my room to lie down for a bit."

Without further ado, Rachael's mum got up and slowly walked back inside the house. Rachael remained seated, watching her mother go. Who was this monster that her mother was turning into? She felt her stomach churning as her mother disappeared from view. She had always seemed slightly right wing in her views and probably had voted Conservative all her life, but Rachael always felt that she was essentially liberal and sympathetic towards difference and diversity. Now she wasn't so sure. Maybe she just displayed a typically English veneer of politeness in public, but in private seethed with xenophobia, racism and goodness knows what else. What if Rachael had announced that she was gay, or had come home with a Muslim boyfriend? She had always assumed that her mother would have been cool about it. Now she wasn't so sure. Who was her mother? Not the person she had needed as a child. Not the person she needed now. Rachael felt bereft. She put her head in her hands and quietly shed a few tears.

"Madam, are you feeling unwell?" said a voice in a heavy Spanish accent.

Rachael looked up and saw the handsome young Spanish care assistant looking at her attentively. His soft brown eyes radiated concern and empathy towards Rachael.

"It's OK. I'm just having a moment. I have had a difficult time with my mother this afternoon." Rachael felt an urge to continue the conversation and continued, "I hope my mother isn't making life difficult for you?"

The Spanish man laughed, a melodious gentle laugh that created superfine air waves that caressed the eardrum. "Do not worry for me, Señora. I am – how do you say in Eenglish? – 'tough as old boots'. Your poor mother is not well; she does not know what she says."

"Still, she is lucky to have people like you to look after her. The staff here are all so kind and caring. I feel so guilty that she has to be here, and I can't look after her at home."

"Do not be unkind to yourself, dear lady. I am sure you are very busy, and she is getting good care here, which maybe you cannot give her in your home. What is your yob if I may be permitted to ask?"

The care assistant sat down in the chair vacated by Rachael's mother, and Rachael started to tell him about her job as a police officer. This then opened the floodgates and she told him about her family and how she got on with her sister and two brothers, what her mother used to be like when Rachael was a child, and even about Martin and their failed relationship. She was professional enough not to talk about the details of any cases, though.

In return, the handsome care assistant opened up about his life and how he'd ended up in this quiet part of Hampshire. His name was Pablo (Pablo Angel Sanchez Ramirez to be exact – in England he just went by the name Pablo Ramirez). He was born and grew up in the town of Medina de Rioseco, just north-west of Valladolid or a three-hour bus journey from Madrid. He had a large extended family with several brothers and sisters, all doing well in their own way, and he seemed to have had a very successful passage through school and university with a degree in biochemistry and biotechnology and a master's in forensic science. Despite having the top grades all the way down the line, he had found it impossible to find a job in

Spain and had looked to a career in the forensic science service in England. Unfortunately, he realised that his standard of English was not good enough, so he decided to take any job he could to spend time in the country to improve his language skills. Rachael paid particular attention to the fact that he was still single. He had had a girlfriend in Spain, but they had called it a day when he decided to come to England. It didn't sound as if he had been too gutted to break up with her.

She finally looked at her watch and noticed that they had been talking for nearly an hour.

"Goodness," she said, "I'd better let you get on. I've kept you from your duties for nearly an hour."

"It is no problem," Pablo replied. "It is part of my yob to talk to the patients and their sons and daughters."

"Even so, I'd best be going."

Rachael stood up and started to move to the house. Pablo also got up and then rather hesitantly called after Rachael.

"Dear lady… Rachael. Would it please you to go out to dinner with me some time…? Rachael stood transfixed and then turned to face him. She could see he was deadly serious.

"Oooh, I wasn't expecting that," she blustered. "I will have to think about it. I'll let you know."

"Forgive me," Pablo added very quickly. "I am sorry that I am so unprofessional. Forget that I ask such a stupid question."

Feeling the heat in her cheeks, Rachael turned and quickly left the scene, driving away from the care home without turning back. All that evening her mind was in turmoil. She had been asked by the nicest man she'd met in ages to go out to dinner. Why on earth hadn't she been brave enough to just say yes rather than send out a signal that suggested she wasn't interested? The night was no better. She could get very little sleep, and when she did doze off, all she dreamed about was Pablo, gaining his love and then losing it again through more and more bizarre circumstances. The morning grudgingly arrived, and she was less refreshed than when she went to bed the previous evening. She had one more day of leave left, and she was resolved to try and remedy the situation. It might already be too late, but she couldn't let this opportunity pass her by without at least making an effort.

As soon as it was a reasonable hour to do so, Rachael rang the care home. Mrs Merkel answered the phone in her usual cheery voice, and although somewhat surprised by Rachael's request to speak to Pablo, went to find him. The wait was interminable and gave Rachael far too much time to think of a hundred alternative ways to make her point.

"Hello? It is I, Pablo. How can I help you?"

"Oh hi, it's Rachael from yesterday," she began, her mouth feeling very dry. "Look, you took me by surprise yesterday, when you asked me out to dinner. I may have given you quite the wrong impression that I wasn't really interested, but that isn't the case. I would love to go out with you sometime."

"Qué maravilloso! It will be my pleasure to arrange something at your earliest convenience. I am so happy."

Rachael sensed the tension evaporating at the other end of the line and indeed she was now almost in a sense of euphoria too. They spent the next twenty minutes happily exchanging phone numbers, discussing what sort of food they liked and when would be a mutually good day and time to meet up. Rachael was sure that Pablo ought to be getting on with some proper work, but she was reluctant to end the conversation. In the end they agreed that they would both have to look at their work schedules before making a decision. Pablo finished the conversation by asking Rachael if he could keep in touch by text and Rachael replied that it would be perfectly okay.

Rachael floated through the rest of the day. Someone liked her enough to want to get to know her better, someone really nice who she wanted to get to know better as well. She had not had this feeling in ages. The grey monochrome of the daily grind had suddenly burst forth into a brilliant and blinding array of every colour you could imagine. That evening Rachael went to bed with a smile on her face and slept like a log.

XVI

IT WAS THE FIRST TIME that Rachael had been to the Headquarters for a while. She breezed in happily only to encounter Martin, also on his way in to start his shift.

"You're in a good mood," Martin commented, almost disapprovingly.

"Yes, I've had a few days' leave."

"Get up to anything interesting?"

"Yes."

Silence.

"Well… are you going to tell me?"

"No."

Not to be deterred, Martin continued, "They're re-establishing the murder inquiry team; not as big as before, but I'm going to be in it, so we'll be working together again."

"Oh well, I suppose every silver lining has to have a cloud."

Rachael quickened her pace to distance herself from Martin and purposefully headed towards Detective Inspector Towgood's office. When she entered the inspector was dealing with some paperwork related to another case. He was clearly delighted to put it to one side when Rachael entered.

"Ah, Sergeant Goodfellow, I hope you had a good break? I've had a chance to talk to the Reverend John Randall, and also the boss has grudgingly agreed to reform the investigation team; not as large as before, but at least we can investigate more efficiently. We'll have a group briefing when I've told you about my chat with the archdeacon."

It transpired that Towgood had been to see Randall the day after Rachael had returned from Peterborough in his office in the cathedral close. His reminiscences had tallied convincingly with those of Daniel Jarvis. Jack Nobel had made an impression on him of being a kind, considerate and intelligent child with a singing voice like an angel. Even when his voice broke it developed into a rich bass baritone and Jack continued to sing in the church choir along with some of the men from the village in the bass section. Apparently, Randall had come to trust him enough that he would let him lock up the church after choir practice and return the key and allow him to use the church room for his school rock band to practice. Then, just as Daniel had recalled, Randall talked of a moment when Jack had changed completely. He suddenly stopped coming to choir practice and attending church events.

"That's interesting," Rachael commented. "That ties in with Daniel's account of a particular moment when Jack's character changed completely. Did you press him about when that was or what might have caused it?"

Towgood smiled and continued, "Yes of course I did, Goodfellow. He can't be precise, and to be fair to him it is a long time ago, but he does recall Jack being fifteen or sixteen at the time and remembers that the last time he can recall Jack singing with the choir was at a big Deanery Festival where all the local parish church choirs came together to sing choral evensong in the cathedral, and then give a concert afterwards.

"Randall seems to have been concerned enough to make some enquiries. He mentioned that after a few weeks he went to see Jack's mother, who'd also stopped attending church, to ask if anything was the matter. He remembers Mrs Nobel being defensive and saying that Jack wasn't very well at the moment but hopefully would be right as rain soon. He never saw Jack, who was either not there at the time or deliberately keeping out of the way. He also remembers a second visit a month or two later when there was still no sign of Jack or his mother in church. He was met by Jack's father at the door and told in no uncertain terms to clear off and mind his own business. Randall says he took the message to heart and had no further contact with the family."

"What did you make of Randall? I mean, after all, he is the nearest thing we have to a prime suspect."

"That's a fair point. He's a family man, mid-forties, married with two young children. I suspect Fenton St Mary may well have been his first parish. He seemed pleasant enough. I didn't sense any matrimonial disharmony, although of course his wife wasn't there in the office, and I didn't detect any signs of shiftiness or discomfort answering my questions. He seemed genuinely shocked to hear of Jack's demise and eager and willing to talk about him. But... as you know, there are some very good actors among the criminal fraternity. I was careful, by the way, not to mention the newspaper cutting. As far as he is concerned, we were just making general enquiries about the boy's background."

"So, what's the next move, sir?"

"Well, I think we must do Mrs Nobel the courtesy of informing her of her son's death before news leaks into the media. Not surprisingly they have found a DNA match between the corpse and Jack Nobel's room in Daniel Jarvis' house. There can be no doubt that Jack Nobel is the dead man. They tell me the body can now be released. There's nothing more they can learn from the remains, and they could do with the space in the morgue. Are you alright to spend a few more days up in Peterborough this week?"

"Yes – but will I be able to get back for Saturday evening please?"

"Have you got a hot date or something, DS Goodfellow?"

Rachael could feel herself going red, because that was exactly what she hoped was going to happen – with Pablo. Towgood realised his quip had fallen embarrassingly flat, and after an awkward moment he blustered, "Yes, yes... I'm sure that will be fine. I can make use of the local Force up there if I need to stay into the weekend."

He stood up and paced around the room. When his equilibrium was restored, he continued,

"Assuming nothing untoward happens when we see Mrs Nobel, we can go public and see if we can unsettle our murderer. We'll release the photo and name of the victim around the area and ask for information. I'm guessing the killer's beginning to think he's got away with it. I'd like to flush him, or her of course, out if we can."

He went over to the window and stared out across to the river. Then turning his head, he continued,

"What do we know so far? Jack Nobel is moved to drive down to Hampshire at short notice, apparently provoked by an article in the local paper concerning the local vicar of his home parish at a time when he seems to have had a life-changing crisis. The car he borrowed is found abandoned at a country park a few miles outside of Winchester with some evidence that he may have encountered the murderer there. It looks increasingly likely that Jack's body was dumped in the river just upstream from 'The Red Lion' and drifted downstream to be mangled in the mill.

"The only linking evidence we have is the car key, which I'm now pretty certain must have dropped out of Jack's pocket when he was already dead, and the hessian sacking, which has appeared at the river, the country park and the mill. Facts, facts, facts – we have some at last, but we also have gaps. In particular our murderer remains a shadowy, almost invisible character. We have only one very tenuous and unlikely suspect, no sure motive, and no real idea of how the murder was committed.

"While we're away in Peterborough, I'm going to get the rest of the team to scour any CCTV footage they can find from around the town to see if Daniel Jarvis' car entered the city at any point prior to the murder. I expect most of the tapes have been wiped after all this time, but you never know. Did Jack go and see someone or was Farley Mount as far as he got? Also, we need to look at those statements from Deanside Lane again, particularly those from № 22 and 23, which mentioned a car screaming away at 2am. And what happened to Jack Nobel's other possessions, a wallet for example? The killer probably disposed of them, but it might be worth checking our own lost property as well as that of other businesses and organisations around town."

Towgood purposefully picked up a pen off the desk and then strode out of his office to address the small team that had dutifully gathered for its first briefing. Rachael followed and made a note of the duties she was to supervise. The rest of the day was then taken up with setting people tasks to do which would keep them occupied for the rest of the week.

And so inevitably, the next day at about 4pm, Towgood and Rachael found themselves outside the house of Mrs Nobel in the village of Fenton St Mary dreading the conversation they were about to have with her.

The village of Fenton St Mary was in fenland that was completely flat from one horizon to the other. The main road through the village was completely straight and the houses were organised in a ribbon development along it with just a few side roads providing extra housing opportunities every now and then. Only at the very centre of the village was there another road of any substance which ran parallel to the main road and led to the parish church and some of the older properties. You got the impression that the village could have been plonked down anywhere along the road in that landscape and it wouldn't have made the slightest difference. Rachael was surprised that Towgood seemed unnerved by the landscape. More than once he had commented on how flat it was and how anyone could live in that environment he didn't know. It didn't worry Rachael who imagined there must be some spectacular sunsets and skyscapes.

Mrs Nobel didn't react to the news of her son's death in quite the way that Rachael was expecting. There was no wailing or gnashing of teeth, merely a stoic acceptance of something she was almost expecting. Rachael almost felt there was a sense of relief as if a painful chapter had closed allowing Mrs Nobel to get on with whatever remained of her life. Towgood asked if she would like the support officer to call by and stay with her for a while. This was politely declined. Towgood then said he would leave and come back in a few days to ask some questions which while necessary, might also be upsetting. Mrs Nobel said she didn't mind if they asked the questions now, to avoid having to make another trip.

"Well, only if you are sure, Mrs Nobel...? And if it gets too much we can always stop and carry on another day. I do insist, however, that my colleague at least puts the kettle on and makes a cup of tea."

Rachael, with some internal irritation at being made the skivvy, took her cue and went out to the kitchen. She was careful to make sure she could hear everything that was said in the living room, nevertheless. She heard Towgood begin his questioning.

"Now as I have just said we believe that your son, Jack, was murdered. I'll be honest, we don't have a motive and we don't really have a suspect. We've only been able to establish that the murder victim was Jack in the last few days. We caught up with a friend of his in Peterborough, Daniel Jarvis. I assume you knew your son was lodging with him? It must be some comfort to know that Jack was getting his life back on track. Daniel told us that Jack was becoming more like his old self."

"I didn't know my son was in Peterborough," Mrs Nobel replied, "and it gives me no comfort at all to hear that my poor son has yet again had his life destroyed by cruel fate. I did have a postcard from him last year saying that things were looking up and he'd come to see me when he could stand before me with some dignity."

There was nothing that Towgood could say to this, so he simply continued with his previous drift.

"It appears that an article in the local paper about the Reverend John Randall taking up a post in Winchester was the catalyst for your son going off to seek someone out. Unfortunately, we think that this action directly led to his demise. I gather the Reverend Randall was vicar here when your son was a teenager. We have spoken to him, and he confirms what Daniel Jarvis also told us, that there was some kind of incident that occurred when Jack was about fifteen that changed his character completely and sent him off the rails. Neither of them could say what had actually happened. I don't suppose you could shed any light on the matter?"

Mrs Nobel was silent for a long time, staring out of the window. Rachael, who had re-entered the room with a mug of tea, thought it quite possible she would say nothing. But eventually she did speak.

"Jack was too pure and fragile for this world. How any god could send such an innocent soul to live and grow up in this filthy, corrupt and unpleasant dimension and be considered loving and good is now beyond me. He did what he was told, he was kind and considerate to people, he worked hard at school and had a bright future ahead of him. He sang in the church choir and helped out with community activities in the village. Everybody said what a lovely lad he was. I was so proud of him.

"I don't know exactly what happened. Jack would never tell me. He went off his usual bright and chirpy self to a church event and came back in a state of shock, shut himself in his room and wouldn't talk to anyone for a couple of days. It was so unlike him that I became desperately worried. I got cross with him, which I wish I hadn't now, and forced him to come out of his room. I begged him to tell me what the matter was but the more I did so, the more he'd go back into his shell, and we'd get nowhere."

"Can you tell me more about this event that seems to have caused the problem? The Reverend Randall mentioned something about a Deanery Festival."

"Yes, that's right… Well, not a great deal to be honest. I didn't go myself. The choir met up at the parish church quite early, about half past eight, and were taken in a minibus that had been hired for the day to Peterborough cathedral. I gather they rehearsed during the morning and early afternoon, gave a choral evensong about half three and then did a short concert in the evening at about seven. There were choirs from all over the diocese there. It was a big event. I think they got back about ten o'clock in the evening. I remember Jack coming in and saying he was tired and going straight to bed. It was only the next day that I began to realise that something was wrong. At first, I thought he was just going down with a bug, but as the week went by and the doctor could find nothing physically wrong with him, I realised something else must be the cause."

"I suppose you can't remember the names of any of the other members of the choir who went on the trip… and do you know if they still live locally?"

Mrs Nobel could remember quite a few names. Most of Jack's contemporaries had flown the nest and some of the adult members had died in the intervening period, but there were still three or four people living in the area. Daniel Jarvis was not among those mentioned. He had briefly sung in the choir but had given up a year or two previously. Interestingly, the Reverend Randall had travelled with the choir in the minibus also.

"Thank you, Mrs Nobel. That gives us some further leads to investigate. Now, if you are feeling up to it, can you carry on describing what happened to Jack after this event. Daniel Jarvis has told us his school work deteriorated and he left school completely when he was in the sixth form."

Mrs Nobel was again silent for quite a period, but she did continue,

"It was horrible to watch really. It was like my darling boy was gradually submerged by a growing hideous monster consuming him. He became moody and sarcastic. Whereas he used to be diligent and organised about doing homework, he wouldn't care less. Whereas he used to help out with all sorts of village activities he would no longer bother, and of course he immediately gave up the choir and told me that he had decided to become an atheist."

"John Randall tells me he called round a couple of times. Do you remember?"

"I remember the one occasion. Jack was adamant that under no circumstances was he prepared to talk with the vicar, so it must have seemed quite rude, me talking to Randall on the doorstep and not inviting him in. I think the second time must have been when he talked to my husband. Dennis would certainly have given the vicar an earful. He never had much time for religion and felt that his lad had been fed all sorts of funny ideas."

"…And your husband, is he still around?"

"No, we got divorced after Jack left home. We had nothing left to hold us together. I never loved him anyway. It was a marriage of convenience. I was desperate to get married and unfortunately Dennis was the only man available at the time. While Jack was thriving and doing well, I could just about bear him."

Rachael was rather startled by this statement, and it became apparent that Mrs Nobel had picked up on this. She continued,

"We all want to marry the man of our dreams, but I'm afraid there are not enough of them to go around. Dennis was useless with Jack, of course. Jack was an empathetic, liberal-minded, intellectually adventurous individual, whereas Dennis was a mean-spirited xenophobe and racist. He thought Jack was weak and should take up boxing and spend less time studying foreign languages. He secretly despised the fact that Jack did so well at school. Jack, I think, came to hate and despise his father with a visceral loathing."

"Do you have any contact details for Dennis? Would you like us to get in touch with him?" Towgood asked, rather gently and delicately.

"I don't know where he is exactly. The day after Jack left, I told Dennis to either sling his hook or I'd walk out and never come back. When he said he wouldn't, and I wasn't going anywhere either, I took the bread knife and threatened to plunge it into his black, malicious heart. I knew he was a snivelling worm, and he packed his things in record time and was gone. He went to Leeds, I think, but whether he is still there or not, I don't know. I don't suppose I should be telling police officers that I threatened to murder my husband, but I would have done it, you know, if he hadn't taken flight."

"I'll pretend I didn't hear about that. We've had no complaint lodged against you," Towgood responded, rather recklessly in Rachael's opinion.

"Well, I suppose if you do find him, he has a right to attend his son's funeral even if it is going to make a difficult occasion ten times worse."

"Yes, well about the funeral, the body can now be released, so as soon as you sort out an undertaker, get him to contact this number and the transfer can be arranged." Towgood passed a business card to Mrs Nobel and then was quiet for a few moments, looking slightly uncertain in Rachael's opinion. He did eventually continue, "And after Jack left home, what became of him? Daniel was able to tell us nothing about that."

"I... I don't..." Mrs Nobel started, then stopped. She tried again, and stopped again. "I'm sorry, Inspector, I thought I was stronger than this. I don't think I can cope with any more questions at the moment."

Towgood reached out and gently held her hand for a second. Rachael was surprised at the empathy Towgood showed in this action as she'd assumed that he was emotionally rather a cold fish. He then said, "That's absolutely fine. We'll leave you be for the moment. This can wait for another day. Are you sure you don't want victim support to call round? Is there a friend or neighbour we can call to come and sit with you for a bit?"

"No, I shall be fine," replied Mrs Nobel with a degree of fortitude.

Rachael then remembered something she'd meant to do. She pulled out a photograph from her wallet folder that she'd been carrying.

"Ooh... Mrs Nobel I almost forgot that I'd brought this copy of a photo for you. Daniel Jarvis lent us the original for our investigation. It was taken a couple of weeks before... well, it's of Jack and Daniel together. I thought you might like it if you haven't got any recent ones of Jack."

Rachael handed the photo to Mrs Nobel who received it mechanically and slowly, without saying a word. She stared at it for a while, still saying nothing.

"They look happy together, don't they?" Rachael commented and then immediately wished she'd kept quiet. Mrs Nobel shot a piercing stare at Rachael which was not exactly aggressive, but not exactly friendly either. She had understood the subtext of Rachael's comment all too well.

"I never saw or heard of a serious girlfriend… and he kept any relationships with boys very secret, if he had any. No, he struck me as being alone in some sort of mental hell which prevented him from forming close relationships with anybody. Do you know, I think whatever it was that started the rot, Jack might have still pulled through if he'd had a sympathetic father and been able to forge a happy relationship with someone."

Rachael shuffled uneasily and made to move towards the door, but Mrs Nobel added unexpectedly, "I'm glad Daniel took him under his wing at the end. He was a good boy and I'm sure he would have been a good influence on Jack. I'd like to get in touch with him if that's allowed?"

Rachael nodded but did not commit herself to saying anything. Towgood hastily added, "Well, we really must be going. Goodbye and take care."

Once outside, big clouds were looming in the west, made more ominous by the big sky and the flat terrain. Rachael and Towgood hurried to the car and within five minutes large drops of rain were aggressively hitting the windscreen.

As they drove cautiously back to Peterborough, they compared notes on the interview that they had just had. Rachael was struck by the character of Mrs Nobel. She presented an austere front and her straggly grey hair and worry lines spoke of a life full of cares, worries and disappointments. She had clearly long ago given up hope on things ever getting better. She had shed all her tears of grief for Jack some time ago. Towgood seemed concerned to track down Mr Nobel and to get some insights from his point of view. They agreed, however, that the next few days needed to be spent finding all the people that Mrs Nobel had mentioned and, if possible, interview them.

The following day was one of those that ought to have been utterly tedious, sifting through records and lists, electoral registers and telephone directories, any source of information you may care to mention. However, the backdrop of the need to solve a murder inquiry gave the whole process an urgency that negated the stifling repetition of searching through name after name. PC Black was once again seconded to help them, much to his evident joy, and their efforts bore some fruit, thanks to the resources of the police headquarters in Peterborough. An archive photo in a local paper taken of the Fenton St Mary church choir standing by the minibus ready to go off to the Deanery Festival had enabled them to identify every single member of the choir who had gone on that fateful expedition. The names had been added in order in the caption to the photo, and Rachael was able to pick out Jack, who indeed looked angelic and maybe a little young for his age, and Reverend John Randall, who was obvious from his dog collar anyway. Addresses and contact numbers were found for ten of them by the end of the day, some still local others scattered to the four winds. Much to Towgood's satisfaction, an address and telephone number for Mr Nobel in Leeds was discovered as well as that for the organiser and musical director of the Deanery Festival.

Towgood decided that he must go and talk with Mr Nobel as a matter of urgency, so he set off the following day having warned the West Yorkshire Police Force of his imminent arrival. He left very precise instructions behind for Rachael about who to interview and what to ask. Firstly, she was to try and see the director of the festival and get an exact plan of how the day unfolded. She was then to find out from him the names and details of as many of the adult supervisors and staff who were involved with the event as possible, including people like caretakers, cleaners and leaders of other groups who were attending. When Rachael asked why only the adults, and not contemporaries of Jack who might have been acting suspiciously, Towgood had simply said that they would be casting the net far too wide at this stage.

"…in any case," he'd continued, "an idea is beginning to come to mind, an unpleasant one I'm afraid to say. Anyway, if you have time after that, work through the choir contacts. Try to interview the local ones in person, and ring the ones that live halfway around the world. Ask them to recall anything they can remember about that day. Anything at all…"

"That's part of the problem. That event may well be the key to what unlocks the whole case. We still haven't got a motive or a credible suspect. By the way, your husband is in the church. You don't think you could ask if there's any gossip in ecclesiastical circles about John Randall? He was the vicar at Fenton St Mary at the time we're interested in."

"Well, I'll have to be subtle. He is very keen that we should not discuss each other's work and break confidences. However, if I put him off guard with some red wine and casually mention that Fenton St Mary Church seems to be involved in a murder investigation, he might let something slip. I'll give you a call at the office in Winchester next week if I find out anything useful."

Just then, PC Black breezed into the office. "Are you off?" he asked Rachael.

"Yes, in a while, I've just got to leave everything in order and then I'm heading back to Hampshire."

"Aww… that's a shame. If you were staying over the weekend, I was going to invite you to join our gang on a night out to the Sunrise Club."

Rachael shuddered and was relieved that she could reply that she had other plans, but hoped that Jeremy would have a nice time.

Almost as she was leaving the room, Towgood made a video call and she had to spend another half an hour updating him on where they had got to with the interviews and what, if anything, they had found out.

Finally, she was able to get in her car and start the long journey home.

XVII

THE TRANSITION BETWEEN OCTOBER AND November seems to bring the most obvious and dramatic change to the seasons. One moment it is still late autumn with the possibility of bright sunshine and reasonable weather, the next it is dark and gloomy winter, either wet and miserable grey or cold and biting frost. That first Sunday in November exemplified the principle precisely. It had rained and blown a gale all day. In the evening, however, Rachael was snug and warm in the company of Gavin and Jacob at their small but well-appointed house made cosy by the candles and soft lighting in the main living space.

"Come on then, don't keep us in suspense," Jacob asked with excitement at the first polite opportunity. "How did your date go with the gorgeous Pablo?"

Rachael smiled and replied, "It went quite well, I think."

This of course was a huge understatement. The whole event had been brilliant from start to finish. Pablo had insisted on picking her up from her house and had arrived just on the slightly late side of on time, just to make sure that Rachael was ready. He took Rachael's breath away as he entered the house. He was immaculately turned out with an open-necked plain white shirt that was fashionably tailored, a light-brown jacket, black trousers with a shiny metal-buckled belt and dark brown boots which came to a slight point at the toes. Rachael was drawn to the beautifully smooth, almost olive skin on his face, and she had to resist the temptation to caress it gently with her hand. Pablo was very continental and greeted Rachael by kissing her lightly on each cheek and then producing from behind his back a small but tastefully arranged bunch of flowers. He also said the right things about how beautiful Rachael looked without going ridiculously over the top.

They had exchanged messages all week about where they would like to go. Rachael wasn't keen on over-spicey food or far-eastern cuisine, and Pablo bemoaned the fact that there was nowhere in the whole of Hampshire that did authentic Spanish cuisine. In the end they settled for a well-regarded Italian restaurant in the old part of Southampton. Pablo's car was small, but he kept it clean and tidy, so the journey was comfortable enough and she was relieved to find that he was a careful and sensible driver.

The walk from the multi-storey car park to the restaurant was a short one and thankfully it was dry. In fact, it was a clear night and the stars twinkled optimistically while a slightly lighter blue was noticeable on the western horizon where the evening star shone brightest of all. How lovely to show off to the rest of the world that she, Rachael Goodfellow, could boast the company of such a handsome and desirable young man as Pablo Ramirez!

The funniest moment came when they were shown to the table by a young waiter trying to put on a phoney Italian accent. Pablo responded by speaking very quickly in seemingly fluent Italian which left the young waiter flummoxed and completely uncomprehending. After that he continued to serve them perfectly well, but now with a characteristic Hampshire bur.

"I didn't realise you could speak Italian as well as English? I feel so useless only being able to speak English," Rachael observed wistfully.

"Spanish and Italian are very much the same. We can understand ourselves almost without studying each other's languages," Pablo explained.

During their meal, Pablo grew in confidence and became increasingly flirty, which Rachael in turn increasingly encouraged. Pablo risked holding Rachael's hand across the table just briefly as he was paying yet another compliment to her beauty which, much to Rachael's shame, gave her a delightful frisson. It was not all Mills and Boon stuff. Rachael found Pablo easy to talk to, despite the language barriers. They seemed to have similar outlooks on life, share similar interests and values, and both hated the same politicians.

There was of course the usual awkward moment when it came to pay the bill. Pablo insisted on footing it completely, however Rachael protested that as she was earning more than Pablo it was only fair that they split it. In the end Rachael allowed Pablo to pay on the understanding that it was a special occasion. In future she expected to pay her way as she was a modern, independent woman.

All too soon the evening was coming to an end. They'd both agreed in advance that they would not stay out really late on a first date, just in case it was a complete disaster, and both were too polite to state the obvious. Thankfully, it was far from that.

And so, at ten to midnight Pablo had pulled up outside Rachael's house to let her go home. Rachael had plucked up the courage to ask if he would like to come in for coffee. Pablo had looked long into her eyes, causing a moment between them which was charged with electricity. He'd finally said, "My mother say to me, 'Pablo, if you are lucky enough to find a nice girl, make sure you treat her with respect, and don't take advantage of her on a first date. You can give her a kiss, but nothing more…'."

At this point, he had leant over and kissed Rachael full on the lips with a long lingering kiss. Rachael had responded enthusiastically, and the kiss extended to a fairly lengthy affair which confirmed to Rachael that they had crossed the Rubicon from being just good friends to potential partners.

With a cheeky glint in his eye he finally added, "… my dear mama, gave me no advice on how to conduct myself on a second date, so maybe we can have coffee and take things further next time?"

"I'd like that very much, very much indeed," Rachael had replied without hesitation. She'd kissed him one more time fairly quickly and then got out of the car. She'd stood on the pavement watching Pablo drive off around the corner, before skipping like a child to the front door and entering in a state of delirium.

OF COURSE, GAVIN AND JACOB were not content with 'It went quite well, I think.' They probed mercilessly until they got the full unadulterated, blissful account of the previous night's proceedings.

"Bloody hell, Rachael, it sounds as if you've found a good one there," Jacob said approvingly as the last little detail had been extracted. "When am I going to meet him?"

"You keep your hands off him. He's mine," Rachael responded with mock indignation. "I'm sure you will get your opportunity to meet him before too long."

Rachael enjoyed the company of Gavin and Jacob. They were very far removed from what she privately classified in her mind as 'girly gays', but nevertheless, she could gossip with them like she used to do as a teenager with her classmates and friends; something she couldn't do with her world-weary married female colleagues and certainly not with her straight male colleagues. It was nice. Sometimes she knew she was lulled into talking about her work, giving far more away than she really ought. However, she also knew that Jacob, being Gavin's partner would be discreet and wouldn't pass on anything that was sensitive or cause Gavin or Rachael problems at work. So inevitably, after a little late evening alcohol had flowed, Rachael opened up about the case she was involved in. (Gavin was not part of the small team that Towgood had been allowed to reassemble, and so was as much in the dark about the most recent developments as Jacob.)

"It's turning into a really sad case," Rachael opined rather blearily. "Jack Nobel seems to have been such a nice kid. Then something happens to turn him into this moody delinquent dropout. He is just getting his life back on track, thanks to his former schoolfriend Daniel, and then – bang, something reminds him of that incident, he goes off to do who knows what, and then is murdered.

"There's this cute photo of Jack and Daniel, just before the end. It reminds me of you two and his mother says Jack never had a girlfriend. I asked Daniel if they were an item, but he laughed and said he was planning to get married to his girlfriend very soon. He admitted that Jack might have had feelings for him though.

"We've spent the last week in Peterborough trying to narrow down when this teenage incident took place. We're pretty sure it happened in the afternoon between 4.30 and 6pm, but what it is or who was involved we haven't really got a clue."

Jacob sighed and then said, "It's obvious, isn't it?"

Rachael looked blank. "What do you mean?"

"Come on, you're being very coy," Jacob continued. "There's a huge elephant in the room you guys aren't talking about. I'm guessing he was sexually abused, most likely by a man. It's the only explanation that makes much sense. Rachael, you've already said that you strongly suspected he was gay, and it seems as if his mother thought the same – they normally know, mothers. Imagine being a fifteen-year-old boy struggling with your sexual identity, wondering why you fancy your best friend and not the girls in your class and constantly asking yourself if you're a freak and the only person in the world who feels like that. That's what most of us have to deal with, which is hard enough, but then imagine that you are abused by an unpleasant and aggressive older man, and all the things you fantasised about sex became a ghastly nightmare. Your whole world would be shattered. The shame would be unbearable. You dare not tell anyone. You'd probably just want to die. Is it a surprise that Jack went off the rails?"

Rachael was taken aback by the force with which Jacob stated his argument. She had, as a technicality, considered sexual abuse as a possible scenario, but as they had found no evidence of it so far, it had remained in the background of her mind, a remote possibility. Jacob had forced it to the front of her mind so that it disturbed her immensely.

"Well, yes, I see your point," Rachael admitted cautiously.

Gavin then decided to chip in. "So, it could well be that in that newspaper article you mentioned, Jack recognised his abuser and decided to do something about it. But what I wonder? Blackmail? Extortion? Maybe just to have it out with him and then expose the culprit as a paedophile? Yes, and then maybe that person got scared enough to do away with Jack before he could spill the beans."

Rachael was very nervous now and she interjected with some force,

"Gavin, you know I shouldn't have told you about the newspaper article. We're keeping that evidence under wraps at the moment. You must not breathe a word to anyone about it – either of you."

The evening came to an end fairly soon after that and Rachael had an unexpectedly disturbed and sleepless night imagining the worst things that might have happened to poor Jack, both on that day in Peterborough and also when he was murdered.

XVIII

MONDAY MORNING ARRIVED ALL TOO soon and Rachael found herself along with seven others desperately trying to concentrate on Towgood's briefing. The office looked a mess, with photos and documents pinned to noticeboards all around the room and a whiteboard behind Towgood scrawled across with barely legible blue marker pen. Towgood was himself looking a little dishevelled for a Monday morning.

"Now it's going to be a busy week. We're going to ramp up the investigation and maybe get some reaction from our murderer as well. We are circulating the photo of Jack in the Winchester area, and it should be shown in local and national newspapers as well as local TV. We're organising a press conference for Wednesday, and we hope to have local and national coverage for that. As well as bringing forward witnesses, we are going to be keeping an eye open for anyone suddenly responding suspiciously.

"While I and DS Goodfellow were in Peterborough last week, you made two interesting discoveries – congratulations on your hard work and diligence in uncovering these.

"Firstly, a wallet was found at the household waste and recycling centre. It contained £30 in cash, a driver's licence and a credit card; both of these were in the name of Jack Nobel. It was discovered in the general waste skip by a keen-eyed worker just before the waste was about to be crushed. He'd noticed the cash poking out and assumed someone had accidently dropped it in as they were putting waste into the skip. He can't remember now exactly when he found it, but he thinks it was shortly after the Easter Bank Holiday. It's been in the site office ever since.

"Secondly, we have two pieces of CCTV footage that have turned up..."

Towgood dimmed the lights in the office and then with a remote control turned on the overhead projector attached to the ceiling which projected on to a yellowing, off-white board fixed to the wall. The footage was in black and white and was rather jerky, like a remastered silent movie from the nineteen twenties. Towgood provided a running commentary throughout and paused the footage at what he considered to be key moments. The first piece showed the entrance to a multi-storey car park, tucked away behind the council offices near the top of the High Street. A rather battered car that seemed vaguely familiar for some reason came up to the entrance barrier. Towgood was able to freeze the footage and zoom in on the number plate. It was now clear that it was Daniel Jarvis' car. Towgood pointed out that the time of this recording was about 10.30am, two days before the most likely time that the body was thrown into the river. The car disappeared inside, but Towgood fast-forwarded the footage to a moment about five minutes later when a figure emerged onto the pavement, looked around and then moved off in the direction of the High Street. Towgood rewound, froze and expanded the picture of the man and, just discernible, was the face of Jack Nobel. He was casually dressed but in clothes that looked clean and respectable. Rachael guessed that one of the 'donkey work' jobs would be to try and find out if the clothes in the picture matched the remnants found on the corpse.

The second piece of video showed the close in Winchester cathedral. It was focusing on the entrance to the cathedral office. A young man was seen entering the main door and coming out again about fifteen minutes later. On freezing the video, once again the features of Jack Nobel could just about be made out. Towgood pointed out that the time difference between the two videos was only about twenty minutes, so it seemed that Jack had wandered down from the car park to the cathedral by a fairly direct route. The CCTV from the exit to the car park had been wiped, so there was no video record of when Jack left Winchester.

"...so, we can see that Jack Nobel went to Winchester with a very specific purpose in mind," Towgood continued. "This involved seeing someone involved with the cathedral. To do what, I wonder? Issue a threat? Seek advice? Meet up with someone who was going to help him?

"We only have one lead with a cathedral link at the moment. The archdeacon, the Reverend John Randall, was the subject of a newspaper article that was highlighted by Jack Nobel and seemed to be the spur for his trip down south. A couple of you know this, the rest of you can now access this evidence on the secure server, but please, this is to be kept only in the team for the time being."

Rachael turned slightly red as she knew she'd already broken this instruction and just hoped that Gavin, and especially Jacob, could be trusted to keep their mouths shut.

"Now, I said that we were hoping to flush out anything or anybody suspicious. When we make our big appearance on TV, some of you, with assistance from outside the group will be watching the offices in the close, and the movements of the archdeacon in particular. I will have a word with Detective Sergeant Goodfellow, and then she will organise your work schedules for the week. You all have plenty to be getting on with until then."

Towgood looked around for a moment to see whether anyone had any questions, then moved efficiently to his office. Rachael instinctively moved to follow him.

"I haven't had a chance to brief you properly on my interview with Mr Dennis Nobel yet," he began as Rachael settled herself down in the chair that was rapidly becoming her default seating position when discussing things in Towgood's office. Towgood shuffled some papers on his desk in a vain attempt to make it look neater and more organised and then settled into his own, rather plush swivel leather chair behind his desk that would allow him to slightly sway from side to side while he was thinking.

"It turned out not to be as useful as I'd hoped," he continued. "Still, it was good to get more context. I can see that Dennis could be considered a difficult man, but not quite as evil as Mrs Nobel was trying to make out. He clearly has very traditional views about a woman's place in the home and family, and also adheres to very stereotypical ideas of masculinity. It's not surprising that his marriage to a strong independently-minded woman with modern attitudes came to grief. They seem particularly ill-suited for each other. He confirmed the events of the day in question and confirms giving Randall a piece of his mind when he came calling that second time. He clearly has no time for religion and thought the boy's head was being filled with all sorts of nonsense. He'd have much rather Jack had taken up boxing than spent time singing in the church choir, just as Mrs Nobel said. However, he was gracious enough to admit that Randall was admired, loved even, in the local community and he almost showed regret for having been so harsh with the vicar on that occasion when they clashed. He tells of his wife going to pieces completely when Jack went off the rails. Neither of them knew how to cope. When Jack left home Mr Nobel says he couldn't stand living with his wife any longer and left himself. Interestingly, he didn't mention being attacked by Mrs Nobel with a knife and he insisted that it was his decision to leave, not hers. Jack clearly took after his mother, but I didn't sense the hostility or hatred for his son that Mrs Nobel claimed."

Rachael nodded appropriately but really didn't understand why Towgood had found it essential to rush off to Leeds to interview him so urgently – unless he suspected Mr Nobel was the murderer, of course.

Towgood now turned to the matter of the interview he wanted Rachael to do with John Randall. He proposed that she should arrange to do it tomorrow before the big news conference planned for Wednesday. Rachael could spend the afternoon preparing after she'd sorted the team's work for the next few days.

"Sir, about Peterborough," Rachael chipped in when she thought Towgood had finished giving his instructions. "Do you think that Jack Nobel was sexually abused at some point during the day?"

"Of course. Why? ... Don't you?" responded Towgood raising an eyebrow in surprise. Rachael was taken aback by the certainty of the response. Had she really been the only one who had not considered this as the likeliest possibility?

Towgood continued, "That's one of the reasons I wanted to see Mr Nobel, to see if there might be any history of sexual abuse in the family."

"I assume you were convinced?"

"He's not going to say, 'I abused my son', but I could detect none of the tell-tale signs that sexual abusers tend to give when being challenged. So, let's just say that idea has moved way down into the 'unlikely' category. Jack probably had a fairly miserable home life with his parents being constantly at war with each other, but I don't think physical or sexual abuse within the family was an issue.

"The only evidence we have is giving a nod and a wink towards Randall as the perpetrator of such an offence. However, when I interviewed him, I really didn't get the sense that he was the sort of man capable of doing such a thing. That's partly why I want you to see him, to get a second opinion on his character. We must be very careful how we proceed. I can't go accusing a high-ranking member of the clergy with rape, let alone murder, unless I am absolutely sure of the evidence. When you go, take DC Roshni Kaur with you. Sorry to be sexist about this, but having two female officers, especially an older one, is likely to keep things calm and non-confrontational. You can mention the newspaper article, but do it in an oblique way so that it looks like we are still just generally gathering evidence rather than treating him as a suspect. But having said that, don't be afraid to follow your instincts if he starts to say some unexpected things. I trust your judgement."

"Thank you, sir."

To say that Rachael was tired by the time she crawled into bed that evening was an understatement. She'd had to organise the surveillance teams that Towgood wanted posted, assign two members to help with the press conference planned for two days' time, ensure that the remaining CCTV footage was being sifted through and arrange someone to follow up on the credit card in Jack's wallet to see if there had been any unexpected spending on it. Having obtained an appointment to see the archdeacon the following day, it had been mid-afternoon before she was able to think about the questions she was going to ask him.

One thing that did happen that was helpful was that Karen Oakley phoned from Peterborough. She'd deviously quizzed her husband about Randall over the weekend. He'd not really come across Randall himself, but did recall having a discussion with fellow priests at the time Randall was appointed archdeacon to Winchester about how much he deserved it. 'It couldn't happen to a nicer guy' he remembered someone saying. Karen also observed that her husband had pointed out that vicars could be as bitchy about each other as any other profession, so it was rare that no-one had a bad word to say against him.

Rachael was intrigued. Was this guy a holy saint who, like a seagull flying across a range finder just at the crucial point of firing, had accidentally slipped into view at the wrong moment, or was he the most devious and evil criminal that Rachael had yet encountered? Rachael was almost champing at the bit by the time she came to interview John Randall the following day.

Accompanied by Roshni, she was shown into a large, wood-panelled sitting room, liberally sprinkled with portraits of former worthies and holders of clerical office dating back several centuries, and sumptuously furnished with well-matched chairs and a settee. The ambience would not have been out of place in a Tudor mansion house that had been turned into a five-star hotel. Randall was standing just inside the door and greeted them hospitably, gesturing for them to sit on the settee whilst he made for an armchair situated opposite.

Randall was fairly short and verging on stocky. His dark hair was thinning on top, but Rachael could see the resemblance to the much younger, fitter vicar of Fenton St Mary in that press photo of the choir waiting to board their minibus. He commenced the conversation,

"Now, I gather you have some more information about poor Jack Nobel… a terrible business that. I was most shocked when the inspector came to see me recently. Under normal circumstances, I'd write to the family and send my condolences, but relationships were so bad in the end between the Church and the family, I'm not sure it would be appreciated. What do you think, Sergeant Goodfellow?"

The concern seemed genuine to Rachael and Randall seemed at ease and in no way shifty.

"I would advise against it, sir," Rachael responded diplomatically. "You're right that neither Mr nor Mrs Nobel take kindly to religion these days."

She paused for a second or two and then continued. "We have been making extensive enquiries in the past week or so in the Peterborough area and we have a particular interest in the events of the day when you and the choir went to the Deanery Festival on July 6th, twelve years ago."

"That's a very long time ago. My memory isn't that good."

"Nevertheless, you did recall the event when my colleague, Detective Inspector Towgood spoke to you previously. Just try to tell us as much as you can about the day from your perspective."

Randall's brow furrowed and he thought for some time. "Well…" he began with hesitation, "I remember we all went in a large minibus. One of the senior members of the choir was a teacher and had been able to borrow the one that belonged to the school. We left reasonably early in the morning and there was very little traffic on the roads. We arrived at the King's School in Peterborough in good time. I left the choir to get on with their morning rehearsal and went down to the cathedral offices where we had a meeting of local clergy. I can't remember any of the details of what we discussed, I'm afraid.

"I didn't see anything more of the choir until evensong in the afternoon. I do remember having a coffee and a sandwich in a café in town during lunchtime. A couple of clergy friends joined me, and I recall we spent a fair old time catching up and discussing how things were going in the diocese."

Roshni was busy taking notes while Randall was speaking, concentrating intently, desperate to capture every little detail however insignificant. A pause in Randall's flow of reminiscence provoked Rachael to interject.

"We are particularly interested in the time period between the end of evensong until the start of the concert, which I assume you attended. Can you remember anything about that period of the day?"

"Well, yes. In fact, that stands out in my memory the most. I took the time to drop in on a very dear old friend and his wife who lived nearby. They were like my mentors at the local church I attended when I was a young man. They were very important in helping me make the decision to train for the priesthood."

"Can they vouch for you?" Rachael asked before realising this was almost suggesting that Randall was a suspect.

"I doubt it," Randall replied with a slightly sardonic smile. "They are both dead now. You're asking me to recall events from a long time ago and they were both in their eighties then."

"I appreciate that. Perhaps you could give us their names and the address they were living at, just so we can get a picture of everybody's whereabouts?"

Randall duly obliged without appearing to feel victimized. He accounted for the rest of the day, which was recorded assiduously by Roshni, but nothing unexpected transpired from the telling. It fitted with other people's descriptions of the evening and return journey perfectly.

"Now one more thing," Rachael continued. "Do you recall seeing Jack Nobel more recently? We believe he visited the cathedral offices in the week before Easter. Maybe he left you a message?"

"Really?" said Randall, genuinely surprised. "He didn't come to see me or leave me a message. Mind you, I probably wouldn't have recognised him even if I'd met him face to face in the street."

Mrs Randall popped in towards the end of the interview to ask if they would like a cup of coffee or tea. Rachael scrutinized intensely the interaction between Mr and Mrs Randall to try and sense any tension or disharmony in their relationship. She was disappointed. Mrs Randall appeared to be an honest and open sort of soul with a cheery disposition and willing to have a chat with anybody. The exchange between her and her husband suggested genuine warmth of affection and mutual respect.

Rachael, rather to Roshni's surprise, accepted the invitation in the hope that some casual conversation might disarm Randall into saying something unwise. After taking a bite out of a chocolate biscuit (kindly provided with the coffee) she decided to make a bold move.

"Forgive me, Archdeacon for asking – it is obliquely related to the investigation – but what is your view on homosexuality?"

Randall almost choked on his coffee before answering. "My goodness, that's a strange question for a police officer to be asking a vicar. Do you want the Church's view or my own personal view?"

"Well, let's frame the question in an example. Supposing a young teenager from your congregation came to you and said they were being troubled by feelings of attraction towards someone of the same sex, what would you say to them?"

"Mmm… what I would say would depend very much on the particular person in question, but in general I'd try to reassure them that they were not alone or a freak of some sort, and suggest places and organizations where they could get help or support. I certainly wouldn't come down heavy with the hell fire and wrath of God stuff if that's what you're thinking?"

"So, you would take a liberal position?"

"Don't quote me on this, but the poor old Church of England has got itself in a right muddle on this issue, mainly to try and keep the different traditions in the Church together. Let's just say that our understanding of human sexuality is a lot more complex than we used to think when I was a teenager, and we have to move with the times or else become utterly irrelevant."

Randall took a sip of coffee and then rather unexpectedly continued,

"Oh, and by the way, if you are delicately trying to probe to see if Jack Nobel ever came to seek personal advice of that nature from me, the answer is, 'no', he never did. In fact, I have never had that conversation with a teenager or adult in my congregation, although you might be pleased to know that I do have the gay switchboard number as a resource if such a situation did arise. Most people go and seek advice from those who are going to tell them what they've already decided to do in their heart, so it's no real surprise that gay people don't generally come clamouring to the church's door for help on that matter. Anyway, the police force has hardly got a proud history on gay rights, don't you think?"

Rachael felt that she had been outwitted in her ploy, but with the gentlest of rebuffs. She decided that it was probably time to go. She thanked the archdeacon for his time and hoped, but couldn't guarantee, that they wouldn't have to disturb him again. Randall very graciously showed them to the door and then said he had to get something from the boot of his car, so accompanied them out into the close where his rather old but well-looked-after estate car was parked. Roshni and Rachael were moving away when Rachael just happened to glance back and see that in the boot of his car, Randall had a considerable quantity of sacking that looked suspiciously like that used at the

Winchester mill and some rope which looked suspiciously like that found close to Daniel Jarvis' car on Farley Mount. An intense spasm of panic momentarily seized Rachael. What was the best thing to do? Should she confront Randall there and then? After what seemed like a month, but was only a few seconds, she grabbed Roshni's arm and said, "Keep walking casually until we're out of sight." As soon as they were through the gate to the close Rachael rang Towgood to explain what she had seen in the back of Randall's car. Thankfully, he answered straightaway. He responded with some excitement.

"Right, you two out of there and back to the office. I don't want Randall getting a whiff of suspicion that what is going to happen next has anything to do with your interview this morning. Time for a devious covert operation, I think."

Rachael found out later that barely ten minutes after leaving the scene, two police cars, sirens blaring and blue lights flashing, had raced into the cathedral close and put blue tape around the area containing Randall's car. A startled archdeacon was asked by one of the constables if he wouldn't mind handing them his car keys as they'd had an anonymous tip-off of a bomb threat and they had to check the vehicles in the cordoned off area very carefully. Several vehicles were checked, but in reality, a full forensic search of Randall's estate car looking for blood, fibres, DNA – the lot, was the objective of the exercise. The event was not inconspicuous. People were evacuated from the nearby buildings and crowds gathered close to the police cordon, speculating on what was happening. The forensic team worked quickly, however, and the close was back to normal by the end of the day. Nothing appeared in the newspaper or the local news, so Towgood had his fingers crossed that he'd got away with a very risky enterprise.

When Rachael and Roshni returned to the office, Towgood was understandably too busy to talk to them. He rushed by them on his way to deal with another crisis and just had time to blurt out, "No time to talk now… Give me a written report of your interview and leave it on my desk by the end of the day… I'll see you both in the news conference studio tomorrow morning bright and early."

As Rachael compiled the report, with Roshni sitting opposite and contributing from her detailed notes, she kept wondering whether Randall really could be a murderer and a rapist. From what she'd seen and heard today it seemed so unlikely. Roshni was of a similar frame of mind. She thought that the archdeacon seemed like a nice man. She was impressed with his wife as well.

And yet, there was the sacking and the rope in the boot of his car, the highlighted article in the Peterborough newspaper, and the video footage of Jack visiting someone in the cathedral offices. None of it was conclusive, but it was all vaguely pointing a finger in the same direction. You had to ask the question, if Jack was not visiting Randall, then who else at the cathedral would he have been visiting? Just as she was writing the last sentence, she was seized by a mini panic attack. Suppose this had nothing to do with Fenton St Mary and the troubles of Jack's teenage years, suppose they were barking up the wrong tree again and they were doomed to have a 'garden gnomes fiasco part 2'? Suppose it wasn't a murder at all, maybe suicide or just a grotesque accident? Rachael steadied her nerves. No, they had demonstrated it couldn't have been an accident. You couldn't tie yourself up in a sack and hurl yourself in a river with the expectation that you were going to get mangled in a mill almost a day later downstream. Even if it was suicide there must have been an accomplice for the same reason. Rachael added the last full stop with a defining tap on the computer keyboard, printed off a copy and then, finding a buff document folder in her drawer, inserted the sheets of paper and placed it prominently on Towgood's very untidy desk.

XIX

RACHAEL HAD NEVER BEEN INVOLVED with such a prominent murder inquiry before, and certainly not one which involved a national press conference. The whole event was therefore novel and somewhat exciting. The conference room in the police headquarters had been turned into a news briefing studio. At one end, there was a long, wooden bench behind which the speakers and the worthies could sit. Towgood was to take centre stage, but Rachael thought that he would be less than happy to have the chief constable sitting on one side of him and the chief superintendent sitting on the other. Both, she imagined, would be in full dress uniform, prominently displaying their authority to the world behind the camera. On the bench, microphones had been positioned at regular intervals to allow up to five speakers to participate. When Rachael entered, technicians were fiddling with them and connecting them to a console that seemed to have a ridiculous number of sliders and buttons. There were also two TV cameras mounted on tripods aimed at the principal seat behind the bench. These also were being adjusted by technicians. On the wall behind the bench where the spokespeople were to sit, there was a banner which the chief constable had insisted must be present, which stated that Wessex Police were 'caring for the community in a diverse and changing world' along with the Force's logo, county badge and a picture of a smiling, helpful PC in a high visibility jacket. Rachael thought the presence of this was slightly distasteful, especially considering the reason for having the press conference. A fair number of chairs had been neatly arranged in front of the bench for members of the press to sit, listen and ask questions. Rachael's task was to 'facilitate the accommodation of the press.' That is, basically act as a glorified cinema usherette.

She wondered how many would turn up and whether she would see any familiar faces off the television. The press conference was due to start at eleven and members of the press started drifting in from about ten fifteen. She recognised a couple of local reporters, fairly shabbily dressed, who had arrived early to try and get a decent seat. The crime correspondents from the BBC news and ITV were amongst the later arrivals. She recognised both from appearances on television news and was rather awe-struck as she led both to prominent positions near the front of the room. She was surprised to see how many foreign news outlets sent a representative as well. By the time Towgood entered the room, flanked by the chief superintendent and the chief constable, with the Force's press officer and crime commissioner also in attendance, the room was nearly full and buzzing with activity. Towgood remained standing while the other four took their places behind the front bench. The room became hushed as Towgood looked around the room, signalling that he was ready to start. Rachael was incredibly impressed with her boss at this moment. She would have been a gibbering wreck standing in front of all those people, yet Towgood looked calm, authoritative and in control. His presence was as convincing as any ennobled Shakespearian actor.

"Ladies and gentlemen," he began, "we've called this press conference today because we very much need the assistance of the general public to help us solve the murder of a young man whose remains were found at the Winchester mill on Easter Monday this year. You may recall the incident was well publicised at the time, but it has proved to be an extremely difficult case to investigate and only in recent times have we been able to ascertain the identity of the victim. He is Jack Nobel, a 27-year-old man at the time of his murder, who resided in Peterborough with a friend from his school days. The most recent picture we have of him has been posted on the Wessex Constabulary website and can be downloaded by press and TV for publication and broadcast purposes."

The now familiar picture of Jack was projected onto a screen at the side of the front bench. Daniel had been cropped out of the image, but nevertheless Rachael still felt a churning of unhappiness in her stomach every time she saw it. It remained displayed until the end of the press conference. Towgood continued,

"We have video camera evidence that Jack was in Winchester on Thursday 12th April. He parked his car in the Castle multi-storey car park at 10.30am and then walked down through the town to the cathedral where he went into the cathedral offices and spent fifteen minutes before emerging again. We believe that Mr Nobel was murdered somewhere in the Winchester area on the 13th or 14th April and his body dumped in the river, not far from 'The Red Lion' pub. I would appeal to anyone who saw him or interacted with him during this period to come forward and talk to us. There will be a dedicated, anonymous phone line that will be posted on the website and can be copied and advertised by the media.

"We are also interested in Mr Nobel's contacts in the Peterborough area where he had been living for at least a year, and we would like to speak to people that knew him as a teenager growing up in the village of Fenton St Mary in Cambridgeshire, if we've not been in touch already.

"You can access a more detailed briefing paper to flesh out your news stories on-line, but if there are any questions, I'll take them now."

A well-dressed man with a good physique but greying hair, suggesting that he was probably in his early fifties, stood up and confidently addressed the hand-held microphone that was put in front of him. He looked familiar to Rachael.

"Ezra Mackay, BBC," he began. "Isn't it the case that this investigation has been shambolic from beginning to end? I gather you spent the first few weeks tracking down the wrong suspects in what was reported in some newspapers as 'The Garden Gnome Fiasco', and it is now six months since the body was found and you are only now releasing the name of the victim? Have you any leads at all? It seems you have very little prospect of finding the murderer."

Rachael thought this was a very mean-spirited question and would have responded in no uncertain terms that the reporter was wrong and didn't know what he was talking about. She also noticed a smirk on the chief superintendent's face. Had he slipped some information to Mr Mackay to discredit Towgood? Towgood remained serenely calm and responded with good grace.

"I don't agree with you. This has been an immensely difficult case where the body of the victim was found so mutilated that it was unrecognisable. It constitutes great progress that we have been able to identify him at all. It is also not true to say we have no leads. I am not sharing everything with you at present, but I will add that we now have an ever-improving understanding of the victim's movements in the days before his death and we know there is a strong link between the cathedral and his murder. In fact, we would be particularly interested to hear from the person or persons who talked to Jack Nobel when he went into the cathedral office on 12th April as we've been unable to track them down so far.

"As for the 'Garden Gnomes Fiasco', as you put it, we were unlucky that a second crime cross-contaminated our murder inquiry. I would point out that we did solve that crime and the offenders were brought to justice. I'm sure the council tax payers of Wessex will be delighted to know that their police force is taking all crime seriously and is not just worrying about the high-profile cases."

Rachael noticed that Towgood looked sharply in the direction of the chief superintendent as he said this and interestingly, the chief superintendent looked away to avoid making eye contact. The BBC correspondent seemed satisfied with the answer and did not pursue his criticism. Several other television and newspaper correspondents asked questions, mainly of a technical nature or to clarify something that Towgood had already stated. The local newspaper reporter asked if the general public in Winchester was safe with a murderer on the loose. Towgood responded that since nothing had happened in the last six months, it was unlikely that there was much danger, but he added a caveat and concluded, "…unless there is anyone out there who actually knows who the killer is, in which case, I would advise them to get in touch with us straight away as they could be in grave danger." That got the reporters' pencils scribbling away furiously. The crime commissioner made some politically slanted points (the election was next May) and the chief constable made some bland reassuring statement once the questions had ceased.

So, after about forty-five minutes the event came to an end. The journalists drifted away, and the technicians started to dismantle the cameras, lights and microphones. It didn't seem such a big deal in the end, maybe even a bit of an anti-climax. That evening, however, Rachael was soon disabused of that notion when she turned on the television news and discovered that the press conference was the lead item. Great prominence was given to the name of the victim and his photo and significant sections of Towgood's address were broadcast, including his assertion that there was a link with the cathedral. They even had their crime correspondent analysing the work that police had done so far and what their next steps should be. Most of this bore no relation to what the team had actually done or what Rachael thought they would be doing in the next few days. Pablo texted very excitedly to say he'd seen her for a few seconds on the TV and was over the moon that he was now going out with a screen celebrity.

The newspapers the following day were just as eye-opening. 'Victim named in gruesome mill murder' was the headline in one of the more reputable ones, 'Killer in the close' proclaimed the most popular tabloid, and 'Wear your stab vest to evensong' shouted the most scurrilous.

Towgood proclaimed himself satisfied with the proceedings the next morning at their daily briefing and was hopeful that the publicity generated would do the job for them.

"Right, now let's hear from the team that was keeping an eye on the cathedral close. Any unexpected movements, especially involving Randall?"

"Nothing out of the ordinary, sir," one of the officers responded. "Randall emerged from the office in the afternoon to go across to the cathedral looking cheerful and relaxed."

"Mm… that's disappointing," Towgood said with a furrowed brow. "Well, keep up the watch and do be discreet. I don't suppose anyone else was acting suspiciously?"

"No, sir."

There was plenty for everyone to do. There was still potential CCTV

~ 136 ~

footage to review, hotlines to set up and maintain, and a follow-up on Jack's wallet. Rachael rang Karen in Peterborough to ask her to check out Randall's friends that he claimed to be visiting at the crucial time on the day of the Deanery Festival.

It came to mid-morning and Rachael noticed an upright and distinguished man leaving the chief superintendent's office. He wore a dark grey, woollen overcoat and had a clerical dog collar attached to his black shirt. His neatly slicked silvery-grey hair and metal-rimmed glasses made him strangely familiar to Rachael. Then she recognised him as the dean of the cathedral. She imagined him as a stern, academic type who would quibble over the exact translation of a particular ancient Greek word in the original biblical text and look down on anyone who did not have a university degree in theology; he seemed very cold, detached and unapproachable. What was he doing visiting the chief superintendent?

"Towgood, my office now," boomed a voice as loud as a town crier.

Rachael quaked and felt she was going to find out very soon what it was all about. Towgood calmly walked across the open plan general office area towards the source of the command as if he hadn't a care in the world. Those working in the vicinity became hushed in the hope that they would be able to hear what was going on. As usual, only the coarse booming voice of the chief superintendent could be heard. The calm reasoned responses of Towgood would not penetrate the walls.

"I don't take kindly to senior members of the clergy complaining to me about police harassment and slander. You better have a damn good reason for telling the world that this murder is linked to the cathedral. Do you realise that there are reporters and television crews from all over the world swarming all over the close at this very moment? Nobody can get on with any work as they are being accosted by people wanting interviews and statements. It's a gross intrusion of privacy."

There followed a period of silence as Towgood evidently justified himself.

"Your head is well and truly on the block here. The dean plays golf with the chief constable regularly – and I've had a round or two with him myself. I don't want you interviewing any of the cathedral staff without my express permission. Do I make myself clear? If you make a balls-up of this one, you'll be out."

A further moment of silence followed.

"Get out! It's no bloody business of yours who I play golf with."

Towgood emerged calmly and returned to his own office, walking carelessly through the open-plan layout as if contemplating somewhere nice to go on his holidays.

Rachael had a meeting with him scheduled for ten minutes later. When she entered her first comment tried to show comradely concern.

"Are you OK, sir?"

"Yes, I'm fine. My arm still aches a little from playing badminton at the weekend, but that's just old age creeping up on me."

This wasn't what Rachael had meant, and moreover she realised that Towgood knew that it wasn't what she meant, so she changed tack slightly.

"It's a bit of a disaster not being able to interview Randall again without the chief super's permission?"

"Au contraire, Sergeant Goodfellow, things have worked out very well. I've obviously stirred things up and maybe our murderer is starting to get a bit worried. It would be very interesting to know who is driving the complaints coming from the cathedral. As for any interviews, there are always ways around the shackles that are supposed to bind us, but we will need to tread carefully.

"Now, we must keep our fingers crossed and hope that something comes in from the Great British Public after the bombshells we dropped yesterday, and also, we need to pay our respects at Jack Nobel's funeral next week. I think we'll take that junior PC that was helping you. He can mix a little more easily with any younger people who might be attending."

After the excitement of the press conference and interviewing Randall with the discovery of the sacking and the rope, the next few days were rather dull and uninteresting. Information dribbled in rather than flowed in, and nothing that was earth-shattering came to light. On the few occasions that she saw Towgood, she could tell he was disappointed by the response. He was clearly keeping out of the way of the chief superintendent and using work on other cases as a front so as not to have his wings clipped. Nothing seemed to be out of the ordinary with the continuing monitoring of Randall's movements (which presumably the chief superintendent knew nothing about) and even more frustrating, a technical glitch meant that none of the clandestinely obtained evidence from Randall's car would be available until the middle of next week. Still, there was another date with Pablo to look forward to at the weekend.

XX

THE FIRST DATE WITH PABLO had gone extremely well in Rachael's eyes and they had texted or phoned each other at least once a day ever since. Finding time to meet up in person had not been so easy though. Rachael was obviously busy with the murder investigation, and she had to do a fair amount of overtime, as well as spending time away in Peterborough. Pablo too, had to take on extra shifts, sometimes through the night, which meant he would be asleep during the day. They did manage to meet up for the odd rushed lunch break or a casual drink in town when both of them felt they had enough energy not to fall asleep. Rachael didn't feel they were quite at the stage where they could just pop around to each other's houses without notice, although she was pleased that Pablo seemed to respect her reluctance about this without appearing to lose interest.

Rachael, of course, also visited her mother at the nursing home frequently. She and Pablo had decided, for the time being, to pretend not to know each other to avoid confusing her. The ploy was not entirely successful. She may have been suffering from dementia but even so, Rachael's mother was still a very perceptive lady and began to be suspicious. One Sunday afternoon when it was wet and miserable and Rachael had dropped by to have afternoon tea with her mother in the common room with the other residents, they were staring out at the large drops of rain splattering on the glass windowpane when quite out of the blue she said,

"That Spanish assistant always seems to be buzzing around when you're here. Look at the way he's fussing over those two in the corner. I hardly see him at all the rest of the time. He isn't making a nuisance of himself, is he? I can complain to the matron if he is making you feel uncomfortable."

Rachael spluttered on her tea and then laughed. "No, Mother, he is no problem at all. I'm sure he is just trying to make an effort when guests arrive."

Thankfully, Rachael's mother was having a spell where she was much calmer. She was on a new medication which seemed to make her happier and more content. There was far less reference to how her older siblings had made much more of their lives or paranoia about people trying to steal her money. Rachael was hopeful that they would be able to attend the carol service at the cathedral again as they had done for twenty years, ever since she was a child.

Both Pablo and Rachael realised that they were going to have to engineer some quality time together if they were going to move their relationship on to the next level, and so Pablo had suggested that they should have a weekend in London, take in a show and have a nice evening meal, and then give themselves a chance finally to spend a night alone together. Rachael insisted that they share the cost. She remained acutely aware that Pablo earned a lot less than her and she did not want him to feel he always had to be the chivalrous alpha male. He had reluctantly agreed, and the date was set for the coming weekend. Rachael was excited and somewhat nervous too. She spent an age on Friday evening after work deciding what she would wear and what she would pack. She knew she must resist the temptation to take too much. Saturday morning arrived drizzly and grey-cloud laden, typical of late autumn. Pablo arrived in his car absolutely at the time he said he would and cheerily bundled Rachael's small case into the boot of the car. Rachael relaxed a little as Pablo in his normal optimistic manner struck up an easy-going conversation. Although the station was within walking distance, Pablo had a colleague who lived literally around the corner from the railway station and had generously allowed Pablo to park on his drive for free during the weekend. This would make the homeward journey so much less taxing when they returned on Sunday evening. London was only about an hour away, but it was still a bit of an adventure to go there by train.

The hotel was nice. They'd got a really good discount on a hotel booking website, probably because the main clients were business people who only required rooms during the week. Having signed in and sorted their room out, they had time to go and wander down Oxford Street and look in the shops. Rachael didn't really need any clothes at the moment, so she didn't try Pablo's patience too long looking at dresses. The cloud had thinned and lightened, and it was mild for the time of year. They went and looked in book shops and a record shop (yes, there still was one open on the High Street). Pablo seemed to enjoy this and was able to suggest some songs by Spanish artists that Rachael might enjoy.

As the show they were going to see started quite late, they decided to eat first. Pablo had discovered an authentic Spanish restaurant just off Shaftesbury Avenue and was keen to introduce Rachael to the delights of his native cuisine. Considering they were right in the heart of London, Rachael was struck by the small-scale nature of the place which was obviously a family-run business, probably handed down from father to son through who knows how many generations. It had a cosy, friendly feeling with photographs and pictures of typical Spanish scenes placed at intervals along the walls. As soon as the staff cottoned on to the fact that Pablo was a native of Spain, the manager came to greet him like a long-lost son and made it his job to serve Rachael and Pablo personally. They spoke to each other incredibly quickly in Spanish, leaving Rachael utterly uncomprehending and resorting to smiling and nodding at what she hoped were the right moments.

Rachael was relieved to find that there were tasty things on the menu which she really liked and of course, the wine helped too.

The theatre was only just round the corner so there was no sense of rush or anxiety to get there. The show was a musical; a modern one about the founding of America. Rachael was not an aficionado of the theatre but nevertheless enjoyed the novelty of the spectacle and the experience of watching live entertainment. She also enjoyed being able legitimately to snuggle up to Pablo during the more romantic numbers. When they emerged into the night air at the end the sky was clear, and the temperature was as cool as it gets in the middle of a big city. They found a bar which was not too busy but nevertheless had atmosphere. The staff were dressed smartly in black trousers and open-necked white shirts and a small trio of young musicians was playing mellow jazz as background music in the far corner. Rachael was neither a fan nor a hater of this music style, but right now it seemed to create just the perfect ambience. They both drank fancy gins and talked easily about how they found the show, how they'd found the food in the restaurant, how life was in Spain, how life was in England, about anything that took their fancy.

Then at about two in the morning it was time to return to the hotel. Rachael was not tired; indeed, she had never been more awake or alive in her whole life. They went to the bedroom. There was an awkward moment when neither of them knew quite what to do, and then Pablo leant over and kissed Rachael, pulling her closer to him. Rachael responded in kind. Soon Pablo no longer had his shirt on, and Rachael had lost her dress. Not long after both were completely naked and lying together entwined and writhing on the bed. First Pablo was on top and then Rachael. The sensuousness and intimacy of their love-making was something that Rachael had rarely experienced before. With Martin it had all been rather cold and clinical.

There was not a lot of sleep in the few remaining hours of nighttime. Breakfast was missed and they just about managed to check out by the deadline set by the hotel. Instead, they found a small café that was doing 'brunch'. They were in no hurry, and it was nearly 2pm before they got up to have a wander around the sights in Central London. It was one of those autumn days of piercing, dazzling, bright sunshine, desperately trying to restore the glory of summer but not having the energy or warmth quite to manage it. Even here in this urban extremity there were golden brown leaves sprinkled across the pavements like forgotten confetti. The bright sunshine suited Rachael's mood which was one of contentment. Her body still tingled from the memory of the physical contact with Pablo the night before. She was happy. She felt fulfilled. Rarely did she have the time just to fritter away an afternoon, and so she luxuriated in the opportunity to dawdle and wander aimlessly with the man she loved. Yes, she had made the decision that it really was love, the real thing, and she desperately hoped that Pablo felt the same way about her.

Eventually, after the sun reluctantly, but all too early, set in the west, Rachael and Pablo made their way across Westminster Bridge in the gathering gloom and walked the short distance to Waterloo station to catch the train back to Winchester. Rachael nestled into the arm of Pablo as they sat together in a thinly occupied railway carriage watching the ever-diminishing number of lights flash by the window as they finally quit the suburbs of the capital and hurtled through the Surrey and Hampshire countryside. Before she even noticed it, they were stepping down onto the platform at Winchester station and Pablo was taking her back to her house in his car.

There was a long and lingering kiss in the car. Rachael asked if he wanted to come in for coffee, but Pablo said he needed to get back as he had an early shift in the morning. Rachael was a little disappointed but appreciated that she could also do with a good night's sleep before work herself. Just as she got out of the car Pablo pulled out a door key and presented it to Rachael. He told her that he loved her very much and trusted her enough that she should feel able to come and go in his house whenever she liked. Rachael stood for a second unable to say anything, then she bent down in through the driver's window to kiss him again. She said she would come over tomorrow evening after work. When she did so, she reciprocated the gesture.

From that time on they came and went from each other's houses as if they were their own. They became a proper couple and Rachael suspected and hoped that it was only a matter of time before they moved in together in a shared house of their own, and then… who knows?

Rachael was resolved on one other thing as well. Her life was going to change and that meant her siblings would have to share more of the responsibility for looking after their mother. With new-found confidence she rang her eldest brother and demanded that they get together for a family conference about how they were going to share the arrangements now that Rachael was in a relationship. She brushed aside the usual excuses about distance, having a family to bring up and a busy work schedule with such force that Matthew was stunned into silence and agreed. Ruth, the second eldest, was of course in Australia, but even so Rachael insisted that she should participate via video link and not just passively assume that the rest of the family would cope. James of course agreed immediately to her request, but she knew he would be utterly ineffectual whatever he agreed to do. A date was set for the New Year when they would get together at a time when it wouldn't be the middle of the night for Ruth and thrash out a new and more equitable plan for looking after and keeping in touch with their mother.

XXI

IT WOULD BE CRASS AND in poor taste to suggest that attending a funeral would make a nice day out, but Rachael suspected that for different reasons her two accompanying colleagues attending the service of internment for poor Jack Nobel regarded it in this fashion.

Detective Inspector Towgood had clearly expected a much better response from the press conference than he was actually getting, and Rachael could sense that he was feeling under pressure from higher authorities to make progress. Even taking into account the relentlessly flat landscape around Fenton St Mary which he hated, Towgood was probably glad to escape from the office for a few days.

PC Jeremy Black probably viewed the event like a school trip, a chance to get away from the mind-numbing daily routine. Rachael had given him a detailed briefing of his role. He was to have his ears and eyes open during the ceremony and the reception afterwards, to pick up any gossip among the assembled mourners, particularly the younger ones. He was to fraternise discreetly with any attendees who might have been contemporaries of Jack. Rachael reminded him that although he was not in uniform, he was to look smart and not look out of place amongst the assembled company. To be fair, he had made a good effort and looked very handsome in his fitted two-piece black suit and polished black shoes. He had even found a sober black tie to go with his neatly ironed white shirt. Rachael had to admit he was probably the most smartly dressed out of all three of them.

The church, which was slightly back from the long, straight road which bisected the village, had some ancient stonework at the east end but was substantially rebuilt in the 19th century. It therefore didn't have that musty air of centuries past and had clean, white-washed walls and flat, tiled floors. At some point the pews had been taken out and replaced with chairs, probably to make the space more flexible and welcoming.

There was a good turnout. A few faces looked familiar from the interviews they had done a little while back. There were also plenty of completely unknown people, a sizeable number of whom must have been the same age as Jack. Rachael did spot Daniel sitting near the front of the church with a very pretty lady with long blonde hair sitting next to him and occasionally grasping his arm. Rachael recognised her as Daniel's fiancée, Julie. Not a pleasant day for them, that was for sure. The three police personnel had decided to spread themselves out discreetly rather than all sit together. Towgood explained that it would make them look less conspicuous and also would allow them greater scope for observation of the congregation. Towgood positioned himself by the door which would afford him an excellent view of who was coming in and who was going out. Rachael and Jeremy sat at the back of the central nave on opposite sides of the aisle and made out that they did not know each other. Mournful music was being played extremely badly on the ill-tuned organ.

Finally, there was a stir and people stood up in a wave starting from nearest the door. The vicar, who was female, entered ahead of the coffin, reading the prescribed biblical texts from the funeral service. The coffin was carried by five men of various ages and one woman who must have been close to Jack's age. It later transpired, thanks to Towgood's digging at the reception afterwards, that these six were co-workers at the supermarket where Jack had been working when he had caught up with Daniel again. Interesting then that Jack must have made a good enough impression that they were prepared to make this gesture. Mrs Nobel came next. She had regained some of her composure since Rachael had last seen her and cut a defiant and commanding presence, but also an isolated and very lonely one. Behind her walked a man and a woman, both of a similar age to Mrs Nobel, followed by two earnest looking ladies in their mid-twenties who were similar enough in appearance to be unmistakable as sisters. Rachael later found out that the woman was Mrs Nobel's sister being accompanied by her husband and two daughters. Finally, a man, again of a similar age to Mrs Nobel, lingered a little behind the others and sat on the opposite side of the aisle when they took their places. Rachael guessed correctly that this was Mr Nobel.

The vicar, who was a calm, reassuring woman and had a way of addressing the gathering as if she were a mother capable of making everything right, was relatively new to the parish and so knew nothing of the events that were of interest some ten years previously. To her, Fenton St Mary was a different world from then and for that reason the police hadn't even bothered to interview her concerning the death of Jack. However, it also meant that her comments about Jack, however kindly meant, were of a very general nature and it was clear to everyone that she knew very little about him.

Rachael was thus pleased to see that Daniel got up to present the eulogy and given the circumstances did a really good job. He even managed to crack the odd joke about things they got up to as kids. It was only when he got to describing the very last time that he saw Jack that his voice cracked, and he had to pause for a moment or two to regain his composure. As the coffin was taken out to the churchyard for burial, Towgood, Rachael and Jeremy joined the solemn procession that led to the graveside. The skies were leaden but at least it wasn't raining even if there was a persistent moisture hanging in the air. The atmosphere was incredibly sad; too sad to be able to bear for long.

Rachael looked intently at the faces of the mourners as the committal took place outside. The vicar, with her solemn but somehow soothing and reassuring manner recited the liturgy as the coffin was lowered into place.

"We have entrusted our brother, Jack, to God's merciful keeping and we now commit his body to the ground…"

Who was being really affected at this moment? Mrs Nobel had a stoical mask of defiance in the face of overwhelming grief. Perhaps she knew that if she was to shed too many tears at this point, she would fall to pieces completely. Her sister with her family in attendance, stood at Mrs Nobel's side offering her comfort and looking appropriately solemn. However, it was perfectly clear that this was only a very sad moment for them. There was no gut-wrenching grief. Mr Nobel's reaction was interesting. He stood as far from his ex-wife as it was possible to be, and he seemed to be squirming and looking for some other hole to disappear into as if consumed by overwhelming shame. Was there some element of guilt here?

"…Earth to earth, ashes to ashes, dust to dust…"

Daniel was clearly feeling deeply moved. He had his arm around his fiancée who also had hers around him. They were holding each other close for comfort. One or two others who were around Jack's age had a tear in their eye and were probably remembering him as a school friend in happier times.

"…in sure and certain hope of the resurrection to eternal life…"

On the edge of the group who had come out for the committal was a young woman, again about Jack's age – maybe a little bit older, but she seemed to be on her own. She did not seem to know the other people there from Jack's peer group. She was dressed very respectably, but cheaply, suggesting to Rachael that she was not well off. She had a handkerchief in her hand, and she seemed unduly distraught.

As the earth was thrown on top of the coffin and the main party moved away from the grave site, Rachael manoeuvred to catch up with the woman to have a chat.

"Hello, are you OK?" she asked in what she hoped seemed a friendly and caring manner. "I couldn't help noticing you seemed very upset just now and didn't seem to have anyone to support you."

"Oh… I'm OK. It's just the emotion, you know. I was overcome for a moment. That's all."

"Are you coming to the reception? It's in the pub in the village."

"Oh… I don't know. I don't really know anyone here. I thought I might just go home."

"Do come," Rachael responded hoping not to sound too desperate, "it will do you good to have a cup of tea and something to eat before you go, and you might be able to share some happier memories. I'll walk with you. I'm Rachael, by the way."

Rachael was relieved that the balance of doubt just shifted in her favour and the young lady, who said her name was Amy, agreed to stay just for a short while.

While they were walking along the damp, grass-tufted lane that led via a shortcut to the pub, Rachael casually asked Amy how she came to know Jack. Over the course of their walk and a cup of tea in the pub, Amy told Rachael that she had come across Jack when they were both in a very bad way, down and out on the streets of London when they were eighteen. Rachael listened intently. This was the missing part of Jack's life that they had never been able to find anything about.

"…I always knew Jack was slightly different. I wondered how he'd ended up in that mess. He was too clever, too intelligent. He should never have been mixing with the likes of us."

"Maybe he felt the same way about you? You seem to have your wits about you."

"Yeah…" Amy laughed. "I owe it to Jack that I turned my life around. It was like one day he decided that enough was enough and he was going to make something of himself. We stuck together as a team and thanks to some really good people at the homeless shelter, we managed to get jobs, first of all in bars then we managed to get some shop work. We both started to save a bit of money and gradually became 'respectable'. Jack suddenly decided he wanted to go back to Peterborough. I was devastated and nearly went with him, but I didn't and am glad I didn't. I sensed he didn't think of me romantically, and if I'd hung around him too much longer, I think I might have fallen in love with him.

"I've got a pretty good job now, working with drug addicts. It's hard work, but I can empathize better than some of the other staff and the clients seem to appreciate it. Poor Jack. I read about his death in the newspaper and just had to come to the funeral and pay my respects."

"Did Jack ever tell you what events led to him ending up in that mess in the first place?" Rachael enquired as casually as possible.

"Oh yes, he told me exactly what happened… and who was responsible."

Rachael got over-excited at this point and said rather unwisely, "Look, I'm a police officer and I'm investigating Jack's murder. If you know something we need to know."

Amy was rattled and after a moment's incoherent mutterings she said, "I've already said too much, I think. I really have to go. I need to get the bus back to Peterborough to catch the train."

"I can give you a lift if you like?" Rachael said desperately, knowing she'd already blown it.

"No... no it's alright," Amy stuttered and turned to run out of the room. Rachael caught her hand and thrust a card into it, specially printed with the phone number of the investigation unit.

"Call us," Rachael pleaded.

It was no good. Amy left the room. She did keep hold of the card, however. That was one consolation, but damn it, she was so close to finding out something really important and she'd managed to mess it up.

Both Towgood and Jeremy had been working the room hard and had been talking to as many people as possible, but gradually, one by one, in twos and threes people departed. When it was more or less just the family left it was time for the three police officers to go too. Towgood accompanied by Jeremy and Rachael paid their respects to Mrs Nobel and her sister's family (Mr Nobel had left pretty quickly, evidently not wishing to cause an uneasy atmosphere as the room thinned out). Towgood, gently and sensitively, spoke for all three of them.

"I do hope you will be alright, and I wish you some peace and contentment in the future. The only thing I can say is that we will do everything in our power to catch the murderer. I know that's not much consolation." He then gave Mrs Nobel a hug and bade her farewell.

Rachael had come in her own car because she was planning to go home to Winchester that evening. Towgood was planning to stay on an extra day and so was taking Jeremy back to Peterborough with him.

"I think we ought to have a debrief before we all disappear," Towgood said as they were standing in the church car park. "I noticed a carvery on the main road just before we got to the island on the ring road around Peterborough. How about we stop there, and I will shout you both an early dinner. I think you have to go that way anyway, Rachael, to get back onto the A1?"

Jeremy was more than OK with that, and Rachael didn't mind either as long as she didn't end up having to drive home in the small hours of the night. An hour later they were sat around a table and making the most of Towgood's generosity. Rachael felt it would be good manners to offer to buy drinks, but Towgood was feeling expansively generous and said he would pay for those too. The pub was a large, open-plan structure with tables of various sizes dotted about with a mixture of bench seating and ordinary chairs with a long semi-circular bar situated centrally. There was nothing original about the place. Its format must have been repeated hundreds of times up and down the country. It was very quiet, being midweek and still quite early.

Rachael related her meeting with Amy. She could see that Towgood was getting very interested when she got to the point where Amy was about to reveal what had happened to Jack and could almost feel his disappointment when she rather tamely had to explain that Amy had then rushed off without spilling the beans.

"Oh well," Towgood said, "at least we know there is someone out there who does know what happened. The only trouble is finding her. Social worker or working in drug rehabilitation? Living in London? Called Amy? Might not be impossible to find her. Very difficult though. A full report on my desk when I get back in a couple of days, please, Goodfellow. Now, PC Black what did you discover?"

"I asked his school friends what they thought had happened to him."

"What was the point of that?" Rachael asked, perhaps a little disparagingly.

"Gossip often contains kernels of truth. I wondered whether anything might emerge that we hadn't considered yet."

"And did it?" asked Towgood.

"Well… no, not really. Half of them seemed to think he must have just been unlucky and met his death at the hands of a random mugger. Most of the others thought it must have something to do with his time when he left school and was on his way down and out. A couple of them who were on that trip to Peterborough with the choir did say that he looked rather dishevelled when they met up with him again for the concert in the evening. They linked that day very strongly to Jack going odd, just as we have."

"Did you get names and contact details?"

"One of them asked me to go out with them, so we exchanged names and telephone numbers."

"DON'T get involved until this case is sorted," Towgood warned. "Arrange someone to interview them professionally, please, and then send a report to me in Winchester as soon as possible."

The waiter arrived with their orders, so conversation ceased while he was hovering about.

"Did you find out anything, sir?" Rachael eventually asked.

"Mm… well, it wasn't as fruitful an exercise as I would have hoped, but one thing arose which I hadn't realised before. I spoke with Daniel Jarvis, and he remembered Jack saying as he drove off that last time that he knew someone down there that could help him out."

"So, he had a contact. I wonder why he's not come forward?" Rachael wondered out loud.

"You assume it's a man; it could easily be a woman," Towgood pointed out pedantically. "Are you sure there wasn't anything else found in Jack's wallet apart from the cash, driver's licence and credit card? I tend to put bits of paper in mine with phone numbers and passwords I'm likely to forget."

"Jack was a young man in his twenties, not some middle-aged guy who's beginning to lose his marbles," Jeremy commented with half a laugh. Rachael almost choked on a potato at his cheekiness in making this comment to a senior officer. Towgood wasn't exactly pleased. He responded rather haughtily,

"Young man, I am far from being senile. You would do well to appreciate that with increasing years comes judgement, wisdom and experience. You are likely to make a lot of rash and irresponsible mistakes if you are not careful.

"Goodfellow, tomorrow have the wallet checked again and make sure the bank notes were scrutinised for scribblings as well. Also, chase up his credit card. I don't think we've had anything back as to whether there were any purchases made on it during his visit to Winchester."

"Yes, sir."

Towgood sort of explained why he needed to consult with the Peterborough police again, but it didn't sound convincing to Rachael. She suspected he

~ 153 ~

fancied another day out of the orbit of the chief superintendent. Their business was concluded more or less as they finished eating. Towgood and Jeremy made their way to Towgood's car whilst Rachael found a quiet corner just to give Pablo a quick call. How nice it was, just to be able to do that. How quickly they had settled into that cosy familiarity with each other.

"Hola, querido. Yes, I'm just setting off now. It will probably take me three or four hours to get home. It depends how bad the M25 is... No, I've had something to eat... Are you at mine? OK, don't wait up if you've got an early start tomorrow. I'll join you in bed when I get in."

The journey home was a long and tiresome one. It was dark pretty much the whole way. The incessant movement of headlights towards her on the opposite carriageway was mesmeric and she needed to keep the radio on to give her some focus to stop her drifting off into sleep. Eventually, she arrived home at about 11.30. With great contentment, she kicked off her shoes, undressed and fell into the arms of her beloved, who only semiconsciously acknowledged Rachael's presence.

XXII

RACHAEL DUG OUT THE FILE on Jack's wallet from the grey-metallic three-drawer filing cupboard. There were photos of the wallet with the contents, the credit card and the driver's licence. She noticed that there were no separate photos of the bank notes, although three, crisp ten-pound notes seemed to be poking out in the picture of the wallet. A separate page in the file informed her that the articles were being held in the forensic science lab, so she decided to go down there in person to sort it out quickly. That turned out to be highly optimistic. None of the more experienced workers seemed free to deal with her. She stood tapping her fingers on the reception desk for twenty minutes before a fresh-faced young woman in a white coat and metal-rimmed glasses, came to her assistance. She had probably only just finished her apprenticeship.

They found the wallet bagged up in the correct cupboard. When opened by the technician, suitably gloved and using various scientific instruments, the contents were in place as shown in the photo in Rachael's file.

"Can you check whether there's any little bits of paper stuck in the lining or anything marked on the bank notes?" Rachael asked as politely as she could.

Fortunately, the young, inexperienced technician was keen to unleash her skills on this unexpected opportunity that had come her way. She was prepared to investigate with enthusiasm. Each ten-pound note was examined meticulously under natural and ultra-violet light. Nothing was found. A close examination of the depths of the individual pockets of the wallet, poked and prodded with dental-like instruments, seemed to be producing nothing either.

Rachael was just beginning to accept that this line of investigation was not going to yield anything new when suddenly the young woman, in triumph, extracted a screwed-up piece of paper.

"Well, look what I've found..." she shouted in wonder. "It was lodged right in the corner of the pocket where the driving licence is kept."

Unfolding it without destroying it was a tricky and quite time-consuming operation, but eventually it was clear that it was an old supermarket till receipt. Scribbled in pencil on the back was an eleven-digit number beginning with zero. Rachael excitedly wrote the number down in a notebook.

"Ah, that looks as if it could be a mobile phone number," the young technician explained with as much interest.

"Make sure you preserve this and keep it with the rest of the contents of the wallet," Rachael commanded authoritatively to the technician who was having one of her best working days so far.

Rachael felt invigorated by this discovery and hummed to herself as she took the short drive back to the police station. As if that wasn't good enough, when she arrived back, she was bombarded by an avalanche of new information that had been gathered by the team during Rachael and Towgood's absence the previous day. It was such a shame that it had to be Martin who conveyed the news. He couldn't help having a condescending air of smugness as he briefed Rachael. 'While you've been rushing around the country like a headless chicken, look at what I've managed to do with proper professional police work,' he seemed to be saying. Rachael tried to ignore this and just behave in a super-professional and detached way in response. She couldn't deny that what Martin had to say was important though.

Firstly, they'd had a call from a lady who said she'd been working in the cathedral office reception when Jack called in. She hadn't realised the significance of this until she'd heard about the police investigation and seen the CCTV footage on the news. Apparently, his behaviour had been rather odd. He didn't ask to see anyone in particular but just left a general note where it could be observed, and left.

Secondly, some of the forensic evidence was finally back from the secretive, not to say rather dubious, sweep of Randall's car. The tyre prints matched a set found near the river where they supposed Jack's body, tied up in a sack, had been dumped. Even more sensationally, a few strands of hair had been found in the boot of the car amongst the hessian sacking whose DNA matched that of Jack Nobel.

Rachael managed to say, "Good work, Martin," through gritted teeth before turning to Roshni who was sitting at the desk next to hers and asking her to find out if the number found in Jack's wallet was a phone number, and if so, who it belonged to. The next step was to get hold of Towgood to find out what he wanted to do. This turned out to be very frustrating. He was not at the police headquarters in Peterborough and his mobile phone kicked through to the automatic answer service straight away. Rachael left messages with both, that he should get in touch immediately.

Martin was getting over-excited nearby and butted in when Rachael had finished leaving a message on Towgood's phone.

"Do you think we should make an arrest? The evidence looks pretty damning now. It's got to be Randall."

"No. Neither of us has got the authority to sanction that, and if we go in like a bull in a china shop, we might wreck the case," Rachael responded irritably.

"But if you can't get hold of Towgood, you're the next in line…"

"No, Martin…" Rachael rebuked him in a louder voice which caused others nearby to stop and turn. More quietly she carried on, "Go and get on with some work and stop pestering me. I'll tell you what's going to happen when I've spoken to Towgood."

Martin went off like a little boy in a sulk, but was soon replaced by Roshni returning with some news.

"Rachael, that number is a phone number and I've found out who it belongs to."

"That was quick. Well done, Roshni."

"Yes, it belongs to a guy called Bakowski, Michael Bakowski. Unusual name, isn't it? Maybe Polish? We've got an address too. A flat above a chemist's shop in the High Street."

A sense of unexplained familiarity came over Rachael with this information, but before she could dwell on it for too long the phone rang and Towgood was on the other end of the line. Rachael quickly relayed the day's developments – probably a little too quickly for Towgood to fully digest them at the other end of the phone.

"…DS Hall thinks we should arrest Randall straight away. Do you want us to act now?"

"No, no, no…" came an immediate and explosive response from Towgood. "If anyone's going to be doing any arresting, it's going to be me."

There was a long pause and Rachael was beginning to think that she had lost the phone connection. Finally, Towgood continued,

"Randall shows no sign of doing a runner. If we are convinced it's him, we can pick him up anytime."

"Do you still, have doubts, sir?"

"I've never known a case like this, Goodfellow. For months, we've struggled to get any facts at all, and now suddenly we are being deluged with evidence that unerringly suggests who the perpetrator is. And yet… and yet the facts seem to be giving us a crazy answer. I've been desperately trying to dig into Randall's past, up here in Peterborough. You would have thought that if he was an abuser, there would be suspicions, rumours and gossip hanging around somewhere. He is unlikely to have done it just the once and to only one person. Where are the other victims? I can find nothing, absolutely nothing bad about Randall. Everyone says what a nice guy he is. Even Jack's family, although they've split with the Church, don't seem to have anything against Randall personally."

"Should we at least seize his car now that we have such incriminating evidence?"

"Have we retained the sacking and the hair fragments in forensics?"

"Yes."

"Was everything fully recorded and photographed?"

"I'm checking with DS Hall later, but I would imagine so."

"Then we'll leave it for the time being. There will be too many questions and suspicions raised if we suddenly impound the car now. The idea we were originally checking out a bomb threat will look very implausible indeed.

"I'll be in in the morning. Can you arrange an interview with that lady who saw Jack in the cathedral office? Tomorrow, if possible… Oh, and I think it might be wise to arrange a venue away from the close, if possible, just to be discreet. Then… what to do about this mysterious phone contact? I think we'll take a risk and try to catch him unawares. We can wander around to the chemist's shop after we've seen the cathedral office worker."

Towgood terminated the call and Rachael thought she'd better deal with arranging the interview herself, but not before she'd had a lunch break. Martin had returned to the office and was strutting around as if he was in charge. There was only so much of him she could bear at the moment, so some fresh air and a trip to the local sandwich shop was a necessary tonic.

On her return, Martin was nowhere to be seen, but a file with recent information on the case lay on his desk and inside was a hand-scribbled sheet headed, 'Woman who called about seeing Nobel at cathedral office', followed by a name and two phone numbers, one a work number and the other a home one. Rachael tried the work number first. The reply came quickly.

"…Hello? Cathedral office. How can I help?"

"Is that Mrs Cooper?"

"No, Miss Cooper only works two mornings a week. It's not her day today. Can I give her a message?"

Rachael thought for a second, particularly about Towgood's reluctance to be seen to be too publicly breaking the chief superintendent's embargo on harassing the cathedral staff, and replied, "No it's alright, I'll try and get in touch with her at home. Thank you for your help."

A call to the home number was more productive. From her voice, Miss Daisy Cooper struck Rachael as being a timid creature, probably a spinster in her late fifties or early sixties. Rachael introduced herself and asked if it would be possible for her superior to interview her the following day. Miss Cooper said that she'd be working at the office if he wanted to drop by. Rachael asked if it would be possible to arrange a meeting up at the station during her lunch hour. However, Miss Cooper explained that she didn't have a car and it would take rather a long time to walk there. Rachael then suggested that they meet up at one of the tea shops in the High Street instead, as that was only a two-minute walk away from the cathedral. Miss Cooper was agreeable to this, much to Rachael's relief.

What to do next? Towgood had wanted some information on Jack's credit card spending during the key period. Roshni had gone away to investigate this and maybe it was time to catch up on her progress. Across the functional office space, with harsh fluorescent strip lighting being required even during daylight hours now that November was rapidly moving towards December, Roshni could be seen sitting at her desk, brow furrowed, deep in contemplation over something she was seeing on the computer screen. Rachael moved across to her.

"Hi, Roshni, did you make any progress on Jack's credit card?"

"Yes," Roshni responded positively. "There were three items listed for the time Jack is thought to have been down here: a petrol station near Oxford, a guest house in the suburbs of Winchester, and some extra credit on a 'pay as you go' mobile phone. These are the last items that were recorded for the card. Nothing more was spent on it after this."

"Did anyone settle the bill?" Rachael asked.

"No. The credit card company have been trying to track Jack down since the credit period elapsed, so they were quite pleased that we'd called so they could finally put the account to bed."

"So, I'm guessing that Jack must have filled up with petrol on his way down, paid for his accommodation and then needed to use his mobile phone for an important call – we never found a mobile phone, did we?"

"No, and the number is now dead. We were able to trace it from the phone company and the account. There is no phone responding, however."

"Mm… what about the guest house?"

"DC Yapp took a statement from the owner. He's over there now," Roshni said pointing to the far corner of the room. "He can probably give you a more detailed account than I can."

Rachael crossed to where DC Yapp was sat. He had a rather distant glazed expression on his face and was obviously suffering an 'afternoon low'. Rachael's approach jolted him to full consciousness.

He had visited the owner of 'Sunny Meadow House' in person. The house was a large, detached residence that may once have been adjacent to a sunny meadow but was now definitely condemned to be surrounded by newer, less charming properties on the edge of a large housing estate on the fringes of the city. The owner, Mrs Evelyn Jones, explained to him that when she and her husband retired, they found themselves with a property that had three spare bedrooms, their grown-up children all having flown the nest. She had decided to start a little 'Bed and Breakfast' business to keep herself busy and earn a little extra cash. She found that she was rather good at it and was attracting a lot of customers, mainly people having to travel for work, but also a growing number of tourists. DC Yapp was very complimentary about the place and said he would love to stay there himself. The price was quite reasonable as well, considering it was located in Winchester.

Mrs Jones had a sketchy memory of Jack. She described him as being a little dishevelled but well-spoken and very polite. She couldn't remember there being any problems with him, and he certainly wasn't one of the clients she gave a 'red mark' to, meaning that she would never allow them to cross her threshold again. She remembered that he had a rather old, battered car, an old Toyota, that looked as if it was in need of some maintenance. She had been able to confirm that he had stayed for three nights, checking out and paying with a credit card on the Saturday morning of the Easter weekend. As the credit card company had honoured the transaction, as they were bound to do, Mrs Jones had no reason to think anything was amiss.

"That's interesting," Rachael said when DC Yapp had paused for a moment. "It looks as if Jack had finished everything he had planned to do and was about to head home."

DC Yapp was sceptical, "Not necessarily. He could still be planning to do something important on the Saturday before making a quick exit, or even just move on to somewhere else to avoid being tracked down."

"Did you ask about how Jack seemed emotionally? Was he worried; was he calm?"

"I did ask, yes, but it was difficult for her to remember details like that. It's such a long time ago now. She says that she can't remember him being nervous or worried and maybe he was even quite jaunty when he left, but she wouldn't swear to anything for certain."

Rachael was beginning to realise there was an awful lot of information that Towgood was going to have to assimilate tomorrow morning before attempting to interview Daisy Cooper or go searching for Michael Bakowski. She decided to get the whole team together for a debrief on what they had found out in the last few days. She finished by saying that in the last hour of their shift they should make sure their files were complete and that a short summary of the key points and facts should be placed on top of all the other insertions. They were then to be left on Towgood's desk so that he could see them first thing in the morning.

Rachael then summoned all her powers of tact and endurance to go and get a more detailed update of the forensic information from Martin. He had returned to his desk following the impromptu briefing and was slumped in a casual manner either deep in thought or daydreaming about something unrelated with work.

"Come on then, tell me more about this forensic bombshell you've gathered," she said in as neutral a tone as she could muster.

Martin responded by opening a file and showing a photo of a set of tyre prints. The accompanying notes identified them as being less than two metres from the water's edge at the very spot Rachael and Towgood had stood all those months ago contemplating the clues of the piece of sacking and the dropped key by the side of the river at the entrance to Deanside Park.

"Do we know which tyre it was?" Rachael asked.

"As a matter of fact, we do," Martin responded with some triumph. "Back right... there's an unusual imperfection in the tread which is unique to that tyre."

"Interesting... the car has to be backed up to the river. There's not enough room for it to be front ways on without falling into the river."

"Exactly. Ideally situated to quickly open the boot, remove the sack and its contents, dump them in the river and then make a speedy getaway."

Rachael was desperately trying to recall the area in her mind's eye. She remembered there was a short stretch of gravel track which had led from the road and then petered out some distance short of the river bank.

"Is there room to turn a vehicle by the river?" Rachael asked.

In response, Martin produced an aerial photograph of the scene showing that it would have been virtually impossible.

"So, the car must have been reversed up the track, which to my mind shows a cool degree of premeditation," Rachael surmised. "Certainly not something you would do in an arbitrary moment of blind panic. What about the hair fibres?"

"They are about as straightforward a piece of evidence as you could hope for. Hair entwined with the fibres of the sacking indicate that the victim must have been in the boot of that car at some point."

"Mm… I agree it looks pretty damning," Rachael responded.

Martin seemed now a little agitated. "Look, I know what you said before, but if the murderer gets wind of the fact that we have this evidence, he could still try to get rid of the car or at least destroy any remaining sacking, change the tyre and thoroughly clean the boot. We ought at least to impound the car now. I don't think the evidence we have has been obtained strictly by the book and I wouldn't necessarily bet on it standing up in court if unsupported."

Rachael had to admit that Martin had a good point, but she couldn't go against the express wishes of Towgood. She decided to level with Martin and hope he would be reasonable.

"Towgood thinks that if the forensic evidence we hold has been properly recorded and photographed it will stand up as evidence without having the car as well."

"Of course, it's been recorded properly," Martin snorted.

"He is in a tricky situation," Rachael pleaded. "The dean has complained to the chief superintendent about the police spreading defamatory inuendo against the clergy in the close. You know what the chief is like. He's told Towgood to back off. I think the inspector feels he has to have an absolute watertight case against Randall before he can move."

Martin just restrained himself from banging on his desk, but with barely disguised frustration he responded, "For pity's sake, how much more evidence do we need? Randall's guilty and any other DI would have had him banged up days ago."

"Alright, alright…" Rachael said trying not to sound panicky. "A compromise… post a constable specifically to watch over the car tonight. It's kept in the street outside Randall's house, isn't it? If anyone tries to tamper with it the officer can intervene and if necessary, make an arrest. If you are still not happy tomorrow, you must take it up with Towgood yourself."

This was just about enough to mollify Martin. "OK, I have someone in mind who can do the job," he said, rather sullenly.

At that moment, much to Rachael's surprise, Pablo made an unexpected entrance.

"Hola, Rachael. They say it is permitted for me to come and find you. It is alright, yes?"

"Hi, Pablo, is it that time already? I'll just get my things and we can go. Oh… this is Martin by the way."

"Ah, your ex novio. I am happy to meet you, Martin."

Martin shook hands with Pablo and grunted in a way that wasn't exactly rude, but not exactly polite either. To avoid further embarrassment Rachael quickly shepherded Pablo away towards her own desk and tidied up as fast as she could so they could quit the scene. As she and Pablo left the room, an ugly look was thrown in their direction by Martin which she didn't like at all. It was full of a murderous mixture of lust, fury, envy and jealousy. Still, she would have been pleased with the detailed instructions given to Martin's chosen constable, which were exactly in line with what Rachael had told Martin was permissible. She would have been more concerned had she known that Martin had then carried on the conversation thus,

"Oh, and Constable, there's one other thing I'd like you to do, as a personal favour to me. I'll see you're well rewarded…"

XXIII

RACHAEL ARRIVED FOR WORK THE next day in a relaxed frame of mind. She'd had a very pleasant evening the night before. With Pablo, they had met up with Gavin and Jacob for a quiet drink in one of the local pubs in the town centre. Being Winchester, it was not surprising that the establishment had tried to be a bit more upmarket than just a pub. It had acquired more of a wine bar feel, nevertheless retaining some of the comfortable features that you might find in a cosy country inn. In particular, on that evening which looked as if it might be the prelude to the first hard frost of the winter, it had situated in one corner a roaring fire with armchairs suitably arranged around it. Gavin had managed to grab these as, being midweek, it had not been busy and the four of them had been able to sit and chat, almost imagining they were sitting in the living room of that old, converted country farmhouse that they all suspected they would never be able to afford. Rachael was so pleased that Pablo seemed to get on with Gavin and Jacob so well. There was none of that forced awkwardness that you get when someone feels they have to be polite just to keep up appearances. Rachael felt that if Pablo had met Gavin and Jacob without being Rachael's partner they still would have ended up as good friends. They'd avoided talking about work too, which was just fine by Rachael. In fact, as far as she could remember Jacob spent a lot of the evening talking to Pablo about their favourite football teams and the relative merits of the English Premier League and the Spanish La Liga. She had been happy just to sit there soaking up the atmosphere with an interesting gin.

Towgood did not look as if he'd had such a relaxing evening. He came in looking careworn and somewhat older than Rachael imagined him. He'd thanked Rachael for organising the information so efficiently for him and then retired to his office for a good two hours or so to read and inwardly digest it. Rachael decided to seek out Martin to find out how the surveillance had gone the previous night. She was pleased to find him somewhat less agitated than the previous evening, sitting at his desk doing some paperwork.

"Well, how did it go last night?" she asked with forced camaraderie.

"Thankfully, no-one interfered with the car," Martin responded. "I told PC Grimthorpe to walk up and down along the pavement if anyone came along and showed any interest in the car. He only had to do that twice during the night, once when Randall returned to the house, and a second time when a tall clerical gentleman hovered about in the road. He was the awkward customer. He accosted the constable and asked him what he thought he was doing wandering around aggressively in the close."

"What did he look like?" Rachael asked fearing the worst.

"Quite old. Probably early to mid-sixties. Tall, good figure for his age, and very imposing. Has grey hair and isn't balding, glasses, and very superior attitude."

"Damn it, that sounds like the dean. He's the one that's been giving us the grief about harassing clergy in the close. Have you told Towgood?"

"Yes, I went in to see him first thing when he arrived this morning."

"And...?"

"He didn't say much. He reckons the evidence we already have should stand up in court whether we impound the car or not. He seemed more interested to know why the dean was wandering around the close at that time of night."

"Mm... Have you still got a watch on the close?"

"Yes. Constables are taking it in turns to do a shift. We have twenty-four-hour surveillance of the area. Towgood is happy for that to continue for the time being. All the officers have been briefed to be discreet."

As Rachael feared, there was a price to pay for PC Grimthorpe's encounter with the dean. At about eleven Towgood was summoned to the chief superintendent's office for one of those shouting sessions that stopped activity on the office floor and was audible to everyone in the usual half-conversational mode.

"Why am I still bloody well getting complaints about harassing clergy in the close?"

(Silence, while a reasoned and calm response was given by Towgood.)

"You better not be trying to pull the wool over my eyes, and the dean has every effing right to be wandering around in his cathedral close at any time he likes."

(Further silence…)

"I want the schedule for every beat officer's round for the last two days and a justification for any patrols through the close. Now, get out of my office."

Towgood looked less buoyant than normal as he emerged from the chief's tirade. He went over to Martin's desk before returning to his own office and Rachael clearly heard him say,

"Well, I'm sure you heard what the chief superintendent wanted. That's your job for today. I'm sure you can find appropriate reasons for our officers being in the vicinity of the close."

At about quarter to midday Towgood emerged from his office again to summon Rachael to their meeting with Daisy Cooper. They decided to walk, even though the weather was not particularly pleasant. Towgood clearly wanted to clear his head with some fresh air after the morning's effort. They arrived before Miss Cooper, and settled themselves in a quiet corner with a view over the High Street beyond the Butter Cross directly below. The café was on the first floor of a Tudor building which had a solid wooden floor that was not precisely flat and walls consisting of black painted wooden beams interlaced with white painted plaster, again diverting slightly from four-square planar geometry. There was a quiet hum in the room as it started to fill up with the lunchtime trade. Along one of the short walls was a display counter with cakes and sandwiches, behind which a couple of female assistants in chequered aprons were taking orders and dealing with payment of bills.

Towgood ordered two coffees while they were waiting and visibly seemed to relax. Ten minutes after they had arrived, a woman looking very much as

Rachael had imagined Daisy Cooper to be from their phone conversation wandered in. She looked around hesitantly. Rachael sprang up and introduced herself before Daisy could change her mind and led her over to their table. Towgood gallantly got up for a second time and ordered a coffee and a sandwich for Miss Cooper. When he returned, he was at pains to keep his interview technique as informal and conversational as possible. Rachael knew her role would be to discreetly take a few notes.

"Now I gather you saw our murder victim in the cathedral office just a day or so before he unfortunately met his end. Can you describe him for me?"

This was a deliberate ploy that Rachael had noted before from Towgood. It ensured that they were talking about the right person and gave Towgood a sense of the reliability of the witness in describing key details and events. To Rachael, Miss Cooper's observations seemed remarkably sharp. She seemed to be the sort of person whose net curtains might twitch should a stranger come walking down her street; a little bit like Miss Marple in an Agatha Christie novel. Towgood seemed satisfied as well.

"Very good. Now there was something about his attitude and behaviour that struck you as rather odd, I gather? Please don't worry if you think you've told us something already, it won't hurt to hear it all again."

"That's fine," Daisy said, looking as if she might relish the opportunity to tell a saga to a captive audience. "Well, this young man entered that I've just described to you. If he'd just asked for someone or handed over a package, I probably would have forgotten all about him by now, but he didn't. He just stood there looking as if he hadn't quite made his mind up about what to do. I remember asking him at least twice if I could help him. Finally, he said he wanted to leave a message for someone. I then said, 'yes, that would be possible,' and asked who the message was for. Well, instead of just telling me, he stood silent again and then said he couldn't tell me. Naturally, I told him that I couldn't very well deliver a message if I didn't know who it was for. Again, after taking an age to think, he asked me if there was a noticeboard in the reception area where people coming in and out would look. I thought to myself, 'That's an odd question,' but actually there was such a noticeboard by the door where urgent day notices could be pinned for the clergy and admin staff who came in and out of the building. I said I'd have to look at whatever he was posting before agreeing to let him put it up. I remember he pulled out a postcard, a large one, almost double the size of a standard one. It had a picture of Peterborough cathedral on one side and he had written a message I didn't understand on the other, but it seemed harmless enough, if a little odd. Well, to be honest I didn't know what to do. In the end, reluctantly, I said he could put it on the noticeboard in the bottom right-hand corner. He seemed happy with this, pinned his card picture side to the wall, bade me good day and left."

"Interesting..." Towgood observed. "You didn't happen to notice anyone reading it in any detail, by any chance?"

"Well no. The rest of the day was very busy, and my attention was elsewhere. I was off for a few days after that, but I do remember that the next time I was in the office the card had gone. Either someone had taken it, or it had been thrown away by one of the office staff tidying the noticeboard."

"...And I suppose you don't happen to remember what was written on the card?"

"It's a long time ago, and I don't want you to get the idea that I regularly go poking my nose into other people's business, Inspector..." Rachael noted a slight smile appear on Towgood's face as they both realised how untruthful a statement this was, "...but it went something like this. 'Hi. It's Jack here. Do you remember Peterborough twelve years ago? I do! I think we need to talk'. There was then a number which began '07' so I assume it was a mobile phone number. Don't quote me. I can't say that was the exact wording."

"Don't worry. That has been most illuminating, Ms Cooper," Towgood reassured her.

Rather to Rachael's surprise, Towgood then engaged Daisy in fairly trite conversation while she finished her coffee and a sandwich. He later explained that this allowed him to get more of a feel for the personality and reliability of his witness and it was also good PR with the public. Eventually, Daisy looked at her watch and, in a fluster, realised that she needed to rush back to work. Rachael and Towgood were left to contemplate the interview.

"It feels like that has brought the events of last Easter into a bit more focus, but I would have been happier if we had seen an image of Randall come into play at some point. He seems conspicuously absent from the events down here so far."

Rachael finished the last dregs of her coffee cup and then felt bold enough to say that she was surprised that they hadn't already taken Randall in for questioning at least.

Towgood sighed, leant back in his chair and said, "I know, I know... It's just I can't afford to be wrong with this one. It's odd. I'm usually the one going on about facts, but this time I have an intuition that Randall is not our man. I agree, the facts all seem to point to Randall. The forensics from his car seem absolutely damning. Come on, let's go and see if we can catch this Bakowski fellow at home. Maybe he can enlighten us further."

The two of them got up and left by the uneven and rather narrow staircase that led from the café, now quietening down somewhat, to the pavement below. It was then a short walk down the High Street and off to the left down an alley to reach the chemist's shop. A sense of déjà vu, which had been troubling Rachael ever since Bakowski's name had emerged, grew stronger as they approached the entrance to the flat above the shop. Then, all of a sudden in a blinding flash, it all became clear. It had obviously become clear to Towgood at the same time.

"Oh, for Heaven's sake, if there turns out to be a link between this case and that wretched business with the garden ornaments after all, I think I'll go on long-term sick leave for aggravated stress. Damn it, if I'd remembered Michael Bakowski was the guy we thought had been murdered, I'd have looked at our interview notes with him this morning. Never mind, Goodfellow, we'll have to just do the best we can. If you think of anything I might have forgotten, feel free to join in with this interview."

Fortune was smiling on them on this occasion. Michael was in. By the look of him, he'd been lounging in front of the television most of the day and hadn't bothered too much about the clothes he was wearing. He was nevertheless immediately recognisable as the thin, gangly twenty-something that they'd interviewed over six months previously. Rachael wondered whether he still had a limp. He was none too pleased to see Towgood and

Goodfellow again and was initially very wary. His mother was out, and he was the only one in the flat.

"We meet again," Towgood said with mock enthusiasm. "Who would have guessed you knew our murder victim after all?"

Michael looked blank. "What do you mean?" he asked suspiciously.

Rachael could see that Towgood was somewhat incredulous by the way he slightly raised his left eyebrow. However, he continued, taking a slightly different line of attack.

"You are not going to deny that you knew Jack Nobel and were in touch with him in the week before Easter, are you?"

"I know Jack. We go way back. He used to help me with a few jobs when I was up in London. Yes, now you mention it, that was the last time I've been in touch with him. He lives up in Peterborough now I think."

"Are you seriously trying to tell me that you've not heard that Jack was the murder victim that we thought might have been you? Haven't you read the papers? Haven't you seen the news on the telly?"

The effect on Michael was unexpectedly dramatic. The colour drained from his face. He stood open-mouthed for a second, and then flopped back into the settee holding his head in his hands muttering, "Fucking hell... Fucking, fucking hell..."

Towgood asked Rachael if she remembered where the coffee was kept from their last visit and instructed her to go and make one for the visibly shaken Michael. When she returned Towgood was taking a kindlier tone with him and had filled him in with a bit of background. Michael was shocked to a degree that slightly surprised Rachael. He was babbling rather randomly.

"I can't believe it. I mean, we were two of a kind. We'd come and go without a word but not think anything of it. So, he was murdered almost as soon as I last saw him. Poor bastard. Here... you're not trying to pin this on me just because I've got a record?"

"You're alright," Towgood reassured him, "we have a suspect with far more cause to do him in than you – unless you have even more to tell us than we suspect?"

"No, I ain't," Michael responded forcefully.

"But we do think you might have some valuable information to help us get the guy who did," Towgood added.

Michael sat contemplating for a moment and then said, "Well, if he's dead now I suppose it don't matter what I say."

"Right, let's start at the beginning. How did you come across Jack in the first place?"

"I used to go up to London quite a lot. Gus Kenwood had stalls at some of the markets south of the river. I started off by going with him as his paid helper. It was all legit, mind you…Well, most of it anyway… After a while, Gus trusted me to do some of them on my own. It was hard work and with some of the stock I really needed another person to help. I was on a stall one day and I was snowed under with boxes trying to put stuff out and serving customers at the same time. These two came along, a man and a woman. I thought they were a couple, but I found out later that they were only friends. I assumed they were just browsing looking for something to buy. We got talking and the guy, who of course was Jack, noticed I was struggling a bit and asked if I wanted any help as he wasn't doing anything for the rest of the day. Now, I wasn't born yesterday, so I was a bit wary that I was being set up for a scam, but they both seemed honest, and I was desperate, so I gave them a try. At the end of the day, I checked the takings, and everything was in order. In fact, the takings were better than normal. The two of them were naturals with the punters and drew in a large crowd, so I thanked them, gave them a few quid each for their efforts and asked if they would like to help out again on a more regular basis."

Michael laughed at this point and continued, "My God, I've never known anyone so grateful. Jack hugged me and said 'thank you' about thirty times and skipped off with his friend as if it was his birthday or something. We got to know each other quite well over the next year and became almost like business partners, except I always held the purse strings, of course."

Rachael now felt she had to intervene, having been given licence by Towgood to do so. "The girl… what was her name, and have you kept in contact with her?"

"She was called Amy. I never got to know much about her. She always came with Jack, and I always arranged work through Jack… A nice girl, but I

~ 172 ~

could tell she was well and truly smitten on Jack… and Jack didn't feel the same way about her. When Jack upped and left, she vanished as well. I never kept her number so I ain't got a clue where she is."

Rachael felt a moment of intense frustration. The one person who seemed to know the whole motivation for Jack's actions in that week before Easter had for a moment become tantalisingly close to being reached, and now had dissipated into the ether once more.

Towgood resumed the questioning. "So why did Jack go? Did you keep in touch?"

"I don't know. I heard rumours he'd decided to leave London and go home. I didn't keep in touch. You could have knocked me over with a feather when he called out of the blue. He said he was in Winchester, and he wanted to see me. I'd changed my mobile, so how did he know my number?"

"Mm… Yes, about that call. Can you remember exactly when it was?" Towgood asked.

"Yeah, Wednesday, sometime in the evening. Maybe Tuesday, but I think it was the Wednesday before Easter. He said he was down in Winchester for a few days and would I like to meet up. I said I was busy, but sure, one evening we could meet in one of the pubs for a drink."

"And did you?" Rachael asked.

"Yeah, Friday evening in fact, in the 'Wessex Arms' at the bottom of the town."

Towgood's eyes glistened. "Tell us in as much detail as you can what you talked about, particularly if he said anything about why he was down in this part of the world."

"Well, that's the bit I remember really. It seemed a bit odd. He said he'd come down for 'resolution'. God, he sounded like some weird guy in a religious cult or something, but he said he was deadly serious and what he had to do was necessary for him to get on with his life. He said he'd managed to contact a man who had done him a great wrong when he was young, and he was going to meet him and confront him."

"Did he say who the man was?" Towgood asked with undisguised eagerness.

"No, it was strange. I asked him the same question, but he wouldn't say. It was almost as if the mere mention of the name would cause him unbearable shame."

In obvious frustration, Towgood slunk back in the chair in which he was sitting. Rachael, then remembering her conversation with Gavin and Jacob some time ago asked, "What do you think Jack was going to do when he came face to face with this guy? Was he going to blackmail him and extort money out of him?"

"Our minds don't half think alike – I asked him that exact same question. I said if this man was guilty enough to pay a regular sum to keep me quiet for the rest of my life, that would be resolution enough for me. Jack went ballistic. He said something like, 'You haven't got the first idea, have you? There is not enough money in the whole world to put right what he did. No, I want him to admit his guilt to my face. Depending on what he says, I may forgive him, I may expose him to the world, I may even kill him if he makes me angry enough.' I told him to keep his hair on. He didn't say much after that for a while."

Towgood and Rachael looked at each other for a second. It hadn't occurred to Rachael that Jack's death might have been the result of self-defence rather than pre-meditated intention. Michael continued,

"At the end of the evening, just as he was about to go, he said to me that he could really do with a wingman, just in case things turned nasty, someone to just wait behind a hedge somewhere, to call on if he needed back up. He was planning to meet this guy somewhere remote the following day after he'd checked out of his lodgings. I said I was sorry, but I had other... er... business to attend to." Michael reddened considerably when he said this. Towgood, however, was no longer concerned with past misdemeanours.

"And how did Jack take that?" he asked.

"He was disappointed, I could tell, but he said something like, 'Oh well, I'm sure I'll be able to manage.' I felt a bit guilty and said he could ring me if things got serious. He shrugged his shoulders and left."

"Weren't you worried about him when you didn't hear anything from him again?" Rachael enquired.

"Not really – we both come and go as we please. He didn't ring so that was that. Ask my mum. The number of times she's gone on about me not letting her know where I am. I just assumed he'd done his business and gone."

Towgood looked at Michael through half-closed eyes for a moment and then, much to Rachael's surprise, he said, almost as a coda to the conversation,

"That's not quite everything is it, Michael? There was one further moment after that when you had some dealings with Jack."

Michael looked startled and responded with some anxiety, "How did you know about that? Well, OK, I admit it, though it's a small thing and I didn't actually see him again."

"Go on…" urged Towgood. "I do wish we didn't have to drag every little detail from you as if we were dentists trying to pull your teeth out. Don't you trust us or something?"

"Frankly, no – but I'll tell you what happened. It can't hurt now anyway. After I ran away, after the disagreement with Ryan, I felt I needed to get away from the area pretty quick. I noticed Jack's mobile was still showing up in the area on my 'where are my friends and contacts?' phone app. I thought I might be able to hitch a free lift with him. So, I rang him, but there was no reply. It was odd that the app was showing him located near 'The Red Lion', but I thought it was safe enough to risk going back to check if his car was there."

"What time was this?" asked Towgood, now showing intense interest.

"Probably about two o'clock in the morning by the time I got there. It was very quiet. No-one was about, but just before I got to the pub, I noticed a car parked at the entrance to a track that led down to the river. Ah, Jack's car, I thought, so I approached it. Just as I was getting close, the headlights came on, the engine started up and it rushed straight towards me. I had to jump out of the way to avoid being hit. It was definitely breaking the 30mph speed limit as it headed towards town. There was no sign of anyone else about and Jack's mobile signal had disappeared. So, after ten minutes I made a hasty retreat and hung around in town to catch an early train the following day."

"Could you see the driver?" Towgood asked, almost straining now to extract information from Michael.

"I was dazzled by the headlights. The driver must have had them on full beam. I can tell you that the car was an estate car. I remember seeing the shape as it went away and thinking that I'd have expected Jack to have a smaller car than that."

"And even now, with everything that happened you didn't think that Jack might be in trouble? When did the signal from Jack's phone disappear?"

"Difficult to say. I noticed it was gone as soon as the car vanished, but I hadn't been checking for about twenty minutes beforehand. I knew where I was headed, you see, and I didn't want to run down the battery... And before you get too moral about what a bad friend I am, I'm sure you remember that I had problems of my own to worry about at that time."

Although this was an impertinent rejoinder, Towgood couldn't help smiling to himself as he recalled the absurd interactions between Fielder, Bakowski and Kenwood. He relaxed the tension and said, "Thank you, Mr Bakowski for your co-operation. You have been most helpful. You're not planning to go anywhere if we need to talk to you again?"

A shake of the head signalled that Michael could think of no practical escape route from further questioning. Rachael and Towgood clonked their way down the wooden staircase to find themselves outside the chemist shop in the cold wintry air with the light just beginning to fade and a red sunset beginning to develop in the west.

"How did you know he'd been back to the river?" Rachael asked with admiration.

"I didn't. It was a shot in the dark. I knew he wasn't telling us everything. Still, that was a bit of a bonus and colours in one more corner of the picture. Let's go for a bit of a stroll. It's been a long day, and I don't think we can do much more before tomorrow. Besides, I want to keep out of the chief superintendent's way."

The days were shortening quite alarmingly now and especially as the sky was covered with heavy clouds, the daylight was almost spent. The street lights were beginning to come on and the lights in the shops were becoming noticeable. Rachael followed obediently in Towgood's wake as he slowly made a progress back up to the High Street and then to the café where they had interviewed Daisy Cooper earlier. They passed under an arch into a narrow street with a mixture of independent shops and old houses, some half-timbered. The massive Norman cathedral then loomed up in front of them and Towgood made for the short, diagonal gravel path that led through the relatively small graveyard to the great west door. However, they continued past this and proceeded down a short alley on the north side of the church which immediately opened out into the cathedral close. It was here that Towgood chose to stop and reflect on matters. He sat on a bench looking out to the close with the cathedral at his back. Rachael sat down beside him. The old-fashioned street lamps that would have been gas lit a couple of generations ago, shone more reliably with modern electricity.

"Out there is the answer to all our problems," Towgood said with a dramatic hand gesture. "If only we could uncover the truth."

"What more do you need to convince you that John Randall is a killer?" Rachael responded with just a hint of frustration. "The facts unerringly point to him, and you are always going on about facts, facts, facts. He is in all the right places at all the right times in Peterborough and the forensics on his car are incredibly damning."

"And yet there were no fingerprints that matched his in Daniel Jarvis' old Toyota abandoned on Farley Mount. There is no positive ID of him being there or at the riverside when we think Jack's body was bundled into the river. His car – yes; him – no. Also, I want to see evidence that he is capable of such a crime. I could not find anything shady in his background. There is nothing. No hint of a misdemeanour or even an argument with a colleague, not even a whiff that he did something that was brushed under the carpet to keep the Church smelling of roses."

He paused and peered into the gloom as if attempting to send X-rays from his eyes to penetrate the secrets of the buildings in front of him.

"Humour me for a moment, Goodfellow. Let's call our murder suspect 'X'. Let's be positive and review the circumstances of the case we do know.

"Sometime on July 6th twelve years ago X encounters Jack at the Deanery Festival in Peterborough. Something so dreadful happens between them that it completely destroys Jack's personality and ruins his ability to get on with life.

~ 177 ~

My money is on a violent sexual assault, but let's not get carried away. That's just speculation. X thinks he's got away with it and Jack moves out of the picture entirely. Time and fate bring X to Winchester.

"Meanwhile, Jack, homeless and in a bad way, is rather astonishingly rehabilitated, along with this woman, Amy – who we still desperately need to interview, by the way – thanks to our garden gnome thief, Michael Bakowski, in London. He returns to Peterborough and starts to rebuild his life. He meets up with his old friend from school, Daniel Jarvis, who takes him in and provides him with a home. Everything is going fantastically well until one day Jack sees an article in the local newspaper that causes him to immediately want to travel down to Winchester and confront someone involved with the cathedral. The newspaper article suggests that the person is indeed John Randall, but let's continue calling our suspect X for the time being.

"Having settled into a B&B on the outskirts of Winchester, Jack then makes his journey into town and leaves the postcard with the cryptic message alluding to the original incident in Peterborough. I think we can assume that the intended recipient of the card found it and acted on the message by contacting Jack. From what Michael told us, Jack wanted to confront X about that incident. My hunch is that they met up at Farley Mount on the Saturday of the Easter weekend. It seems Jack wasn't interested in blackmailing X; maybe it would have worked out better for him if he had."

Rachael looked at Towgood with a disapproving raise of the eyebrow.

"Oh, yes," Towgood continued. "I suspect Jack was threatening something much worse; to expose X and share all the sordid details with the world. Imagine the shame, the destruction of X's reputation, the loss of his job and influence, the turmoil that would probably end his marriage. A regular bribe payment would be far better than that.

"Things get desperate, and X drags Jack into the bushes and strangles him with the rope we found there. He backs up his car and bundles the body in to the sacking that he fortuitously happens to have in the boot, and then carries it away. Does that sound convincing to you, Goodfellow?"

"It all seems to fit together well with the facts. Jack's car is left abandoned while X makes his getaway with the body in the car he is driving."

"Does it indeed? Well, there's a couple of things that worry me. It was Easter Saturday in a popular beauty spot within easy travelling distance of Winchester. Is it really likely that X could have strangled Jack without being seen by anyone? Consider this also. If X is Randall, how would you consider his physique?"

"Fairly short, rather plump and probably not someone who goes out for a run every day," Rachael had to concede.

"Exactly," Towgood exclaimed with a certain degree of triumph. "Jack had had his problems, but he was still a fairly tall, fit, young man in the prime of his life. Who do you honestly think is going to come out on top?"

Rachael felt confident enough these days to respond contrarily to her boss' hypotheses and felt obliged to do so now.

"If the weather was bad, then there could easily have been times when no-one else was up here, even on Easter Saturday, and even the fittest person can be caught unawares by an unexpected turn of events."

Towgood was silent for a moment before continuing.

"That's a fair point. If you can convince me that the weather was atrocious up there, I might bow to your second point too.

"Anyway, to conclude the scenario, X drives away and leaves the car with the body in somewhere we do not know. Maybe he was bold enough to leave it parked in plain sight. Then late at night, when he thinks there will be no one around he drives to the river down by 'The Red Lion' and dumps the body in the river. Jack's car key falls unnoticed from his shirt pocket, the sacking gets torn in the process of being moved from the car, Jack's mobile is discovered and disposed of along with his wallet and other possessions. Unfortunately, just as he is driving off, X encounters Michael walking towards him, so X drives towards him and then makes his getaway. We find the body mangled in the mill on Easter Monday."

"We know the estate car involved in dumping the body belongs to John Randall. That to me is a fairly damning piece of evidence."

"I agree," Towgood said with a sigh. "That would need some explaining away and so I can only leave it another couple of days before I bring Randall in for questioning, whatever the dean or the chief superintendent have to say.

Let's take a stroll around the back of the cathedral and then back up through the bottom of town to the station. By then it'll be time to go home."

The last thin azure streak was visible on the western horizon and Venus was a piercing pinprick of white light low in the sky. The lantern-like street lamps were now necessary to see their path. They walked through the arch of a ruined wall and down a path that led to the east end of the cathedral, clearly showing the signs of sinking into the bog that the Normans had unwisely built it upon. It wasn't often that Towgood simply had a conversation about mundane issues other than work, so Rachael felt slightly awkward when he asked about the wellbeing of her mother and how things were going with Pablo. She answered formally and in a non-committed way. She politely asked how he was keeping out of working hours, not expecting much in response. Towgood was politely ambiguous, saying something but not revealing anything about himself at all. It suddenly occurred to Rachael that she knew nothing at all about her boss' life outside of the police station. She'd always assumed he was married, but what was his wife's name? Was she younger or older than him? Did she have a background in the Force? Did they have kids and if so, how many? She felt rather ashamed that she had worked closely with this man for eight months now and knew hardly anything about him as a person.

Her train of thought was interrupted by a brooding sense of a growing, dark shadow behind them which quickly grew to the sense that they were being approached at speed by a presence that wasn't entirely friendly. She turned sharply just in time to see a figure looming behind them holding a glinting metallic object at head height. Just in time she realised it was a knife and the figure was poised to strike Towgood in the back.

"Look out," she screamed, pushing Towgood sharply to the right.

The figure struck, but thanks to Rachael's action, the blow fell on the shoulder and not his back. Towgood let out a howl of pain and surprise and slumped to the ground clutching his shoulder with the opposite hand. The malevolent figure also let out a growl of frustration, the deep growl of a man's voice of some maturity before running off.

"After him, Goodfellow. Don't let him get away," hissed Towgood, obviously in some pain.

Rachael's first inclination had been to kneel down and check her boss' injury. She wavered for a second and then followed her chief's command. She ran to the end of the path where it met a small road which connected the High Street to one of the main arterial roads out of the city. She looked both ways, but could see no one. A slight mist that was beginning to form didn't help. She imagined that she heard a door slamming nearby, but she was unable to detect the direction accurately. She gave up the pursuit and returned to where Towgood remained a slumped pathetic figure, a dark red stain on the back of his jacket now becoming all too apparent. She quickly got to her knees to examine the wound and to assess the victim's general demeanour. Towgood was conscious but strangely quiet. Rachael quickly got out her radio and spoke to the centre.

"Request urgent assistance. Colleague injured requiring medical assistance. Ambulance required. Passageway behind the cathedral near the east end."

"Okay, I'll get the nearest patrol car to you with a first aid kit. I'll pass you over to the ambulance controller."

There was a pause as she was transferred to the ambulance control room.

"What's the nature of the injuries?"

"Bleeding profusely from a stab wound in the shoulder."

"Is the patient conscious?"

"Yes."

"Can you pass the radio across so I can talk with the injured person?"

Rachael did this while continuing to apply pressure to the wound using a handkerchief that she happened to have in her pocket (she tended to wear trousers for work even when in plain clothes). There seemed to be an interminable series of questions and she could sense Towgood becoming more and more irritable as the inquiries seemed more and more pointless. At least she could now hear the siren of a police car getting nearer. Finally, the phone was handed back to Rachael and she resumed the conversation with the ambulance controller.

"Hello? Are you applying pressure to the wound? How is it looking?"

"It's difficult to tell," Rachael admitted. "It's dark and I can't see how bad the wound is under his clothing."

"Have you got police back up there?"

Two officers were rushing up the alley towards them as these words were spoken.

"Yes," Rachael responded. "They're just arriving."

"Look, it's going to take about forty-five minutes to get an ambulance to you, so I know it's not ideal, but it might be better if you take him yourselves to A & E in the police car rather than waiting in the cold."

Rachael was rather stunned by this, expecting an ambulance to be there within minutes. She could only say, "OK," in a shocked voice and hang up.

The arrival of the two young officers stirred Rachael into action, however.

"Quick," she said. "We'll need to take him to hospital in the car. The ambulance will take too long."

Checking that Towgood was still conscious and able to respond to questions, she helped him to his feet. The male officer supported him on the side with his good arm, taking most of his weight. The female officer supported him more gingerly on the side where he had his injury. Rachael maintained a firm pressure on the point where she assumed the wound was most severe. Towgood looked dreadfully pale, even in the darkness of the dimly-lit passageway. However, he was able to move forward slowly with relative ease. The fifty metres that remained to the police car, its blue flashing light still automatically but silently working, seemed to take an eternity to cover. Finally there, the female officer opened the back door and laid out a thin plastic sheet protecting the whole of the seating area. Rachael carefully manoeuvred Towgood in as delicately as she could. Even so, there were a few grunts and groans as he finally found a comfortable position.

"OK, as quick as you can. It should only take a few minutes to get there."

Rachael was sat in the back with Towgood, while the male officer was driving, and the female officer was in the front passenger seat. The driver was confident and proceeded quickly, but without giving any sense of panic to the passengers. Even though the city streets were still busy with the homeward-bound rush hour, the siren and the blue flashing light allowed them to forge a clear path up to the Romsey Road and the Royal Hants County Hospital.

"I'm sorry... I don't know your name," Rachael said, addressing the female officer.

"PC Stephens."

"PC Stephens… could you radio the station and request the passage where we were attacked be cordoned off and guarded immediately. I'll get in touch later to discuss getting a forensic team there in the morning. Oh… and make it clear that there should be a minimum of two people on duty there. A potentially dangerous attacker is still at large."

PC Stephens obliged immediately. However, there was clearly some problem at the station. She turned around to address Rachael directly.

"A DS Hall is querying my authority to request this."

"Tell him DS Goodfellow has requested it…" Then thinking that might not be sufficient she added, "…acting on behalf of Detective Inspector Towgood."

That seemed to do the trick. She looked sheepishly at Towgood who seemed to give a little chuckle. His eyes were closed most of the time now. Thank goodness they'd arrived at the reception entrance to A & E. PC Stephens jumped out of the car to find someone inside. She returned immediately with two paramedic orderlies with a stretcher. Rachael quitted the back seat gratefully to allow them to take over. They efficiently laid him on the stretcher and took him inside.

"I'll stay here with him. My shift is over anyway. Could you two go back and just check that they do close off that path completely from one end to the other? It's in your patrol area, I gather? If there is any nonsense, can you just let me know and then I think you can resume your regular duties?"

Rachael walked into the waiting area as the police car moved away swiftly. The severe neon lighting, the hard functional chairs and the smell of disinfectant on polished, unforgiving floors and whitewashed walls hardly made the atmosphere encouraging or welcoming. She texted Pablo to warn him that she would be late. He seemed to have boundless reserves of patience, but even so she worried that the unpredictability of police life might eventually cause a rift between them. The minutes ticked by slowly and eventually after an hour of waiting, Rachael went to the reception desk to ask if there was any news. The receptionist was civil but brusque in her manner. She'd obviously had to develop this demeanour to cope with the constant barrage of demands and requests that came her way in her daily routine. Following a quick phone call on the internal system, she told Rachael that Towgood was being seen to and that a doctor would come and give a progress report shortly. Rachael went back to the same chair and sat patiently for a further twenty minutes.

Eventually a doctor dressed in a green jump suit, cap and mask appeared with a clipboard and asked for Detective Sergeant Goodfellow.

"How is he?" enquired Rachael as she eagerly jumped up and moved towards the doctor, who had removed his mask.

"He's okay now. We initially thought he'd lost more blood than he had, and we nearly wheeled him off for a blood transfusion. However, most of the worrying symptoms were down to shock and once we stitched him up and bandaged him, he soon improved. Nevertheless, we're going to keep him in overnight for observation."

"Can I see him?" Rachael asked.

"Sure. He's in the cubicle that's right at the end of the emergency admissions area. We'll move him if a bed becomes available in one of the wards, but I'm not promising. He might have to spend the night down here. We're pretty full at the moment.

"Not too long please. I don't want you tiring him out. He's still quite weak and I don't think he realises he's not as young as he used to be.

"Oh, and there's one other thing…"

Rachael looked expectantly at the doctor who definitely had a furrowed brow.

"…The inspector refused to give us the contact details for a next of kin. When we said he had to give us the details of someone we could contact he eventually said that you could act as his next of kin. Are you okay with that? You'll have to give us your home details as well as your work ones."

Rachael thought this was all very odd but, in the end, she couldn't really see a problem in complying and filled in the relevant form. The doctor pointed her in the right direction and then headed off towards reception, presumably to file his forms.

There were groans and sighs from some of the cubicles as she passed, silence from others. She resisted the temptation to be too nosey about the afflictions of others as she went by and finally, she came to the last cubicle and found Towgood sitting up in bed, dressed in a surgical gown, his clothes neatly folded on a bedside table. He looked pensive and rather pale. His shoulder and upper arm were heavily bandaged.

"How are you feeling, sir?" she asked.

"Washed out," Towgood responded rather feebly.

"Is there anyone you want me to contact? Your wife or other relatives?"

Towgood looked somewhat shifty and then said quite emphatically, "Good God, no... no!" He obviously realised that Rachael was taken aback by this and added very quickly, "I'll be alright in a day or two and I don't want to worry people unnecessarily. I hope you didn't mind me nominating you as a next of kin. They insisted on me specifying someone. I don't expect you to do anything."

To Rachael, this raised as many questions about the circumstances of Towgood's private life as she'd ever considered, but she let the matter drop. Now was not the time to interrogate her boss.

"Are they looking for clues down by the cathedral?" Towgood asked.

"Don't worry, sir. We've cordoned off the passageway and we'll get forensics down there as soon as we can in the morning."

"Who's covering the night shift?"

"DS Hall is manning the office tonight."

Towgood gave a little grunt that was hard for Rachael to interpret.

After an awkward silence in which Rachael thought Towgood was going to drift off to sleep, his eyes suddenly became clear and with renewed energy he declared, "We must be getting close, you know. That was a deliberate if not very effective attempt to assassinate me. Thanks for saving my life, by the way."

"Do you think it was Randall? He could have followed us from the close."

"Come on, Goodfellow. Think. How tall is Randall and what sort of stature does he have?"

"Well, he is short and rather plump."

"Exactly, and what about the person who attacked us?"

Rachael suddenly got the point. The attacker had cast his blow in a downward fashion which would suggest that he was taller than Towgood, who was about six foot. Also, she had seen enough of him in the gloom to grasp that he had a thinner physique than Randall and besides, Randall would never have been able to outrun Rachael and escape.

"I see what you mean," admitted Rachael. "Do you think Randall has an accomplice?"

Towgood snorted. "That would make everything ridiculously complicated. Have we discovered any other evidence to suggest more than one person is involved in killing Nobel? No. I am more convinced than ever that he's not the killer. However, I can't put off bringing Randall in for questioning much longer. He knows something about who's done it, even if he doesn't realise it himself."

"… But not now," Rachael insisted. "You need to rest. All of that can wait for a day or two."

Towgood suddenly looked weak, and pale and he had to admit that Rachael was correct.

"Yes, you're right. Go home and get some rest. I'll need you to be my eyes and ears in the station for the next couple of days. Oh… and do be careful going home. My attacker is clearly desperate. He will know by now that he failed in his assassination attempt. He may try again and lash out at anyone he thinks has information about the case."

Rachael left the lonely figure of Towgood lying in the bed. She suspected he was probably asleep before she closed the door. She considered for the first time that the danger might not be over. She rang Pablo and asked if he wouldn't mind picking her up from the hospital even though it was only a short walk from her home. Pablo of course was very worried about her and said she was not to move until he got there. Despite everything Rachael couldn't help giving a little smile to herself. What would she have done if she hadn't met him? Who would she have turned to for help in this situation?

Her thoughts then turned to Towgood. If her life was in danger, his was more so. Who was to say that the attacker might not sneak into the hospital and try and finish the job? She rang the station. It would have to be Martin who was in charge that evening.

"Hello? Has there been any progress down at the cathedral?"

"Yes, we've got it all taped up and I've managed to get a forensic team out there tonight."

Rachael could imagine his chest puffing out, expecting to get a gold star for efficiency.

"Have they found anything yet?" she asked.

"Well… no, but give them a chance."

"Never mind. Listen, it's struck me that the attack was a deliberate attempt on Towgood's life. We ought to have an armed guard up here just in case he tries again."

"Okay. I was going to send an officer up there to relieve you anyway. Do you want me to come over and see you home?"

"No thanks," Rachael said emphatically. "Pablo is coming to pick me up shortly."

There was silence at the other end of the line, so Rachael continued, "I'll be in first thing in the morning. Can you hold the fort 'til then?"

"Of course," came the curt reply. The line went dead, and Rachael was left to her thoughts while she waited for Pablo to pick her up and the police guard to arrive.

XXIV

THE FOLLOWING MORNING RACHAEL WAS struggling to concentrate. She had not slept well. A misty figure emerging from the shadows and chasing her with a knife kept haunting her dreams and forcing her to wake up in a cold sweat. Poor Pablo had not had much sleep as a consequence either. At least he didn't have to start his shift at the care home until two in the afternoon. He was probably enjoying an hour or two of blissful sleep at this very moment. She was suffering one of those debilitating moments when she really could not decide what she needed to do next.

She had phoned the hospital first thing and enquired after Towgood only to find out that he had discharged himself, somehow evaded the armed guard that was protecting him, and gone home against the advice of the doctors. Irked but not surprised, Rachael was at least relieved that he had not attempted to come into work. Looking around the office, everywhere seemed a hive of activity but incredibly mundane. The casual observer might think they were in the office of an insurance company or a local government department if it hadn't been that most of the workers were wearing police uniform.

She saw Martin busy talking to a couple of colleagues in the corner and realised she could not put off discussing the events of last night with him any longer. As she wandered over reluctantly, Martin caught her eye and quickly dismissed his companions.

"I wondered when you were finally going to talk to me about yesterday," he said in a less than friendly manner. "In the absence of Towgood, the chief super has put me in charge of investigating last night's incident. I trust you will give me your full cooperation."

Rachael was taken aback by this. She'd not really thought through the consequences of Towgood being incapacitated and had just assumed routine intelligence gathering and analysis would continue until he was back.

"Of course," she finally replied. "I have, amongst other things, been writing up a statement about last night."

"Good, but as one of only two witnesses to the event I would like to take you back to the crime scene and get an account from you in person. You can walk me through it. I can pretend to be the knife wielder if you like."

Rachael sensed there was a power struggle going on between the two of them, who were equal in rank, and that Martin was taking the opportunity of Towgood's absence to push for supremacy. She had no option but to go along with it though, and ten minutes later they were standing in the alley where the attack had happened the previous evening.

For the end of November, the morning was bright and cheery and even the vast numbers of dead leaves littering the grass and the edges of the paths were vibrant in colour rather than a soggy mess. The area where the incident had taken place was still cordoned off and various marks had been highlighted with coloured ring markings. Most of these were spots or patches of Towgood's blood. Rachael dutifully re-enacted the progress of Towgood and herself adding a commentary which, to be fair to him, Martin paid close attention to, taking copious notes as they proceeded. Having concluded the dramatic part of her account detailing the actual stabbing, she was pleased to see that both she and Martin were keen to consider where the attacker could have come from and where he could have gone afterwards.

"Unfortunately, there are many places he could have emerged from; there's a side door from the cathedral, there's the red brick house on the right just under the arch or he could have followed you from the close... or he could have been tracking you for longer than that."

Rachael had to admit to not being terribly aware of her surroundings the previous afternoon. The last thing she was expecting was to be followed.

"Where he went is a more limited option, I think," Martin continued.

"Unless he is incredibly athletic and jumped over the high flint wall to his right, he must have either gone to the road or managed to get out through a wooden door in the wall just where the path turns left through ninety degrees. Of course, if you were really slow, he might have got such a head start on you that he'd managed to reach the corner of the road or entered one of the many houses down there before you got to the end of the path yourself."

Rachael ignored the implied criticism and asked, "Was that wooden door locked and what is on the other side?"

"The door was locked this morning and there's a path that leads to the playing fields of the choir school and the back of the ruins of the old bishop's palace."

"Have you found out who's got the key, and have you found out who was in the redbrick house yesterday?"

"No, that's what I'd like you to do now, please."

Rachael opened her mouth to say something, and then realised she couldn't. It felt like Martin had achieved his *coup d'état* and she was powerless to do anything about it.

"What are you going to do while I'm doing that?"

"I have various things to follow up and discuss with the team," he replied vaguely but with intended haughtiness. "But one thing I am going to do later today is haul Randall in for questioning."

Rachael was horrified and could not help herself from saying something.

"You know Towgood doesn't want that to happen yet. You can't do that without his permission."

"Oh, yes I can," Martin retorted with some vehemence. "It's relevant to MY investigation and that overrides any sensibilities that Towgood might have. He should have had him banged up days ago anyway."

He walked off briskly before Rachael could say anything more. After watching him disappear into the close, she decided the only thing she could do for now was carry on with the tasks Martin had given her. She headed for the redbrick house which turned out to be offices rather than a domestic dwelling.

The person assigned with the role of receptionist tried to be very helpful, but it was clear that the number of people who had been in and out of the building yesterday had been many and various, ranging from the dean down to a young man who did a couple of hours' gardening a week. There was no formal list of people going in or out, so the roughly thirty names that were supplied was far from being a complete manifest for the day. The key was also a frustrating matter. Yes, the building did retain a key to the door in the wall, but no, there was no record kept of who used it and when. Moreover, the receptionist knew the key was not the only copy, but she was not sure who else had one or how many there were. Some of the clergy might have one and even the choir school might hold several.

She sat down on a bench in front of the cathedral, intending to rest for ten minutes before returning to the station. The last twenty-four hours had been disconcerting and depressing. However, no sooner had she sat down than her phone rang. It was Towgood. Irritated at having a moment to herself ruined, Rachael was uncharacteristically sharp with him, chiding him for having discharged himself against the doctor's wishes and telling him that he should stay away from the office and work until he was properly fit to return. She couldn't help revealing what Towgood really wanted to know though, which was to find out what was going on and whether any developments were proceeding from the previous night's attack. There was a long silence when Rachael told him that Martin had been given the lead in the investigation and was planning to take Randall in for questioning.

"…Well, that might not be such a bad thing," Towgood said hesitantly.

"But we worked out last night that he couldn't have been the attacker," Rachael responded with a degree of exasperation.

"True, but there is the damning evidence of his car and his associations in Peterborough and Fenton St Mary with the victim of our murder inquiry. I would have had to give him a grilling at some point, even though I'm convinced he's not responsible for the killing – or last night's attack. No, it would be rather nice for someone else to take the rap for annoying the chief superintendent's golfing friends for once. If DS Hall wants to be in charge, he will have to learn to take all the brick-bats as well as the plaudits.

"Keep me posted with what happens. I need to know as much detail as I can about the interview, if it happens."

"I don't know, sir… You should be resting and not getting involved. Besides, the way things are at the moment, DS Hall is not going to let me anywhere near the interview room," Rachael responded with hesitancy.

"Please… It's really important. Find out anything you can. I'm getting a lot better… I really am."

Rachael ended the conversation by agreeing to find out as much as she could about any interview that took place with Randall and to keep in regular contact with Towgood.

Feeling even more disconsolate that she was now being dragged into office politics as well as everything else, she made her way reluctantly back to the station. Martin was predictably scathing about the vagueness of the information she had discovered, but asked her to write it up and include it in the case files for the knife attack investigation.

Across the office space that she had to share with her colleagues of equal and lesser rank, she watched Martin strutting about like a prize turkey. She didn't know how much more loathing she could summon up for this man that she had foolishly fallen in love with when she knew no better. At least he had not been so overblown with self-importance that he had tried to take over Towgood's private office located in the far corner. At the moment he seemed to be in animated conversation with a young male constable. Some of the words drifted across in what seemed a weird conversation.

"Why have you done it now, when we're in the middle of a murder inquiry and an attempted murder of a senior officer? I said do it discreetly when it was quiet and nothing else was happening."

The constable seemed to be indicating that Martin had been very far from clear in his intentions about whatever it was. Martin dismissed the constable abruptly and then threw a suspicious glance over in Rachael's direction as if he'd forgotten that she was there for a moment.

Rachael soon forgot this and resigned herself to the boredom of writing up reports and catching up on the never-ending backlog of paperwork. At noon, the weather began to deteriorate and heavy showers, which never entirely stopped, led to a gloomy end of the day with darkness setting in well before the end of Rachael's shift. Nevertheless, Rachael was determined to take her lunch break and leave the station for at least half an hour to go to the café in the High Street and get away and reflect on things by herself.

For the second time that day her contemplation was interrupted by a phone call. This time it was Pablo, and he was in a distressed state.

"Hi, darling," Rachael said. "I thought you were at work. What's up?"

"No, I am detained with the police," Pablo responded querulously.

"What?" Rachael exploded in disbelief. "Where are you at the moment? Why are they holding you?"

"They say I have a broken rear light on my car, but I did not notice this. I did not understand to have a broken light was such a serious crime in this country."

"It's not. Where are you now?"

"I believe that I'm in the police station in the middle of town."

"I'm coming straight away to sort this out. Try not to worry."

With a mixture of rage and anxiety, Rachael quickly gathered up her things and walked aggressively, at a pace that was almost a run, back to the police station. She burst through the public entrance and headed to the reception desk. The duty sergeant looked up somewhat surprised. Rachael knew him and fortunately, because he was one of the nicest and kindliest people you could imagine, it took the heat out of the situation for a moment.

"Hello, Rachael, we don't see you down here very often. Is there anything wrong?"

Rachael came straight to the crux of the matter. There was no point in beating about the bush.

"Are you holding a Pablo Ramirez in the cells at present?"

"Ah, the Spanish gentleman. Yes, he is in cell three. I let him make a phone call about fifteen minutes ago to his partner."

"What has he done and why has he been locked up?"

The desk sergeant, a man of Asian descent, called Harjinder Sandhu, in his mid-fifties and nearing the end of his time in the Force, did not know off-hand. Pablo had been brought in before his shift had started. He had to look in the logbook to see who had signed the prisoner in and for what reason.

"Well, I have to say, that sounds a bit extreme. 'A defective vehicle and abusive behaviour towards an officer' are what is recorded here."

"Why wasn't a rectification notice issued? That's the standard practice if you're going to make an issue of it. I can't believe Señor Ramirez would be abusive. Who was the officer who made the arrest?"

"It was PC Grimthorpe."

"And has there been a formal charge yet?"

"No, there's a note here to say that he is going to be interviewed later before a decision is made about a formal charge."

"Who is doing the interview?"

"DS Hall... I have to say I'm surprised he's got the time considering everything else that's going on at the moment!"

"Has there been arrangements made for a solicitor? He also should have an interpreter."

"Yes, I was going to get around to that shortly. I'll get on to DS Hall now and ask if he really wants to go through all the expense of getting an interpreter and solicitor in for such a minor infringement. I guess it all depends on the level of the abuse. Why are you so interested in this case? It's not your usual territory. Is there something more going on here?"

"Let's just say I have a personal interest in the case."

Rachael waited while Harjinder went to the phone and seemed to have quite a long conversation. She noticed that he looked over in her direction a couple of times indicating that she had become a topic in the discourse. Remaining at the counter with her elbow grounded and her hand propping up her head, she looked around at the public area which was very quiet. In fact, no-one was sitting on the cheap plastic chairs which backed to the walls, available to those having to wait for long periods to be seen or find out news of those detained or arrested. The room, like the rest of the building, was typically box-square nineteen-sixties corporate-style architecture and in desperate need of modernisation and renovation.

"Martin's coming down to have a word with you."

Rachael was jogged back to the moment by this statement and was intrigued anew as to why Martin was taking any interest in this case at all.

She was even more surprised a few minutes later when he swept in oozing unctuousness and a forced joviality.

"I'm so sorry," he began almost trying to conjure up a false tear, "I'm afraid PC Grimthorpe has been over-zealous. He should never have taken things this far. Sergeant, can you release Mister Ramirez immediately and bring him here?"

Harjinder raised an eyebrow, but carried out the instructions without further comment.

Poor Pablo was escorted to the desk looking like a stunned animal just before it's slaughtered. Although her instincts were to rush to Pablo and hug him to death, Rachael was determined to maintain a professional demeanour in front of her colleagues. Martin continued his embarrassingly false display of sympathy and contrition, apologising profusely but nevertheless informing him that he had to fix his tail light within fourteen days and bring the receipt in to be inspected by an officer. Rachael made the tart comment that she would be accompanying Pablo when he did this to make sure everything was done by the book. She followed this up by saying that she would be working from home for the rest of the day to make sure that Pablo was not troubled by any further aggressive policing.

She was surprised that Martin took this jibe without comment. She would have been even more surprised to see how sweaty and shaky Martin was immediately she and Pablo had left the building.

XXV

RACHAEL WONDERED HOW MARTIN WOULD behave the next day. She was somewhat surprised to find that he went out of his way to be reasonable and collegiate. He brought up the question of interviewing Randall himself and actually invited her to sit in with him on the interview. Towgood and Rachael had been in contact since Martin had taken control of the case and they had anticipated that she would have had to worm the information out of people or risk accessing the interview tapes in a way that was not altogether 'official'. Martin explained that he'd invited Randall down to the station tomorrow on the pretext of filling him in on the investigation of his car following the 'bomb scare' a week or so back. He had accepted it without any hesitancy or suspicion. Rachael graciously thanked Martin and said that, of course, she would only observe, for the sake of the Nobel murder enquiry, and allow him to ask all the questions.

Later in the day, when she was alone and certain that no one was listening, she rang Towgood on his mobile to give the update.

"Mm... DS Hall is not daft. That's quite a good ruse to get Randall in without him becoming suspicious," Towgood responded after Rachael had given him the details. "A good move on your part, too, to say that you would only observe."

"Is there anything in particular you want me to listen out for?" Rachael asked.

"No, not really... anything unusual... any contacts he mentions with people who might be of interest... Oh, and if the chief superintendent intervenes because he is getting an earful from the dean about harassing cathedral staff, melt into the background and let Martin deal with it all."

Rachael had other problems too. Pablo had been really shaken up with the events of yesterday. They had gone back to hers, as she felt it was a safer environment than his place. She was dying to find out in detail what had happened, but Pablo was not keen to talk about his experience and she did not want him to feel he was being interrogated further. He seemed unusually lost and unable to think ahead. In the end, it was Rachael that rang Mrs Merkel to explain why Pablo had not made it into work. She didn't tell the whole story and also made out that Pablo had not been well and would need a day or two to recover. Pablo did not object to this, which in turn convinced Rachael that all was not well. He had such a strong work ethic that he would normally have struggled into work, come what may.

The whole business was making Rachael re-evaluate her life priorities. Until recently, the Force and her career had been her number one goal, but now, since she had been with Pablo, forging a happy life with him that would stand the test of time seemed much more important. Both of them had a weekend free coming up which was quite a rare occurrence. Rachael decided that they needed to get away for a few days, despite the fact that it was now early December. With Pablo's consent, she booked a hotel room in the outskirts of Weymouth. It was near enough that it wouldn't be a hassle to get ready and travel there, but far enough away that they would be away from the vicinity of work.

However, before then, there was the question of the interview with Rev. John Randall, the Venerable Archdeacon of Winchester. He arrived about ten o'clock the following day dressed in black trousers, black shirt with dog collar, and a tweed jacket. He looked relaxed, just as Rachael remembered him from the interview she had done with him previously. Randall acknowledged her presence and recalled that he had already spoken to her. Rachael engaged cheerily in conversation, trying not to give the game away that they were likely to drop at least one bombshell on him soon. Martin bustled in from some other part of the building and greeted the archdeacon, inviting him to follow to an interview suite. Rachael tagged on behind trying to be as inconspicuous as possible. She may not have liked Martin as a person, but he could do his job well and she was impressed with his confidence and manner with which he dealt with proceedings.

"Now, we are going to record the interview," Martin announced when they were all settled around the table in the middle of the room.

"That sounds very formal. Am I under arrest?" Randall asked suspiciously.

"No, not at all," Martin responded soothingly. "But you may say something that is relevant to serious on-going investigations and so it's in everyone's best interests to have an accurate record of what has been said."

Randall shrugged his shoulders and seemed to accept that this was reasonable. Martin proceeded with his questioning.

"Now, I'm responsible for resolving an incident that happened a few days ago, close to the cathedral. A senior officer was stabbed with a knife on the path that leads past the south side of the cathedral. Have you heard about it?"

"Yes, I saw something on the news, and I saw the incident tape and policemen investigating the following day. I didn't realise it was a policeman that was stabbed. They didn't say that on the news."

"No, well we've deliberately kept some of the details out of the media for the time being. Have you heard any rumours or gossip about the incident from staff? Has anyone claimed to have witnessed it?"

"A few have made the 'what is the world coming to?' type comments, but nothing more specific than that. I haven't heard any speculation about who it might have been, and certainly, no-one has claimed to have witnessed the event."

Martin paused for a moment as if processing the underlying significance of this apparently bland statement. He continued,

"The attack took place sometime between 4pm and 5pm on the day in question. Can I ask where you were at this time?"

"Yes, certainly. I would have just finished officiating at evensong. At that time, I would have been tidying things away and de-robing in the vestry before returning home."

Martin intensified his gaze on the archdeacon and continued,

"So, you were very close by to the incident, then. Isn't there a door that leads straight onto that path where the attack took place?"

"Yes, the quickest way out from the vestry is through that door in the south transept. In fact, that's the way I would have gone home."

"…And you really saw nothing as you left the cathedral?"

"It's not surprising. I saw where the police incident tape was the following day and it's around the corner and out of sight from the door from the vestry. Besides, it was getting dark when I left, and I turned in the opposite direction to go into the close and return home."

Rachael made a point of going to the cathedral later and checking this for herself before contacting Towgood. Randall was absolutely right. The path bent sharply to the left and then straightened out behind a wall that hid the path. The crime scene would not have been visible.

Martin continued without any sign of being thrown off-track.

"Who else was at evensong apart from yourself?"

"The dean was there and gave the sermon, there were two of the canons who were assisting and of course the choir, choirmaster and organist were in attendance. The congregation for weekday evensong is never large but there were about fifty people present. A list of those officiating is kept in the cathedral office, but who knows who was in the congregation. Of course, there may have been a few tourists in the main nave, plus the duty vergers and one or two volunteers; probably not many at this time of year."

"Thank you. We will be following this up. Now, you may be wondering why we have asked you specifically about this rather than, say, the dean."

"I can think of one very good reason why you didn't interview the dean," Randall responded with the hint of a smile on his lips.

"Nevertheless," Martin persisted, "there are two reasons why we thought you might be a more appropriate person to ask. Firstly, the senior officer who was attacked was dealing with the Jack Nobel murder case. You may remember we asked you some questions about this previously."

Any flippancy in Randall's demeanour vanished immediately at the mention of poor Jack Nobel. "And you think there's a connection?" he asked with apparently genuine concern.

"It's possible," Martin responded vaguely. "Anyway… Secondly, you may remember that there was a security incident a little while back and we had to check your car for explosives. We've just had some very surprising information back from forensics as a result of that. We found hairs in the sacking that's in the boot of your car. The DNA analysis shows they belong to Jack Nobel. Oh, and by the way, the sacking matches the type in which his corpse was found at the mill. Furthermore, the tyre tread matches exactly a print found at the scene where we believe the body was dumped in the river. Would you care to comment?"

Randall looked genuinely dumbfounded.

"I don't understand. That can't be right. I explained… I haven't seen Jack since he was a teenager. I told you that. This can't be true."

"…And yet you always seem to be around at the crucial moments. You knew the victim when he was young, you happen to be here in Winchester when he arrives to confront his attacker, your car has evidence of the victim's presence in it, your car is also present at the site where the body is dumped in the river, and you happen to be close by when the detective inspector leading the case is attacked and narrowly avoids death. You have to admit that it all looks very suspicious."

Randall's demeanour had changed completely over the last few minutes. He was now nervous and fiddling with his hands. Rachael couldn't decide whether this was due to being found out or suddenly realising that he was facing some serious accusations.

"Look, I have no idea about any of this… but I agree, it sounds serious. I really think I need some legal representation if your questioning is going to carry on in this fashion."

"Very well, we'll take a break, and you can call whoever you wish. We can get the duty solicitor in if you don't have someone else to represent you. DS Goodfellow, perhaps you could get us some coffees while we are waiting?"

Rachael would normally have bristled with indignation at the idea of being cast as the servile woman who was charged with doing the domestic tasks, but she was stunned that Martin was proposing to carry on with the interrogation. He was taking a serious risk. She gave him a momentary glance of surprise and then asked Randall if he took milk and sugar in his coffee. While waiting for the kettle to boil, she saw a tall figure neatly dressed in a black suit with a clerical collar. He was elderly but still in good shape. It was the dean and he was making for the chief superintendent's office. Rachael remembered Towgood's injunction to avoid getting involved in a confrontation with the boss and decided to take much longer over making the coffee than was strictly necessary. Her instincts were right. Less than two minutes after the dean had knocked on the office door, the chief superintendent burst forth, pushed open the door to the interview room and shouted for the whole office to hear,

"Hall... my office... NOW."

Unusually, those working in the office could not work out the shouted reprimands that DS Hall was being subjected to. Perhaps the presence of the dean was modifying the chief superintendent's behaviour. Rachael lurked as invisibly as she could, pretending to be looking for some papers on her desk. Only a few minutes passed before the chief superintendent, followed by the dean, and then very sheepishly by Martin, reappeared and marched back across the office to the interview room. The chief superintendent apologised to Randall, whilst the dean gathered him up, like a mother hen protecting her chicks, and ushered him out of the building. Martin was left looking forlorn. Rachael actually felt sorry for him. She wondered whether she ought to go over and offer some consolation. To be fair, he had done everything rather well. His only failing was perhaps to have over-reached himself without being aware of the underlying political constraints of the situation. However, they made eye contact for just a second. It was a very meaningful moment, but it was unclear to Rachael exactly what the meaning was. Martin immediately turned away and deliberately left the room.

Although she was not to know it at the time, that day was the last time Rachael was to have a rational conversation with Martin. Only through rumours and gossip over the next week or so did she get any insight into what had just happened in the chief superintendent's office. Apparently, Martin had started out confidently enough, stating his case with reference to the evidence that he had put to Randall, and the chief superintendent had listened. However, Martin lost his nerve when he was asked directly if he was going to arrest the archdeacon there and then. When he floundered, the boss laid into him calling him useless and even more of a pain in the arse than Towgood.

When Rachael phoned Towgood later, he was intensely interested in the proceedings of the morning. He particularly wanted to know how Randall had reacted to the revelation of the forensic findings in his car. He was curiously also interested in the dean.

"He always seems to be hanging around like a bad smell when we find out anything interesting around the cathedral precincts. What do you make of him, Goodfellow? The chief seems keen to keep him safe from our enquiries. We haven't been able to interview him properly yet."

"I know my mother doesn't like him much," Rachael responded, somewhat lamely.

"Why's that?"

"She says that he's one of those 'academic priests' who's more concerned with flaunting his superior knowledge of religion and making everyone else feel inadequate, rather than trying to practice in real life what the Gospels were telling him to do. Now if you ask her about the bishop, that's a completely different story."

"Mm... interesting."

"You must remember that my mother is suffering from Alzheimer's, though," Rachael hastily added, worried that Towgood might give too much credence to this intelligence.

"Anyway, that all gives me something to think about. I'll be back in next week. You've got the weekend off, haven't you? Enjoy yourself."

XXVI

THE WAVES WASHED SMOOTHLY AND rhythmically onto the pebble beach, making a constant background sound, ebbing and flowing, that became noticeable when the talking stopped, especially as a soft, grey mist was enveloping the entire landscape. The sound of anything else that was going on was absorbed in the uncertain stillness and haziness of the surroundings. Rachael and Pablo were trudging along the beach with wet weather walking gear. Although it wasn't exactly raining, they were wet through from the excessive moisture in the air.

Despite the unpromising nature of the day, Rachael actually felt more optimistic and relaxed than she had done for a couple of weeks; just to get away for a few days in a different environment was having a positive effect. She felt that Pablo was beginning to be more like his old self again too. The last few days had been quite tense and difficult. Rachael had insisted that he stayed at hers when he wasn't in work. Since the business with the police, he had become very nervous and withdrawn, and Rachael felt she had to tread on eggshells around him. Wisely, she had not tried to interrogate him about what happened as it was clear that, for whatever reason, he didn't want to talk about it.

As they were walking along slowly and with difficulty as the pebbles shifted under every step, Pablo complained that only the English would be mad enough to consider a walk along a stony beach in these conditions as a fun thing to do. Rachael laughed and said that he was an old misery guts and was just as happy as she was to be out in the fresh air and away from things for a few days. They struggled on for half an hour or so before turning inland and heading for a pretty little village with thatched-rooved cottages and narrow irregular streets. At its centre, opposite the ancient stone church with its square tower and surrounding graveyard, was an archetypal village pub. It had started to rain properly now, and Rachael and Pablo needed no further incentive to enter. There was a table near an open fire, crackling away merrily with two enormous logs well ablaze. They eagerly grabbed the spot and divested themselves of their wet outer garments which they hoped would dry off by the heat of the fire. Pablo felt confident enough to buy drinks at the bar and then they thought they might as well make the most of it and order lunch while they were at it.

"You know the worst thing about last week was what that horrible policeman said," Pablo suddenly said as they sat contentedly warm and comfortable after eating with a second drink in their hands.

Rachael, realising that Pablo was now in a relaxed enough frame of mind to talk about things, said nothing and just let him continue.

"He say that people like me have no right to be in this country, and we must not be having relations with their women. He say he could easily find an excuse to send me back to Spain."

Rachael was genuinely shocked. She knew that some of her colleagues were still capable of expressing xenophobic views in private, but she did think that they were all professional enough these days not to allow such sentiments to impinge on their work-related duties. She still allowed Pablo to continue without interruption, however.

"I cannot bear to be parted from you like that. We would be in different countries, and I would not see you every day. You would forget me, and I would never find anyone like you again."

Rachael took hold of Pablo's hand and squeezed it reassuringly. There was a tear in Pablo's eye.

"Mi querido," Rachael said softly and soothingly, "the policeman was talking rubbish. There is no way you would have been deported just for having a faulty brake light. I wish you'd told me this earlier."

"But then you would have got mad and done something stupid at work and got into trouble."

The fire continued to crackle, and the quiet, carpeted bar area of the pub remained as calm as it had been. There were very few people in: an elderly couple who'd decide to take a trip out for lunch just like Rachael and Pablo, an old codger sat at the bar nursing a pint probably wishing that the pub still had a stone floor and only sold beer as it had done in his youth, and a small group of reasonably well-dressed people of various ages who might have been work colleagues out for a lunchtime drink.

"Listen, don't worry about me handling things at work. I can handle my emotions and remain calm, even when provoked. Who was it who said that?"

"It was the nasty young policeman who stopped me and told me I had an illegal car."

"Did anyone else talk to you at the station?"

"No, the nasty policeman says that his boss will give me a 'good grilling' – What is that? I thought it was something you did with meat – but your former lover comes and acts all sweetly and lets me go."

Rachael winced at the reference to Martin as her 'former lover', but knew that Pablo didn't mean anything by it. The whole incident was still shrouded in mystery, however. Why PC Grimthorpe had taken leave of his senses and ridiculously overreacted to a minor motoring offence remained opaque. She did log it in her memory though that she needed to have a word with him at some point to get an explanation.

"It would be the worst thing in the world if they split us up and we had to live in different countries," Pablo continued.

"I wouldn't let them split us up. I'd follow you to Spain rather than allow that to happen."

Rachael was quite startled to hear herself say this, but then she realised that this was only clarifying what had been churning over in her mind for a little while now. Her career in the Police Force had always been the most important thing in her life and she was ambitious to get to the top, if at all possible. However, the most important thing now was her future life with Pablo. She suspected that it would not be long before they got engaged, and then who knows how much longer before they considered getting married. Yes, she would give up the Police Force in an instant and go to live in Spain with Pablo if that's what it took to have a happy, contented life together.

"After Christmas, when I go home to my family for a holiday, I'd like you to come with me – at least for some of the time – so you can meet my parents and other relatives. Also, you can meet my friends in Spain."

"I'd like that very much," Rachael responded, giving Pablo's hand another little squeeze.

They had intended to remain in the pub for no more than an hour and then continue with their walk to take them back to the hotel in Weymouth. However, the weather outside was getting worse and the fire inside remained inviting so that they were still there two hours later. It was beginning to get dark by then too, so they chickened out and ordered a taxi back to town. It was supposed to be a holiday after all, not a weekend's endurance training.

Refreshed by the change of scene, Rachael returned to the fray on Monday morning. She had expected Detective Inspector Towgood to have returned to the desk in his office, but there was no sign of him. The department still had that listless air of indecision and lack of focus that had set in after Towgood had been knifed. Rachael did not have long to dwell on this as she was confronted by an unexpected handwritten note left in a prominent position on her own desk. It was from Gavin. 'Meet me in the briefing room as soon as you get in. I need to speak with you urgently', was the terse comment scrawled hurriedly across the paper. Rachael raised an eyebrow and examined the paper as if the explanation to this summons was somehow engrained in the fibres. She rushed off to the briefing room where she found Gavin on his own with a laptop set up and open on a video file.

"Oh, hi, Rachael. Sorry to be so mysterious, but I thought you ought to see this. We came across it by chance when we were investigating a robbery from one of the shops."

Gavin explained that they were looking at CCTV footage taken from the High Street. The grainy black and white footage was paused showing a still picture of the roadside. Nothing particularly noticeable struck Rachael. Gavin pressed a button, and the video sprang into life. A car came in from the right and parked almost centrally. A man got out. The sense of familiarity finally burst into clear recognition.

"That's Pablo getting out of his car!" Rachael exclaimed.

"Indeed," Gavin responded while freezing the video yet again, "and look at the rear lights. Do you notice they are in perfect condition? Watch what happens next."

Gavin restarted the video. A minute or so after Pablo had quit the scene a police constable came into view from the left. He paused beside the car and looked furtively behind the car, and then around generally in all directions, before swiftly taking out what looked like a truncheon and delivering two sharp blows to the rear lights on either side. The policeman then hastily returned to the pavement and exited to the right.

"What the...?" expostulated Rachael. "Who the hell is that?"

Gavin fast forwarded the video and then paused it again.

"All will be revealed in just a minute. I think you're going to find the next bit upsetting, I'm afraid."

The video recommenced at a time about twenty minutes further advanced. Pablo entered and was about to get into his car when the policeman also re-emerged and accosted him. It was quite clear this time that the policeman was PC Grimthorpe. He led Pablo to the back of the car and showed him the damage to the lights. Pablo clearly was clueless as to the cause of this damage and appeared to be explaining his ignorance of the damage. Then without apparent provocation, Grimthorpe seized Pablo's right arm and twisted it behind his back, forcing him face forward against the car. Pablo was clearly in some discomfort and Grimthorpe was shouting something at him while using his free hand to radio for assistance. Within a minute a police car with its lights flashing sped into view and Grimthorpe unceremoniously bundled Pablo into the back with himself following behind. The car then sped off.

"The little shit. I'll go and find him now and rip his head off," Rachael exclaimed, not concerned to show her anger.

"Much as that may make you feel better, I don't think it's going to get you the answers you want. Grimthorpe is merely the monkey. Who is the organ grinder? That is the much more important question. If you confront him at work you'll get into trouble, and he'll probably stay silent to protect others. Listen, I've worked in stations where there's rogue cops who think they can bend the rules to get their way. They stay tight and loyalty to one another is their overriding principle. To strike back I've found from experience it's best to employ some of their tactics against them in return. Bullies don't like being stood up to and will often crumble or give in if robustly resisted."

"I'm not sure I like the sound of this. What had you got in mind?"

"I happen to know that some of the PC's meet regularly after work at one of the pubs in town. Grimthorpe is likely to be there this evening. I suggest you and I see if we can find him and present him with the evidence of his wrongdoing. We can explain the consequences for him personally should that evidence become public. That might just persuade him to talk. I might also bring Jacob along too. He can assist us if things get a bit physical."

"If it was just me, I'd say forget it, but no one is going to mess with Pablo and get away with it. Just be careful, though. I don't want you or Jacob getting into trouble over this."

Rachael found it very hard to concentrate for the rest of the day. Towgood was nowhere to be seen, and in the absence of specific leadership in either the stabbing of Towgood or the murder of Jack Nobel, she found herself being reassigned to deal with a backlog of unsolved burglaries and assaults. She found this so frustrating because she felt they were so close to unravelling the whole mystery. If only she had been more patient with Amy at the funeral, she might have revealed the name of the killer. Where had she gone? Why was she so difficult to find? And more recently, what if Martin had been allowed to continue his interrogation of the archdeacon? She was no fan of Martin's, but she felt he was asking the right questions, and that Randall might have had more to say.

That evening, Rachael lied to Pablo about why she was going out. She hated doing it, but the last thing she wanted was to worry him any further with this wretched affair. She met up with Gavin and Jacob at their house first and they went over the plan of action. Gavin insisted that he would take the lead and Rachael was to remain primarily as an observer. They entered the 'Jolly Sailor' together, but Rachael and Gavin went to find a seat while Jacob went to the bar. Their choice of seat was premeditated and thought out in advance. There were a number of tables tight to the wall by the large window with bench seats either side. They may well have been church pews at one time, with high wooden backs as well as the seating plank. The effect of the arrangement was to create a number of cosy nooks for small groups to gather around in intimate conversation. Rachael and Gavin sat on the same side of the table with Rachael nearest the wall. Gavin had his laptop computer with him and got it set up. Rachael looked around. The 'Jolly Sailor' was in the suburbs rather than the centre of town, but the city was compact, and it was still within easy walking distance of the police headquarters. It was popular with police staff, possibly because the landlord was an ex-copper himself, but also because it didn't get the tourist and party crowd and so remained conveniently inconspicuous.

Grimthorpe was there with some of the other PCs playing pool in the more public part of the bar area.

"Right, are you ready?" Gavin asked. Rachael nodded but thought he looked unusually nervous.

Gavin got up and strode purposefully across to where Alex Grimthorpe had just finished playing a game of pool and was talking to a couple of the other off-duty PCs who were relaxing after work. The plan was to lure him over on the pretext that they had some important information that might be useful for a job he was doing at the moment. Grimthorpe did not have any dealings with Gavin at work, so Rachael was not surprised to see a look of suspicious surprise when Gavin spoke to him. However, Gavin must have been convincing enough as Grimthorpe followed him back to the table where Rachael remained seated. Grimthorpe made an involuntary wince when he recognised Rachael. This was the first time they had encountered each other since the incident with Pablo. She remained calm.

"You know Detective Sergeant Goodfellow, of course..." Gavin explained. "...Please, take a seat."

Grimthorpe hesitated, but realising that to make a run for it now would look extremely suspicious, he sat down opposite Rachael. Gavin sat next to Rachael and as if by extreme coincidence, but actually carefully coordinated, Jacob arrived with some drinks and sat next to Grimthorpe effectively blocking him in the corner.

"I don't think you've met my partner, Jacob?"

Jacob went through the ritual of introducing himself and shaking hands.

"Excellent," continued Gavin. "Now I thought... well, to be honest Rachael and I thought you ought to see this."

Rachael opened up the laptop so that Grimthorpe could see the screen. She then set in motion the video sequence that she had seen herself earlier in the day. Rachael studied the reactions of Grimthorpe carefully. Initially he became more and more tense, saying nothing, but at the point where Rachael knew that the identity of Grimthorpe would be revealed unquestionably and irrefutably, she saw the colour instantly drain from his skin. He was in shock. At the end Rachael dramatically closed the laptop and Gavin sarcastically commented, "Well, it looks like someone has been a very naughty boy."

"Where did you get that? It's a fake. Someone's trying to set me up," Grimthorpe blustered.

"It's verified footage from a CCTV camera. You should be more careful if you're going to pull stunts like this," Gavin responded. "You know this could end your career. How long have you been in the Force? ...Six months?... Do you know how difficult it would be for an ex-copper of your age, disgraced and dismissed to get another job?"

Grimthorpe tried to get up to leave, but Jacob put a very strong restraining arm on his shoulder and Grimthorpe gave up the attempt. Rachael was glad she was not there on her own. Her rage was boiling inside. If she had had her way, she would have torn Grimthorpe's limbs, one by one, from his body, finishing with his head. However, the calming presence of Gavin and Jacob coolly and methodically demolishing him allowed Rachael to remain outwardly placid.

"So, what do you want?" Grimthorpe asked realising that if they had just wanted to shop him to the authorities they would have done so by now.

"Ah, well there's the point. I'm sure lurking inside your psyche there's a warped sense of patriotism that gives you a deep-seated hatred of foreigners. You would probably also like to stick me and my boyfriend in a gas chamber, but I don't think you've got the bottle or the skill to have tried this stunt without help and without being told what to do. Whose orders were you following and why?"

"I can't tell you that... I'd be in even more trouble. God, Inspector Towgood has already given me a grilling today about this business. Has he seen this footage?"

Rachael raised an eyebrow. This was an unexpected turn of events. As far as she knew Towgood had not been in the office today. Gavin seemed unfazed though.

"As far as I know he hasn't, but he certainly will do first thing in the morning if you don't tell us what we need to know."

"OK, OK... but you didn't hear this from me. It was Detective Sergeant Hall. He said that it wasn't right that DS Goodfellow here was going out with a foreigner. She should be sticking with her own kind, and she should show more loyalty to the Force. He told me what to do. The idea was that we'd put the frighteners on this Spanish guy and warn him off. He was going to come in and interview him and threaten to deport him to Spain if he didn't leave DS Goodfellow alone. I got the timing wrong though. I was supposed to do it when it was quiet and there wasn't a lot going on. DS Hall didn't expect to be in charge of an attempted murder inquiry at the time, and when DS Goodfellow came into the station all guns blazing to find out what was going on, DS Hall told me to make myself scarce and he abandoned the second part of the operation."

Everything suddenly became very clear to Rachael now. It had to be Martin behind it. Why would he not take 'no' for an answer? Why wouldn't he stop meddling in her life? But also, how dare he? What gave him the right to think he could control who she was with or what she did?

"What are you going to do with the video?" Grimthorpe asked anxiously.

"Nothing for the moment," Gavin replied. "I won't be the one to dob you in, but these images are part of a burglary investigation. Someone else could easily put two and two together and if that happens, I'm not going to lie to protect you. That's the best I can offer."

"And you, Detective Sergeant Goodfellow, what are you going to do?"

This was the first time Grimthorpe had addressed her directly. Rachael looked at him directly in the eye and finally broke her silence.

"What you have done to me is worse than assaulting me physically. You've broken your oath of office; you've perverted the course of justice and you're an utter disgrace to the Force. You deserve no favours from me, and you'll get none. Now get out of my sight please. You're making me feel ill."

Jacob loosened his grip so that Grimthorpe could get up and leave the table. Quickly gathering up his coat, he left the building without a word to anyone else.

"Well, now you know what happened, Rachael. What do you want us to do next?" Gavin said as soon as the door had closed behind Grimthorpe.

"You've done more than enough, both of you. Let me sleep on it. I need to think."

XXVII

RACHAEL FOUND IT HARD TO sleep that evening and even worse, Pablo could tell something was not right. Rachael was determined not to tell him what had happened that evening, at least until a resolution of some sort had been achieved, but of course Pablo knew Rachael well enough by now to know when she wasn't being entirely straight with him.

It was therefore not surprising that she was already in a febrile mood when she went into work the following day. Martin was talking to one of the other members of the team in the far corner of the office where everyone of lower rank than detective inspector had to share a work space. Rachael's blood was boiling, and she went over and curtly interrupted.

"Excuse me, DS Hall, can I have a word?"

"Can't it wait? I'm in the middle of something important here," Martin responded irritably.

"No, it can't," Rachael riposted with firm defiance.

The person that Martin was talking to took the hint and moved away mumbling something about returning in ten minutes.

Martin fixed Rachael with his eyes, daring her to challenge him for this impudent interruption. Rachael, however, met his gaze and fired daggers of contemptuous looks back at him.

"I had a chat with PC Grimthorpe last night," she began.

"Is that the reason why he's ill and not at work today?" Martin responded sarcastically.

"Probably," Rachael countered, "because he was forced to admit that my Pablo was set up deliberately. There's video footage of Grimthorpe smashing the rear lights of the car before making the arrest."

Martin started to look shifty. He continued,

"So, what's that got to do with me? I'm not Grimthorpe's line manager. You know the disciplinary procedure."

"You really are a loathsome snake, aren't you? So, you're just going to abandon your faithful little stooge to his fate. Grimthorpe told us that you put him up to it and gave him his instructions. He's not got the experience or the intelligence to do what he did unaided, but no-one in the office would be surprised to hear that you are the mastermind behind the operation. I know why you did it too."

Martin hesitated, perhaps wondering whether to bluff it out, but in the end, he decided he might as well own up and go on the offensive.

"Well, so what if I did? I was doing you a favour. If you don't want to be with me, at least you should be with someone on the Force – or failing that with one of your own kind. What the hell you're doing with a greasy Spaniard who's only good for looking after old biddies, I don't know."

This was too much for Rachael. She flew at Martin and grabbed him by the throat. Martin, shocked and surprised, lost his footing and fell to the floor with Rachael on top of him. There was stunned immobility from everyone in the office. Pens and documents were dropped. A cup of coffee fell on the floor, and everyone looked on, frozen in astonishment. Rachael ended up beating Martin on the chest and trying to slap him around the face, while Martin held his arms up to guard himself, shouting phrases like 'get off, you stupid woman' when the battering diminished long enough to allow him to speak.

"You do not have the right to interfere in my life like this," Rachael screeched at the top of her voice as she continued to pulverise him. "When are you going to get that through your thick skull? I hate you, I hate you, I hate you... It's not a thin line between love and hate; it's a bloody long and thick one... and I hate you."

At that moment, the door to Towgood's office, where they seemed to have just ended up, opened and he appeared serenely in the doorway as if nothing were particularly amiss. Rachael immediately stopped hitting Martin and rose to her feet.

"Can I see both of you in my office now, please?" he said, calmly and softly. Rachael smoothed down her ruffled clothing and followed Towgood into his office. Martin followed her and they both avoided making eye contact. People in the office gradually went back to their duties in an embarrassed fashion, trying, but failing, to pretend that nothing out of the ordinary had just happened.

Rachael felt like she was back at school and had been summoned into the headmaster's office. She felt a mixture of mortification for having lost control and anxiety at the serious consequences that could follow. Towgood's tone, when he finally spoke, was uncharacteristically cold and distant and enhanced the impression of a school principal about to administer a severe punishment.

"When I left this establishment last, I thought I was in charge of a well-organised, professional outfit. Yet, when I came back yesterday it seemed to resemble a badly written episode from a cheap 'cops and robbers' TV series from the nineteen seventies. Instead of getting on with the pressing work in hand, I had to spend yesterday getting to the bottom of what's been going on. Would either of you like to comment on the disgraceful scene going on outside my door just now?"

Martin remained silent. Rachael, close to tears and realising that she was staring at the abyss of her career going up in flames, nevertheless felt she had to do the decent thing.

"Sir, I apologise for my lack of control. It was inexcusable and I'll go and tender my resignation immediately."

The hint of a thin smile invaded Towgood's features. "Fortunately, that won't be necessary," he said dryly.

"...But I've been assaulted," Martin protested. "Surely there must be some disciplinary measures against her?"

In retrospect, Rachael thought that of all the horrible things he'd said or done, this ranked almost top of the list of Martin's meanest things. Towgood remained icily cool and continued,

"You know the procedures DS Hall and I'm sure you are quite capable of filing a complaint if you so wish. However, I think you ought to hear what I've got to say before you decide to do that. You see, I think you've forgotten that I'm a detective, and if I may say so without blowing my own trumpet, a rather good one. I made a lot of progress yesterday. Have you wondered why PC Grimthorpe isn't in this morning? Well, he's been suspended for misconduct. I know all about his attempt to pervert the course of justice. I've seen the CCTV evidence of him in the act and, DS Hall, I know about the link to you and your motivation for putting him up to it.

"DS Goodfellow, I'd like to talk to DS Hall on his own now. Perhaps you could go with DC Yapp to investigate the burglary in Bishop's Waltham that was reported last night. It will keep you out of the office for a few hours so you can avoid the gossip. I'll catch up with you this afternoon when hopefully we can resume trying to apprehend Jack Nobel's murderer, as well as my assailant too."

Rachael left the office like a murder suspect who'd been given a last-minute reprieve from the gallows. She was curious to know what happened in the office after she left, though. This curiosity only increased as the days went by because Martin was never seen again, and neither was Alex Grimthorpe for that matter. No convincing official reason for their departure was ever given and so the rumour and speculation were rife, some of it being extremely wild and lurid. At the time Rachael didn't dare ask Towgood outright what occurred, not least because it would also bring to the surface again her own failings and misdemeanours surrounding the affair.

In fact, it was not until many, many years later that Rachael caught a glimpse of what really occurred when she left the inspector's office that day. By this time, Towgood had retired and by a strange twist of fate was now being cared for in the same nursing home that Rachael's mother (now long dead) had been residing. Pablo and Rachael had been married for a long time at this stage and had three children, the eldest of whom was now in the final year of university. They spent most of their time in Spain, where they had decided to make their permanent residence, but they would both return to England three or four times a year to catch up with relatives and friends or just to relive good times from the past. Rachael made a point of keeping in touch with Towgood. He was physically frail and needed a frame to get about on, but mentally he was as sharp as ever. She felt sorry for him because apart from her occasional visits he seemed to have no friends or family visiting and appeared a very lonely figure. He was always cheerful when Rachael called by however, and on this occasion, they were sat in the bright May sunshine of the well-tended garden while Pablo caught up with some of the staff he knew who were still working there.

"Do you remember that time I caught you and Martin Hall rolling around on the floor, fighting each other outside my office?"

"Don't remind me, Daniel. I think that has to be the most embarrassing moment of my entire police career. What happened to Martin after that? It was all very hush-hush at the time."

"Yes, well we had to keep it quiet because things weren't exactly done by the book. When you left the room, I presented him with all the evidence I'd gathered showing what he'd done and what he'd got Grimthorpe to do – it was scandalous how he'd tried to incriminate your husband.

"I gave him a choice; we could either go through the procedures which would inevitably lead to him being charged with perverting the course of justice and losing his job, or I could arrange for an immediate transfer to another Force with a demotion and a black mark on his record. I made it clear I would not have him on my team any longer under any circumstances. Not surprisingly, he chose the latter option and ended up at the Met."

"I see," said Rachael, not quite knowing what to think.

"I gather you're not entirely impressed," Towgood continued, with a faint smile lighting the corner of his lips. "What would you rather have had me do? Throw the book at him and go through the official channels? Just think for a moment what the consequences would have been. It might have taken six months or more to complete all the disciplinary and legal hearings and procedures, during which Hall would have been still hanging around the place like a bad smell. He had friends, you know. The office would have been split into factions; those who were your supporters and those that were his. There would have been infighting and unpleasantness – probably more stunts like the one Hall tried to pull. Morale and team spirit would have plummeted, and you would have felt more uncomfortable at work than you already were. Believe me, I had your best interests at heart when I did what I did. Besides, you have to admit he was good at his job when he was being professional. Was it so terrible I gave him a chance to redeem himself, while getting him out of our hair?"

"That's all very well, but he could have gone to prison for what he did," Rachael interrupted with a slight tone of irritation.

"And what good would that have done anybody?" Towgood continued. "Prison destroys people and very few come out better people. Most of the inmates are mentally ill and should be in hospital anyway, and those that aren't just learn to be better criminals. Long gone are the days when we even pretended that we were trying to rehabilitate people. Meting out the violent stick of vengeance in squalid Dickensian conditions is what it's all about these days."

"For Christ's sake, you're beginning to sound like a bleeding-heart liberal. Suppose he had become obsessed with another woman in London and used his position to do something even worse?"

Towgood paused for reflection before continuing.

"Then I'd have had to carry the can and take the consequences for being wrong. You can still snitch on me if you like. There isn't that much difference between my life here and prison. Admittedly, the food and the surroundings are more pleasant in the home, but I suspect the company might be more interesting behind bars. You must realise from your time in the Force that the line between right and wrong is sometimes not so easy to define. There have just been a couple of occasions when I've had to tip-toe gingerly across that line for the greater good."

"Well, all I can say is that I'm glad I didn't know this at the time. I definitely would not have been happy that Hall didn't have to fully take the consequences for his behaviour. Still, it's a long time ago and we've been through too much together to fall out over it at this stage. I won't press charges and I'll still come to see you."

"I'm glad to hear it. I just wish you were able to come more often," Towgood concluded with a touch of melancholy.

Back in the present-day, Rachael had to endure a surreal meeting with Towgood that afternoon where the elephant in the room – namely the incident that morning – was studiously avoided. Indeed, the name Martin Hall seemed to have been expunged from the record as efficiently as that of a disgraced North Korean dissident official.

"Perhaps we need to look at this from a different angle," Towgood said. He seemed frustrated, almost defeated and it was clear that he wasn't really recovered from his injury. "Instead of trying to find evidence to incriminate Randall, maybe we should be looking for evidence to show he's innocent."

"That is going to be very hard," Rachael timidly replied. "He knew Jack very well; he was around all day when we think Jack was abused. There's the article in the paper, mentioning Randall by name, which seemed to spur Jack into action; then most damning of all, there's the forensic evidence from his car which puts it at both the likely murder scene and the dumping site by the river. What have you got in his defence to counter all that?"

"Oh, it's hopeless, hopeless, hopeless…" Just for a moment Towgood seemed to let down his guard and let his true emotions show through. "Have we made no progress in finding that girl you talked to at the funeral? How hard is it to find a drugs counsellor called Amy who works in London?"

"To be fair, she didn't say she worked in London. I only assumed that because she said she didn't move away when Jack returned to Peterborough and she said she had to catch a train, which was probably going to London."

"This won't do…" Towgood exploded. "All of this becomes more speculative every time I hear about it. The train could equally be going the other way to Edinburgh." There was a pause while Towgood restored his equilibrium. "…I'm sorry, that was uncalled for…" There was a further pause while he thought intensely on the conundrum facing him. "…Right, we will throw one more shake of the dice to find Amy, and if that doesn't work out, I'll have no option but to arrest Randall, whatever the consequences."

XXVIII

TOWGOOD'S LAST THROW OF THE dice seemed to Rachael to be a very odd one. He went to see Michael Bakowski, still living with his mother and leading as chaotic and disorganised life as ever. As a result of the discussions, Rachael was summoned to the railway station the following day to catch the ten o'clock train to London Waterloo. When she arrived, she was surprised to see Michael standing next to Towgood, obviously expecting to travel with them. On the train, Towgood explained that Michael was going to show them all the places where he'd met Jack and Amy so that they could visit any clinics or outreach centres nearby in the hope that Amy really had stayed local, and they could find her.

Rachael made the comment that it sounded more like a job for uniformed branch, to which she got the frosty response that they didn't seem to have done a very good job so far.

Towgood had been careful to avoid the rush hour, so Waterloo was busy, but not manic. Michael was disconcertingly helpful, revelling in his newly found importance. They started off in the streets near Southwark cathedral. There was a spot close by where Michael used to meet Jack and Amy, particularly in the early days. Towgood took an intense interest in every aspect of the place, noting the streets that led off and the nature of the businesses and buildings. Towgood had already asked Michael if he'd ever been to the place where Amy and Jack had lived, but had drawn a negative answer. He kept probing, however, asking whether they always arrived on foot, whether they mentioned having to catch a bus or take the tube. Although Michael's answers were vague and uncertain, Rachael got a feeling that they couldn't have lived too far away.

Michael showed the two detectives several places where they had set up market stalls and then they travelled further east towards Greenwich where they would also meet less frequently for a market in that area.

After half the day was gone, Towgood finally thanked Michael for his help, presented him with a return rail ticket and bade him farewell.

"Aren't I going back with you?" Michael asked, clearly disappointed that his role as police consultant had come to an abrupt end.

"Detective Sergeant Goodfellow and I still have a lot of work to do. You can go back on any train you like. You can even spend a few hours in London this evening first, if you want. Besides, it wouldn't do your image much good to be seen being too pally with police officers, surely?"

Bakowski sloped off sullenly making for the nearest bus stop. Rachael felt perhaps there was still just the slightest hint of a limp in the way he walked. She had no time to ponder on this as Towgood immediately launched into his plan for the rest of the day. Rachael was to return to Southwark and investigate any clinics or outreach centres that were within easy walking distance of the spot Michael had shown them earlier. He would do the same in Greenwich.

"Now if I recall, Goodfellow, you told me that Amy said she was working with drug addicts. There again, that doesn't necessarily mean she's working at a dedicated drug centre clinic. She could be based at a health centre or a church-based community centre, or a dozen other types of outreach organizations, so keep an open mind. Also, remember that as well as trying to find Amy, it wouldn't be a bad thing if we came across any hostels or homeless organisations who might have helped Jack and Amy when they were homeless here. You never know, there might still be people who remember them. We'll meet up at nine at Waterloo to catch the train back."

Rachael's heart sank. This was the dreary mind-numbing information-gathering exercise she thought she'd left behind in her uniform days. Still, with a sigh, she left Towgood and took the Jubilee Line back to Southwark where her first call was to the Citizens Advice Bureau, housed in a modern, efficient, low-rise office block.

A very confident receptionist was able to furnish Rachael with the information she was looking for, and moreover her local knowledge was able to provide Rachael with a bit of background to some of the establishments as well. There were nine local organizations to visit within a sensible distance: five health clinics, a hospital, a youth advice centre, a hostel for the homeless and a dedicated drugs drop-in centre. It could have been a lot worse. Rachael thanked the receptionist who suddenly became slightly wary.

"Surely you could have got all of this information down at the station?" she said. "You must have details of all these organizations?"

"Oh, we're not local. I'm from the Wessex Constabulary. We're trying to find evidence to solve a murder on our patch."

Rachael was trying to sound professional and convincing, but she could tell it wasn't entirely working.

"But surely you would be liaising with the local Force? We have a very good relationship with the local community officer there."

Rachael mumbled something about how she was sure her senior officer had cleared it with the local Force first, but she was finding it hard to convince herself that Towgood had not gone off on an unofficial venture of his own. She rapidly concluded her conversation with the receptionist and left, knowing full well that a phone call would be made to the local station as soon as she left. Still, it was Towgood's mess, not hers.

Rachael didn't expect to learn much from her visits, and she was not disappointed. The turn-over in staff was such that hardly anybody was around when Jack and Amy would have been wandering the streets of London, and any 'Amy' who was currently on a staff list turned out not to be the one she wanted. At each venue she visited, she left a poster to be displayed in the most public place possible. It showed a picture of Jack and the text pleaded with the reader for any information that might lead to the conviction of his murderer.

Dispirited by what seemed a totally pointless day, Rachael finished her appointed tasks and then settled down at a table in a coffee shop with a large americano and a slice of fruity flapjack. The brown carpet, designed to hide the mud, had seen better days while the chairs and the tables, crammed in to maximise the capacity of a limited space, were flimsy and cheap. She got out her phone and rang Pablo.

"Hola, mi amor. ¿Cómo estás?"

"Hi, Rachael," Pablo replied. "I'm well thank you. When are you going to be home?"

"It's going to be late. Don't expect me any earlier than half ten. How was Mother today?"

"She was a little difficult this morning. She said her family stole her money. The usual thing. She was calm by this afternoon."

Rachael sighed to herself. There would be a run of several days when things would seem well; occasionally she would even delude herself into thinking her mother might recover. But always something would happen to shatter the pretence; reality would reassert itself with the grim certainty that demise was inevitable.

Rachael eventually made her way back to Waterloo station where she had arranged to meet up with Towgood. The evening rush hour had subsided so at least they were easily able to find places to sit in a sparsely populated carriage for the journey home. It was Towgood who voiced Rachael's thoughts on the day's escapade.

"I suppose you think the whole day has been a waste of time?"

"It's not my role to question the judgement of a senior officer," Rachael replied.

"My goodness, that's a politician's answer… and moreover, the response of one who's about to stab his leader in the back."

Rachael considered this comment very tasteless in view of recent events and replied rather icily,

"Well, I didn't find anything remotely useful. Did you? Oh, and by the way, I hope you cleared all this with the local police, because the Citizens Advice Bureau in Southwark is certainly going to be informing them that we have been asking questions."

"Don't worry about that," Towgood responded somewhat dismissively. "As it happens, I may have discovered something that could be useful. I discovered a social worker who'd been working in the area for thirty years. She remembered coming across a couple of youngsters at the homeless hostel she visited called Jack and Amy. She remembered them moving into sheltered accommodation and gradually getting their lives back together. She remembered when Jack left (she didn't know that he'd gone back to Peterborough), and she recalled that while Amy remained for a few months she then successfully applied to do a BTEC in health and social care at the local FE college and moved out. Moreover, she remembered seeing the application form and noticing that Amy's surname was something like Lightwood or Lightfoot."

"But that's not enough, is it?" Rachael responded with exasperation borne out of tiredness and frustration.

Towgood looked startled, but then continued in a composed manner,

"No, it's not enough… but it's something. I have the name of the college and maybe they'll have records of where she went next. We ought at least to get the full name of this girl, which will make it easier to find her."

"And what if there are two Amy Lightwoods at this college or an Amy Lightwood and an Amy Lightfoot… or an Amy Lighthouse… or whatever? When we discover something about this case, there's always something unknown lurking over the horizon that's preventing us from solving it. Personally, I'm beginning to think that DS Hall was right, and you should have thrown the book at Archdeacon Randall as soon as all that incriminating evidence was found in his car."

"You know I'm going to have to do that soon if nothing further comes to light. I'll get everyone scouring college records, electoral registers, staff lists, and goodness knows what else tomorrow. But if nothing comes of that… well, I'll have no option although I still feel Randall has nothing to do with it."

"You're the one who's always going on about 'facts, facts, facts.' Why are you paying so much store by 'gut-feeling'?"

"You're in a very down-beat mood this evening, DS Goodfellow, if I may say so. Is everything alright with your mother?"

"She's the same as always. It's not a condition she's going to recover from. Do you have elderly parents that need care?"

"No, both my parents died a long time ago. We weren't particularly close, so I can't say it affected me much."

There was something in the way that Towgood said this which made it clear to Rachael that he was not prepared to discuss his relationship with his parents any further. The rest of the journey was spent discussing the technical details of who was going to do what in their fact-finding mission in the morning. Rachael was going to have to liaise with the Metropolitan Police to try and find further information about Amy; something she felt they could have far more usefully been doing today.

XXIX

THE CHRISTMAS LIGHTS SWAYED BACK and forth in the High Street as a gale was blowing in from the English Channel. Rachael and Pablo, either side of Rachael's mother, were guiding her as best they could in these treacherous conditions towards the cathedral. It was the evening of the carol service, an event Rachael and her mother had been coming to for years. Memories were clearly flooding back, and Rachael's mother's face looked brighter and younger than Rachael could remember for some time. Fingers crossed that the evening was going to be a good one without incident. Even the questions about why Pablo needed to be there stopped. Rachael had explained to her mother a million times that Pablo was her boyfriend, but the concept seemed too difficult to grasp.

It was a Wednesday evening, a week before Christmas Day. The beginning of that week had been spent feverishly trying to track down Amy, with limited success. Yes, they had discovered that she had registered at the college unambiguously under the name Amy Lightwood and that she had completed her BTEC in health and social care with distinction (they even had a passport photo of her which Rachael was able to recognise), but after she left, the trail went surprisingly cold again. The college had no record of further establishments that Amy attended nor any requests for references on file. The Met were not able to provide any further information from other sources either. They had enough to track her down now, but it might take days or weeks.

The three of them settled on chairs about two-thirds of the way back down the nave. Rachael's mother was seated next to the central passageway up the nave so she could get a better view of what was happening and also get out easily if there was an emergency. The choir and the clergy in their finest and most ornate vestments made their way discreetly down to the west door and eventually after a few minutes of expectant anticipation, the lights were turned out, leaving just the feeble, soft glow of the candles sited at various points around the cathedral building. The pure, innocent tones of a boy soprano started singing the first verse of 'Once in Royal David's City', unaccompanied and with unadorned simplicity. Rachael, with a tear in her eye remembering singing the verse herself as a child chorister, squeezed her mother's hand. How wonderful she felt when she got a reciprocal response. The organ came in with verse two, the soloist had maintained the pitch accurately, the lights went on and the choir and clergy began their slow procession up the central aisle towards the choir stalls. With the precision of years of repetition everyone had taken their place just as the last verse of the carol came to an end. Amongst the clergy, Rachael recognised the bishop, the dean and the archdeacon. At least half a dozen others were present, presumably canons and vicars of the diocese.

Following an opening address and prayer by the dean, the choir sang a couple of numbers, one she knew, the other being unfamiliar. As the service proceeded, Rachael became aware of a growing disturbance at the west end of the church. Initially it was just the occasional sound of a footstep and a whispered voice, but then it became more frequent and intrusive. Turning around from time to time, it was difficult at first to see what was the cause. Eventually she caught sight of a uniformed police officer, standing just inside the door. She presumed that maybe some drunken revellers had got carried away outside and were causing a nuisance, but then on her next backward glance she saw Towgood in hushed but animated discussion with a verger. What on earth was he doing there…?

* * *

… Back in the office Towgood had continued to weigh the balance of evidence after Rachael had left for the day, and had steeled himself to arrest the archdeacon the following morning as the only option left to him.

He was just about to call it a day himself when the phone rang on Rachael's desk. He might have been inclined to let the answerphone cut in, but maybe some sixth sense warned him that it might be important. It was a woman's voice on the other end.

"Is that Detective Sergeant Goodfellow?"

"No, I'm afraid she's not here at the moment," he replied. "Can I help? I'm Detective Inspector Towgood, DS Goodfellow's boss."

There was a long silence and he thought she might ring off. Then a long-shot occurred to him.

"That's not Amy Lightwood by any chance?"

There was a further silence which convinced him that he was indeed speaking with Amy.

"Look, if you can trust my colleague, you can trust me. If you know who abused Jack Nobel when he was a youngster, you've got to tell me now. I'm about to make an arrest and that information is crucial. Was it Reverend John Randall?"

The woman unexpectedly laughed, finally responding,

"No disrespect, but honestly... call yourselves detectives? You're completely barking up the wrong tree..."

* * *

... As soon as Rachael realised that Towgood was present, she felt more and more anxious to go and find out what was going on and assist if necessary. A congregational rendering of 'While shepherds watched their flocks by night' allowed her the cover to move to the back of the cathedral relatively unobserved.

"What's going on?" she whispered to Towgood.

"We've finally got the breakthrough we needed," Towgood whispered excitedly back, like a wolf who has cornered his prey and anticipates a good meal. "We're here to make an arrest, but it's delicate. I'll tell you about it later.

It's best you go back and look after your mother. We need to keep this as low-key as possible."

Rachael rather hurt that she was being excluded from the climax of the investigation and being kept in the dark, returned to her place in the congregation. To her horror, the seat occupied by her mother was empty and she was nowhere to be seen...

* * *

... As soon as Towgood had finished the conversation with Amy, he went to the filing cabinet where documents and photographs relating to the case were now stored, and pulled out an enhanced photostat of the newspaper article that had caught the notice of Jack when he was living with Daniel Jarvis. He read it slowly and thoroughly, finally hitting his forehead with his hand in frustration. Why didn't people read things properly? Why did they always focus on things at the beginning and never notice things at the end? Why had HE not read the article properly? He should have known better. Most of it was utterly irrelevant. It was only the last two sentences that had triggered Jack Nobel's decision to precipitously travel to Winchester and confront his abuser...

* * *

"Pablo, where is Mother?" Rachael hissed.

"I thought she was with you? Didn't you take her to relieve herself in the women's toilets?"

"No, oh my life, where's she gone? Come on we've got to look for her."

Rachael pulled Pablo to the back of the cathedral once again. Towgood had moved away, but a young female constable was clearly guarding the west door exit. Rachael enquired of her whether an old, frail woman had left the building. Rachael was recognised by the constable and so was let into the secret that all the entrance and exit points were being guarded so it was very unlikely that anyone could have got in or out in the last twenty minutes.

"She must still be in here," Rachael said to Pablo, not hiding her concern.

"You go slowly up the north aisle, and I'll go up the south one and we'll meet behind the high altar."

The clergy conducting the service now were beginning to notice that something was going on. The dean seemed to lose his thread in a prayer momentarily, taking a few embarrassing seconds to find his place and carry on. He returned to his seat afterwards but continued to look with a frown towards the disturbance that was going on at the back of the church…

* * *

Towgood was able to get in touch with DS Karen Oakley at Peterborough Police Headquarters. His suspicions were now reinforced by what she had to say, not only from police records, but also the gossip from her husband who he recalled was a vicar in the diocese. He looked at his watch. He might just be able to catch John Randall before he made his way over to the cathedral for the carol service. He dialled the number and was rewarded with the archdeacon's voice.

"Hello? Is it urgent? I have to get to the cathedral in a few minutes."

"I'm sorry to disturb you. It's Detective Inspector Towgood of the Wessex Constabulary here. I just want to ask a couple of quick questions… it won't take long."

Towgood could almost feel an icy cold atmosphere ooze from his phone; hardly surprising in view of the aggressive interrogation he had suffered at the hands of DS Hall. He continued,

"…Your car. Does anyone else drive it apart from you and your wife?"

"I very occasionally let other members of the clergy borrow it, as long as they have insurance."

"Can you recall if anybody borrowed it over Easter earlier this year?"

"That's a long time ago now… I have my desk diary here. Let me see if there is anything down in there that jogs my memory…Well that's interesting, I did lend my car, several times, to someone that week. Yes, I remember… because theirs was being repaired in the garage."

"Archdeacon, who was it?"

* * *

Rachael and Pablo were slowly working their way up the cathedral on opposite sides, scanning every nook and cranny for signs of Rachael's mother. Trying to stay calm, Rachael felt surges in equal measures of panic, worry and embarrassment at the thought of where her mother might be. She had reached the entrance to the south transept, when unexpectedly a tall figure in ecclesiastical robes rushed by her. For a moment, the shock took her back to the attack on Towgood with the swift approach from behind of the assailant and then the rapid departure ahead. On this occasion, however, she had time to see that the figure scurrying away was the dean. A quick glance across to the other members of the clergy, with their astonished and dumbfounded expressions convinced her that the dean's extraordinary behaviour was not part of the intended ceremony. Before she could round the corner to see where he had gone, she heard a familiar voice shouting at the top of her voice.

"You're a bad man," her mother screamed. "You deserve to be defrocked, flogged and thrown in jail."

"Stop it," a male voice replied angrily. "Let me get by, you stupid old woman."

Rachael hurried around the corner to see her mother standing in the narrow doorway that led to the vestry and then to the outside world. She was absurdly trying to bash the dean over the head with a small telescopic umbrella, but because he was so tall most of her blows landed on his chest or shoulders. She was preventing the dean from passing through the door which he was clearly anxious to do.

"Mother!" Rachael shouted. "Stop that at once."

"He's up to something wicked. You can tell it in his eyes," Rachael's mother responded fiercely. She then returned her attention to the dean. "Why are you deserting your post halfway through the service? You're supposed to read the collect for Christmas Day at the end of the service."

Rachael forcefully grabbed her mother by the arm and pulled her out of the doorway to allow the dean to pass.

"I'm very sorry. My mother's not really in her right mind. Don't take it personally."

However, before the dean could pass by, Towgood followed by two uniformed constables burst through from the opposite direction. Surprisingly, he addressed Rachael's mother rather than Rachael herself.

"Ah, Mrs Goodfellow, thank you for assisting us. It's much appreciated."

He then turned gravely to the dean and said,

"Dean John Michael Pretorius, I am arresting you on suspicion of the murder of Jack Nobel. You have the right to remain silent. Anything you say may be used in evidence against you. You have a right to have a lawyer present while you are questioned. If you cannot afford a lawyer, one will be appointed for you."

The dean rose to his full height and riposted with aggressive energy,

"This is ridiculous. You do know that I am good friends with the chief constable? When he hears about this, you'll be clearing your desk."

Towgood stood his ground and returned a withering look.

"I expect to be able to add wounding a police officer with intent to kill to the charge list soon. Unfortunately, I don't yet have enough evidence to charge you with rape and sexual abuse of a minor, but I know for certain that you are responsible for destroying the life of that poor, young man you murdered. What does Matthew's Gospel say? 'Whoso shall offend one of these little ones which believe in me, it were better for him that a millstone were hanged about his neck, and that he were drowned in the depth of the sea.'? Look to your conscience and your soul, Dean."

The effect on the dean was dramatic. To Rachael, he seemed to crumple almost physically. He said nothing more and became totally compliant. The two uniformed officers led him away through the small door in the south transept and out into the close where there was a waiting police car.

XXX

THE CLERGY AND CHOIR HAD doggedly managed to complete the carol service, with the archdeacon stepping into the breach to cover for the dean. Although there was a murmur of consternation rumbling through the congregation, no one really knew what was going on until they heard about it the following day on the news. It made the national TV bulletins and the front pages of the newspapers. 'Dean detained and questioned about unsolved murder' was the headline in the most sober edition, whilst the most scurrilous tabloid screamed 'Killer vicar uncovered in carol service terror'.

The office was a buzz of excitement and activity when Rachael went in the following morning. One little cameo that she observed and which stayed with her involved the chief superintendent storming across the floor to harangue Towgood. Towgood unexpectedly stood his ground and before the chief superintendent could utter a word, Towgood barked at him,

"Don't say a word. He's confessed to everything and we're sending the paperwork to initiate the trial today."

He then pointedly walked past the chief superintendent into his office and definitively closed the door. Lost for words, Towgood's boss sheepishly made a retreat to his own office on the next floor up.

Rachael was still very much in the dark as to how the focus of guilt had swung so suddenly and decisively towards the dean. Finally, in mid-afternoon she had the opportunity to have a full debrief in Towgood's office.

"Well, it just goes to show how wrong you were about our trip to London being such a waste of time," Towgood began, almost smugly. "Amy Lightwood saw one of those posters we left around the place and rang the office here not long after you left to go and pick your mother up. She told me it was Michael Pretorius, not John Randall who Jack had accused of abusing him. The good news is that I now have her contact details and she is prepared to testify in court. After I finished the call and got over the shock of that unexpected revelation, I went back to the news article that had seemed to motivate Jack's ill-fated excursion to Winchester. Most of it, and all the stuff about Randall, is totally irrelevant. It's only this last bit here which is key."

Towgood passed a photocopy to Rachael. The final sentence read, 'Rev. John Randall's promotion to archdeacon means he will join the former dean of Peterborough, Rev. Michael Pretorius, who moved to be dean of Winchester three years ago.'

"I was fortunately able to find Karen Oakley still at work in Peterborough," Towgood continued. "She confirmed that whilst there hadn't been a hint of any gossip regarding Randall, the same could not be said for Pretorius. He was not well liked by his colleagues, according to her husband, and there were raised eyebrows about the reasons for his sudden decision to make a sideways move to Winchester. She is going to search through case files to see if any other abuse allegations can be linked to him.

"The final clincher came when I just managed to catch Randall himself, just before he left for the carol service and he confirmed that Pretorius had borrowed his car extensively during Holy week, because his own was out of action."

"I wonder if that's why he was so difficult and did all he could to stop us investigating in the close and interviewing the clergy? I suppose it was the dean who attacked you. I guess he must have had a key to that door in the wall," Rachael mused.

"Yes, I think he must have been getting pretty desperate by then. We've gleaned quite a lot from the interviewing we've done so far, although he's not told us everything.

"It appears that he saw the notice that Jack left on the Diocesan office noticeboard and arranged to meet at Farley Mount. I think Pretorius thought that Jack would demand money to keep quiet, and I also think that he might have been prepared to pay up, if the sum had not been ridiculous. The tragedy for both of them was that, according to Michael Bakowski, Jack wanted something very different. He wanted a public confession of guilt from Pretorius, and that was the one thing Pretorius was not prepared to do. The weather was not good the day they met and there was probably no one else about, so Pretorius took his chance and killed Jack there and then. He hasn't stated exactly how he did it yet, but he has confessed to murder. He then had to improvise quickly. He bundled the body into a sack which he found in the boot of the car and tied it up with some thick string which was also there. After removing Jack's wallet and loose change, but not his car key, which I suspect was in a breast pocket on his shirt, he must have driven off in a hurry. He must have parked the car out of sight until the dead of night, and then decided to drive to the Itchen where we began our examination, and dump the body in the river. The key must have fallen out at that point, and some of the sacking snagged on some brambles and tore off. As he drove off, Pretorius would have had a scare when he encountered Bakowski coming to rendezvous with Jack, but he got away and had the luck to have his deeds become muddled with all that nonsense over the garden gnomes."

"So, it all unfolded just as we thought, except we have finally unmasked the true principal actor in the drama. It's a very sad state of affairs," Rachael added at the end of the explanation.

One thing that Towgood was a stickler for was to keep victims and other key players involved in the investigation updated with the outcome. He personally went to visit Randall to give a grovelling apology for the way he had been treated by the police and tried to make him understand why he had been such an obvious suspect. He also went and visited, in person, Jack's mother. Rachael could only imagine what a difficult conversation that must have been. She herself was charged with conveying the news to Daniel Jarvis. He was very quiet on the other end of the telephone line, so it was difficult to gauge what he was actually thinking.

The former dean's trial occurred in due course with widespread media coverage for a day or two before everyone moved on to the next sensational story. The proceedings were relatively straightforward. Pretorius pleaded guilty to murder and wounding a police officer with intent to kill. The resulting life sentence with a minimum tariff of twenty-five years was not unexpected. However, the police were never able to gather enough evidence to pursue child abuse charges and Pretorius would never say anything about what happened between him and Jack in Peterborough.

Back in the present, the solving of the case allowed Rachael the opportunity to spend Christmas Day with her mother in the care home. Her youngest brother, James, also managed to be there, cheering Rachael's mother up no end. Mrs Merkel and her staff were fantastic, putting on a decent Christmas dinner with crackers and party hats as well as games and singing in the afternoon for the residents who weren't too far gone in infirmity or mental decline. Pablo had to work, but he was allowed to take half an hour to join Rachael as they ate their meal together. Rachael's mother predictably had to ask why Pablo was sitting with them while all the other staff were working so hard. Rachael, yet again, tried to explain that Pablo was her boyfriend and so now part of the family. Rachael's mum even more predictably said what a shame that was, and hoped that there was still time for her to find some nice doctor or lawyer to marry. It was a good job that Pablo was such an easy-going and understanding character. How much was Rachael looking forward to her two-week holiday in Spain with Pablo in January!

Eileen Pennyweather never got over the shock of that fateful day in the Old Mill. Her manager had been sympathetic and allowed her time off on compassionate grounds. But after a couple of weeks, she still couldn't face going back, and thinking about it, she realised that her volunteering at the mill didn't make much difference in the grand scheme of things. She therefore resigned and lived on her pension comfortably enough. She continued to suffer mentally for a couple of months, finding it difficult to go out in public, especially after dark, but gradually the gruesome images of the corpse and the terrifying nightmares faded from her consciousness. Six months on she plucked up the courage to volunteer at the local foodbank two mornings a week. And so, by the time she heard about Pretorius' trial and conviction on the television news, she was able to do so with a degree of disinterest and detachment.

THE END